# DUGGAN'S DESTINY

# DUGGAN'S DESTINY

## SÉAMUS MARTIN

POOLBEG

Published 1998
by Poolbeg Press Ltd
123 Baldoyle Industrial Estate
Dublin 13, Ireland

© Séamus Martin 1998

The moral right of the author has been asserted.

A catalogue record for this book is available from the British Library.

ISBN 1 85371 867 X

All rights reserved. No part of this publication may be reproduced or transmitted in any form or by any means, electronic or mechanical, including photography, recording, or any information storage or retrieval system, without permission in writing from the publisher. The book is sold subject to the condition that it shall not, by way of trade or otherwise, be lent, resold or otherwise circulated without the publisher's prior consent in any form of binding or cover other than that in which it is published and without a similar condition, including this condition, being imposed on the subsequent purchaser.

Cover photography by Brigid Tiernan
Cover design by Ruth Martin
Set by Poolbeg Group Services Ltd in Goudy 11/14
Printed by The Guernsey Press Ltd,
Vale, Guernsey, Channel Islands.

## AUTHOR'S NOTE

Séamus Martin was born in Dublin but moved to his father's birthplace, Derry, at the age of two weeks. The thirteen changes of residence which followed in the next twenty-five years included a mountain cottage in Donegal, the top room in a Dublin tenement and a corporation house in Ballyfermot.

Séamus has worked for *The Irish Press*, *Independent* newspapers, *The Sunday Tribune* and *The Irish Times* as sports reporter, sports editor, features editor, columnist and foreign correspondent. In Moscow he covered the fall of the Soviet Union, in Johannesburg the rise of democracy. He has an abiding interest in history and linguistics and speaks Irish, French, Italian, Russian and, in his own way, English. He now edits the electronic editions of *The Irish Times* but "commutes" regularly to Moscow.

He is married with two grown-up daughters.

*Duggan's Destiny* is his first serious venture into fiction.

## ACKNOWLEDGEMENTS

This novel was inspired by Gabriel Garcia Marquez's *The General in his Labyrinth* which I read in Moscow when I was a foreign correspondent for *The Irish Times*. I read too that Garcia Marquez had been a foreign correspondent and that Bolivar, the General in Garcia Marquez' novel, had been called, like O'Connell, the "Liberator." O'Connell's son Morgan had fought in Bolivar's army. O'Connell and Bolivar had admired each other and briefly corresponded.

Both men had made a physical as well as a spiritual journey to death. Both had been great men who disintegrated physically and mentally as they travelled to the places where geography and mortality coincided.

The chronology of this book is based on the sparse diary of Duggan, Daniel O'Connell's manservant, and I have tried to keep within certain historical bounds. The places named, for example, are the actual places through which O'Connell and his party travelled. Many of O'Connell's words are his own. I have used "Darrynane", rather than Derrynane, throughout as the name of O'Connell's house and estate, as that was the English title favoured at the time in which this book is set. O'Connell's Dublin residence has been described as "No 30 Merrion Square" throughout as that was its number at the time. Following extensive re-numbering over the years, the O'Connell House has become 58 Merrion Square.

I am grateful to the library of the Royal Irish Academy in

Dublin for allowing me to read Duggan's diary. The National Library of Ireland, and its staff, were as courteous and efficient to me as they have been to all those who have consulted them. In the case of my research their efforts were doubly appreciated as they managed to work as normal during a major renovation. Oliver MacDonagh's *O'Connell* was an indispensable reference book.

I would like to thank *The Irish Times* for allowing me a generous sabbatical to research this book in Ireland, France and Italy. I thank Mr Martin Fitzpatrick who lent me his books on O'Connell.

My editor, colleague and friend, Mary Maher, deserves more thanks than anyone. Her forbearance, patience and advice during the gestation of this novel has been exceptional. Her unswerving devotion to the accurate and concise use of the English language has been both a challenge and a benefit. Any circumlocutions are most certainly mine.

FOR ANITA AND RUTH . . . AGUS DO ÐHEIRDRE.

*Go where you will on the Continent: visit any coffee house: dine at any public table: embark on board of any steamboat: enter any diligence, any railway carriage: from the moment that your accent shows you to be an Englishman, the very first question asked by your companions, be what they may, physicians, advocates, merchants, manufacturers, or what we should call yeomen, is certain to be "What will be done with Mr O'Connell?" Look over any file of French journals: and you will see what a space he occupies in the eyes of the French people.*

Thomas Babington Macaulay.

*No man is a hero to his valet.*

Mme Cornuel

# CONTENTS

# DUGGAN'S DESTINY

# CHAPTER ONE

## I am Firefly Duggan

I am not surprised many think me mad. I have every reason
to be so and I frequently behave as if I am. This is especially
the case on cloudless nights when the moon is strong and
there is breeze enough to whip up a ripple on the river.

Each of these circumstances occurs frequently enough in
itself; to have all three happen at the same time is not so
common as to make me a near-permanent night-watcher at
the bridge, but not so rare that I have not been noticed by a
large number of people.

The bridge runs across the Liffey. I stand with my elbows
on the parapet on those moony, breezy nights when the
clouds are absent. I face westwards, my back to the centre of
the city. To my right is a great pilastered drum holding up a
massive copper-green dome. The drum, in turn, is held up by
a pediment, held up by a set of Corinthian columns, held up
by a short flight of steps, held up by the street that overlooks
the river. In the middle-height of the ensemble stands a

massive statue of Moses to indicate that this is a majestic palace of the law.

To my left is an undistinguished complex of stone buildings marked as unusual only by an Italianate facade flattened into a North European terrace as though pressed in by the smoothing iron of a seamstress. Small images of Christ, the Virgin and St Francis are there to show that this is a palace, albeit a humble one, of the Lord. Straight ahead on normal nights lies a stretch of river, but on nights when the clouds are gone and the moon is out and the breeze causes ripples, it becomes, for me, a field in Tuscany fifteen years ago before my life began to fall apart.

The Law as represented by the huge pile of the Four Courts at my right hand and the Church as seen in the small frontage on Merchant's Quay to my left, had their part to play in all this. The man with whose life my life was inextricably bound was a giant in both spheres. While he lived, I moved in a privileged world; when his life ebbed away my life faded into an insignificance, which yet was filled with horror.

I was, I should explain, the manservant of Mr Daniel O'Connell, the Liberator of Ireland, the toast of continental Europe if not of London; and perhaps the most famous man of his time. When he died and my employment in his establishment came to an end, my life was turned away forever from the salons of the great, to the living hell of the destitute whose manservant I now am. It's not surprising, is it, that I like to remember the fireflies I saw in that field near Sienna in the summer of 1847? There's no madness in that, is there? But there's surely some insanity in seeing them again, not in the Italian summer but in the icy cold of a northern night when the frost falls from the clear sky.

And I do see them, I really and truly do. I knew at the start that the faint flickerings of light thrown in my direction when the moonlight struck the little waves were merely fireflies of the mind, glistenings without substance. Each time my deepest sentiments moved me to visit the bridge the lights flashed more brightly, their movements became more sudden and unpredictable, the chill dissipated and the air warmed and I truly was in Tuscany again, away from the washing of corpses and the moaning of the hungry. The fireflies slowly, gradually, night by night, have become real. They have become my escape from the evil place in which I now live.

A mile or so to my right Mr O'Connell lies in peace under his giant Round Tower in Glasnevin. His corpse was the first one I washed. With the utmost care I cleaned his giant white body but his was a hollow corpse then. His heart ripped out and placed in a silver urn, his innards minutely inspected by the doctors and then cast into a rough sack to be eaten by the dogs of Genoa. A mile or less to my left is where I now wash corpses daily. These cadavers are starved and skeletal, some blackened by the typhus, others yellowed by the jaundice, all buried together. All, at least, are buried whole, their organs intact with no need for re-assembly at the call of the last trumpet.

I have been going to the bridge to tend my fireflies for the past ten or twelve years or more. The appropriate nights do not come often but they add up to quite a number. Each night a carriage or two crosses the bridge, each night lovers stroll past and paupers and drunks and thieves and vagabonds. By now I have been seen and noted perhaps by thousands. I have become known, marked out as one of the city's eccentrics. The common people have dubbed me "The

Moon Man" perhaps or, more sympathetically, by those who know me, I am simply "Poor Duggan" who has gone downhill since his master passed on.

I work at the South Dublin Union: "The Workhouse" to some, "The Poorhouse" to others, to most "The Union," to all the most reviled, the most despised, the most feared and frightful place in this city. There are many even in this time of pestilence who would rather die on the streets of hunger or disease than walk through its gates on James's Street. The charity dispensed there is so sharply edged with austerity as to bring with it, for certain, an immediate humiliation and an inevitable death.

By law the Union of Parishes in the southern half of this city is bound to provide for the poor who live or have lived within its boundaries. Whole families should be admitted as units. No individuals should be accepted unless they bring with them their immediate kin. According to the law it's all or none. Again, according to the law, as soon as these families are admitted they are separated by the sexes and sent to the male and female wings.

In practice the law is very rarely observed. The sexes are indeed separated, husbands from wives, sisters from brothers, but the famine and pestilence that began two years before Mr O'Connell's death caused the other rules to be ignored. Thousands came in barely alive, thousands left, some improved slightly in their physical condition, some still barely alive and most of them in cheap soft-wood coffins destined for mass graves.

It has been my job since the summer of 1847 to be a porter at this, the most hated place in Dublin. My responsibilities are concerned entirely with physical work. I clean lavatories and carry loads from one part of the workhouse to the other. I remove filth and excreta. I fumigate newly-admitted "objects of charity" as they are called, to rid them of their lice. Most of my work, though, involves the washing of bodies and their preparation for burial.

Sometimes I am called in to stop fights among the women inmates, when they have the strength to fight. Some time ago two young women threw their gruel on the floor because they did not like the taste of it. A different type of meal had been used with a new type of taste. Having been raised in the Union and spent all their lives in it, the young women had become accustomed to the yellow maize-meal brought in from America in famine times.

Gradually the native oatmeal porridge, with its blander taste has begun to replace it. The older people remember it well and welcome it like an old friend. Its arrival was a marker that the days of starvation were coming to an end but to the younger inmates it was an unwelcome change. The two young women I spoke of threw their gruel on the floor and were attacked by their elders for doing so. When I arrived their ragged clothing had been torn to ribbons and their bony arms were red raw from the wrestling.

This type of insubordination is severely punished by the master and it is our duty, myself and the men I work with, to put down any such mutinous acts.

These men who work with me in James's Street have become fiends. They have been in the workhouse long enough to have lost that sensitivity which sometimes, though not always, distinguishes the human from the beast. Some have worked there since the time when famine filled the place with walking ghosts from the countryside who barely crossed the threshold and died.

The horizons of these men's minds run for a mile or two in any given direction from the gatehouse of the house of horrors in which they work. Their education is limited, their minds are circumscribed by what they have seen in this world and what they have seen has been brutal, devilish and disgusting to an extent not seen in this part of the world since the dark ages. They laugh at death and its horrors. A corpse can break wind, for example, or it can belch. When I experienced this for the first time I shuddered but my colleagues appeared to think of it as a source of great amusement.

They stood on the bellies of the dead wretches; they pushed their boots into the numb flesh to make the corpses fart and belch as they lay in the oratory for the priest or the minister to send them on their way to the grave.

But those indignities were committed upon those who felt, and who could feel, no slight. Worse things have happened to the living. Those who come to James's Street in the first place are the most absolutely destitute persons in a city that has been overrun by the poor. That is the way it has been ordained.

The conditions in the Union are deliberately planned to be so horrible that only those who live in even direr straits are tempted to consider going there for what is called "relief." Supplies of food and clothing are kept to a minimum not only to keep the costs down but to discourage those not in the most absolute need of sustenance and shelter from approaching the workhouse gates. My fellow workers have made things worse. The policy of not replacing clothes has left hundreds of half-naked young women in the female wing. The famine and the pestilence have put so much pressure on the organisation.

Discipline has collapsed. Rough whiskey and poteen are smuggled in by some porters to corrupt the more impressionable young women, some of whom have not known life outside the workhouse. Scenes of the most horrible debauchery have taken place. Those placed here through the indignity of poverty and disease are forced to suffer further wrongs. There has even been talk of unnatural acts of buggery against young boys in the male wing. I have not encountered any real evidence of this, though I would not be surprised if it were the absolute truth.

I work and live, as you can see, in what is truly a most horrible place but its reputation for evil is even greater than its ability to inflict it.

The people of Dublin in general, and the Catholic people in particular, believe that not only one's body is placed in danger there. They are convinced there are those in the Union who will steal one's soul.

This notion stems from older times when the foundling children left here were instructed in one religion only, regardless of the faith of their mothers.

The young women left their babies at the "cradle at the gate" a contraption peculiar to the establishment. The cradle was attached to a revolving door. The unfortunate mother rang the bell. The gate porter turned a wheel. The baby was wound inside. The mother departed unseen by those to whom she had committed her child. A baby placed in the cradle as a Roman Catholic was taken from it as a Protestant. The simple faith of even the most derelict young women left them stricken with grief and fear of damnation. They had not only lost the infants they had brought into the world but were told by their priests that they themselves would suffer for all eternity.

For nearly twenty years now those of the Roman Catholic faith have had their own chaplain and have had no pressure put on them. No proselytism exists even to the very slightest degree. But the old reputation lives on, undeserved and untrue. And that reputation attaches itself to those who are associated with the place. I am one of those persons and it has affected my life to a great degree.

When Mr O'Connell's glory rubbed off on me I was one of the most sought-after and most respected men of my class. I was a hero of my faith, a living symbol of the struggle for Repeal of the Union with Britain. I was a man who met and spoke with Mr O'Connell many times every day, as a matter of course, when everyone else had to squash into a great throng even to catch a glimpse of him.

The common people had no chance to meet the man himself, but they could meet me. Had I accepted every offer of a drink made to me by the working people of Dublin I would not have drawn a sober breath for decades.

Now I represent something else. Poverty, hunger and pestilence have attached themselves to me, the stigma of the "cradle at the gate" has adhered to my being and I am also, to make things even worse, the madman who comes to the bridge when the moon is out. Those who once stopped me and asked for Mr O'Connell's health now turn their faces and rush past.

Our country has been stricken by the most awful catastrophes. Not long ago the Irish had nearly matched the English in numbers. The extension of the franchise to Catholics made us almost their equals. Now the famine and the pestilence, disastrous in their direct consequences, have also caused our numbers, and therefore our power, to collapse.

The death of Mr O'Connell was a tragedy too, as much for the generality of the people of Ireland as it was for myself.

These tragedies have affected us in different ways. They have driven me to the bridge on the nights when the skies are clear and the moon is strong and the wind is up. They have coarsened those who work with me to an extent that the horrors of death, starvation and disease are to them but cause for merriment.

But I have been in the Parliament House in London. I have seen the Champs Elysées in Paris. I have dined with the owners of a fine hotel in Lyons and I have seen lizards play among the Roman graves in Arles. I have strolled on the Cannebière in Marseilles and along the waterfront in Genoa and I have been inside the palace of the Quirinale in Rome.

I have seen the Pope.

And I have seen fireflies in that field in Tuscany just as I see them now in my half-madness on the river. "Firefly Duggan" is what they call me in the Union. My colleagues, God bless the mark, call me "Firefly Duggan" because I told them I had seen those fireflies and they laughed and ridiculed me because by telling them I had stepped outside the bounds of their mean lives.

Had I told them of Paris or the Pope, of the broad Cannebière or the lanes of Genoa I would have distanced myself further from them and, they would have ridiculed me even more. They might have driven me further from reason. I might now look for the fireflies not only at the bridge but also in the streets, in daylight, in Dublin for the Pope or for the Comte de Montalembert or in Dublin Bay for the flamingos of the Camargo.

It was when I was with my fellow-workers, "shifting

stiffs", as they described the removal of the corpses of the impoverished wretches from the infirmary to the chapel, that I felt I should write down my story. I wanted to tell you how I came to step from the world of the powerful and the "people of quality" to the dark domain of poverty. I determined to recount my travels to the land of powerlessness and disease that I now inhabit.

I wrote some of it down in my diary at the time and added to this later from my memory of the events which took place. I did it to detail my misfortune which I now believe to have been visited upon me because of the ambitions I harboured above my station. This is my story: the narrative of how I travelled to my destiny as Mr O'Connell journeyed to his death.

# CHAPTER TWO

## My Journey, my Master

In those times I hungered to be out of servitude. It was my great ambition to be a man of my own, and at least once Mr O'Connell promised me real assistance in achieving my aims. But Mr O'Connell was a politician; promises to him were like the down of dandelions blown on the wind. Only one in thousands would take root and even that by accident.

My struggle to leave the service of others and have the self-respect to work for myself has been with me since childhood. My father was a servant too and my mother a kitchen-maid in a large house in the county of Tipperary owned by the Hacketts, a family from the Catholic gentry.

It was a happy house set on elevated ground with an avenue of birch trees running up from the road. The Master, Mr Charles Hackett, was a jovial, easy-going man who allowed his own children and those of his servants to mix freely together. The same schoolmaster who taught the

Master's children was paid also to give the basics of an education to the children of the servants' hall.

In this house it was that I learned to read and to write. Being literate was rare for children of the servant classes at that time. I was a good student and loved to read. In fact I became something of a pet to Mr Hackett who often picked special books for me from his library. I managed the long and hard words at first with a dictionary and then on my own. I listened carefully to the speech of my master and his friends and by the time I was twenty I could speak as well as any of them.

I dared not show this accomplishment in public, of course, for fear that I should be regarded as being "forward," a trait no master wished to see in a servant. I simply did my chores with a "Yes, Sir!" and a "Yes, Ma'am!" and nodded my head in acknowledgement of the orders given.

Mr Hackett all the same regularly checked the standard of literacy I achieved. He was proud of me and took me to fairs and horse races and made me read and say my recitations to the other gentry as though I were a turn from the travelling players. Sometimes I would, deliberately, pronounce a word badly or with a strong accent of the countryside in order to show that I knew my station. This would start them all laughing, confirmed in their easy superiority as our "betters."

But I knew that I read more than most of them, that I had acquired knowledge which they had not. I knew too that I could never be one of them, that I could never cross that chasm which divided them from us.

My parents could see a similar chasm opening up between them and me because of my bookishness. My mother welcomed it as a sign that I might better myself and perhaps go into a trade. My father took the opposite view. Servants had their difficulties, he kept telling me, but they never went hungry and it was his view that won in the end. Through the influence of Mr Hackett I was recommended for an interview for a position on Mr O'Connell's staff at his townhouse in Dublin.

Mr O'Connell was very different from the men at the fairs and the horse races; from the landlords who idled their time placing bets on the prowess at hurling and weight-throwing of their servants and tenants. Mr O'Connell encouraged me to read more and left me a key to his library. He encouraged me too in the use of polite speech, for he wished me to be able to convey messages to his parliamentary and legal friends without his having to commit his views to paper. But he too made it very clear as to where I belonged socially. He didn't say it directly to me but it was obvious that while I was to become the servant closest to him in his everyday life, I was to be a servant none the less. Even the clothes he had made for me by his own tailor from the most expensive and finest stuff marked me, by their style, as a man in service.

So my literacy and my speech set me apart from the servant classes and my birth kept me strictly apart from the gentry. I inhabited an almost empty middle ground between the two, meeting few if any of my rare kind. I never married, for I could never converse with a scullery-maid. Those women with whom conversation, due to their intelligence and education, would have been a pleasure were of the class forbidden to me.

My desire to escape from service kept growing. I read of people who had been set up in business by their masters but knew this could not happen to me. Mr O'Connell never had money enough for himself, let alone for his manservant. There is no doubt, though, that he sensed my ambitions and played to them at times by holding out hopes of reward in the distant future. Those ambitions stayed with me over the years only to die with the Liberator in Italy. It was then that I moved instead from the service of the mighty to the service of the destitute. There was no option at my stage of life other than ending in the Union as an inmate myself.

The symbolic journey from one status to the other was also a real journey, a long voyage by sea and land through England and France and Italy and back to Ireland. I departed from Dublin as a denizen of one world and arrived back to be moved to the other. My companions on most of that journey were Mr Daniel O'Connell himself, his youngest son Mr Dan O'Connell and his chaplain, Rev Father John Miley, a curate at the Pro-Cathedral in Marlborough Street in Dublin.

* * *

Mr O'Connell had been ill for some time. His first symptoms showed themselves as some slight pains in the head during one of his visits to his family estates at Darrynane in the county of Kerry on the south-west coast of Ireland.

He was a giant of a man, mentally and physically if not, as many would argue, morally. His own people loved him to the extent that their adulation created a world of myth and mystery around his person.

Although he eschewed violence more than any other Irish leader, his followers dreamed of him with a sword in his hand vanquishing their English conquerors. Though he was a devoted husband and father, the peasantry who loved him painted him as a conqueror of women and a heroic father of thousands. Yet his wife and daughters regarded him as a loving husband and father, faithful to them in all respects.

In those final days as we travelled through France and Italy his strength ebbed. His sharp mind was blunted to the degree that at times he was unable to recognise those who spoke to him or even the very country in which he found himself. The great booming voice had been reduced to a mere whisper, the religious faith, which he had so gallantly defended, had responded by attacking his mind, besetting it with the most obsessive scruples. In this latter he submitted himself completely and without question to Father Miley.

A man of sparkling intellect, a conversationalist who captivated the minds of all who met him, Father Miley became a favourite of the people of Hastings and St Leonard's-on-Sea during Mr O'Connell's stay there.

He was a fluent speaker of the French language and a historian too and has been rewarded since Mr O'Connell's death with his appointment as Rector of the Irish College in Paris.

There was another side to him though. I feel free to say this, now that a decade or more has passed and telling this takes a weight from my mind for I have thought about it almost every day since Mr O'Connell died. It is my solemn view that Father Miley saw the Liberator's last journey as a chance to further himself. Daily on our travels he pushed us onwards towards Rome to a degree that exhausted the healthy members of the party and frequently brought the illustrious patient to the point of collapse.

Mr Daniel O'Connell Junior, my other companion on the journey, was the youngest and indeed the most pleasant of Mr O'Connell's sons. He was a sweet young man of just over thirty years at the time we set out. As the Member for Dundalk he was part of the group in parliament known as Mr O'Connell's "tail," for they followed him into the voting lobbies when told to and pursued him also through the warren of corridors in the palace of Westminster. Mr O'Connell had become very fond of his youngest son, mainly because he did what he was told. He behaved with a compliant good humour at all times and was, in general, an obedient and solicitous son to his ailing father. Mr Dan was a naturally friendly young man who would rarely take issue with another.

But our journey changed him. It left him and Father Miley as adversaries and it banished the natural openness from his character.

* * *

There were more than the four of us when we originally set out from Kingstown on January 29th, 1847, on the paddle-steamer to Holyhead. Another of Mr O'Connell's sons, Mr John, the member for Kilkenny, led a large party of Irish members of parliament to what promised to be a major political event. Our procession of carriages through the city of Dublin had drawn the people onto the streets. At the great pier of Kingstown a crowd of several thousand had gathered to see the Liberator off on his journey to parliament where he had promised to attempt to impress on the English, Scotch and Welsh members how dire the situation in Ireland had become. His golden voice, his great oratory appeared to be the last hope for his country, weakened though that voice had been by his illness.

As the steamer reached the end of the pier Mr O'Connell

went across the deck and stood on the paddle-box. This was placed above the great wheels and considerably higher than the rest of the starboard deck which was nearest to the landward and to the crowd which had walked to the pier's end to wish him bon voyage.

He simply stood there, a wry grin on his face, waving feebly as they cheered. He was still there, still waving when the land of Ireland disappeared over the horizon; the tears which rolled down his cheeks engendered as much by his frustration at the weakening of his mind as by his feeling that he had seen his native land for the last time.

Mr Dan and I climbed up to the paddle-box and brought him down to the deck. He was whimpering like a child and repeating the words "I detest my sins above every other evil."

The Dublin doctors had described his illness as a "softening of the brain", a physical deterioration of the matter from which the brain is composed. The main symptom was a sudden and pitiful deterioration in the very process of thinking. At one moment he would be lucid and at the next his thoughts muddled and unclear. His great booming voice was at times reduced to a pathetic whisper, to a crackling sound like brushwood when it first takes fire.

Crazes and delusions came and went. On this, the occasion of what was to be his last departure from the country he loved, and for the defence of whose people he had used every ruse his fertile imagination could invent, he lost himself in an attempt to make what is known as a "perfect act of contrition". His mind was fixed on the fear that he might suddenly die without the grace given by the last rites of the Church.

Mr Dan comforted him while I fetched the others who had gone to the saloon with Mr John. Their arrival on the deck calmed Mr O'Connell but not before he had, to the great humiliation of all of us, attempted to prostrate himself before a young priest who had been walking on the deck. The last voyage to parliament began therefore in the most inauspicious of circumstances, with the Irish Tories who saw him aboard ship sniggering to themselves and revelling in the misfortunes which had been visited upon their enemy.

At Holyhead the Liberator had fully recovered from this collapse of his dignity and seemed to have returned to his old strength of mind if not of body. By the time we reached Birmingham he was able to show himself strong and smiling to the Irish people, and to his English supporters, who crowded there at the railway station whence he was to travel to London.

But the diarrhoea struck him on the train and weakened him badly. His meals refused to stay inside him and failed to give him any nourishment or sustenance. For a short while the idiot smile returned to his face and he sang out the *Stabat Mater*. This caused much discomfort and embarrassment to his fellow passengers, many of whom regarded his faith as no more than an evil superstition on the one hand and a slight to the faith of the Queen on the other.

He loved the Queen, mind you. "Our dear little Queen" he called her. Even when repeal of the Union would be achieved he wanted Victoria to be Queen of an Ireland which ruled itself from its own Parliament on College Green. The Young Irelanders and many of the Republicans hated him for these views and regarded him as a "fawning Irishman" ready to belittle himself to the powerful for the smallest favour.

Some were more understanding. The rebel republican John Mitchel, who hated England, may have regarded Mr

O'Connell's previous appeals to parliament on Ireland's behalf as hopeless expeditions. But Mitchel admitted that Mr O'Connell never begged alms for Ireland. He owned that his wonderful life could not fail to impress his people. He agreed that Mr O'Connell had broken and "flung off, with a kind of haughty impatience, link after link of the social and political chain that six hundred years of steady British policy had woven around every limb and muscle of his country, down to that supreme moment of blackness and darkness for himself and for Ireland, when he laid down his burden and closed his eyes".

At this time his eyes were open but only just. He travelled in a land in which his enemies were less forgiving than was Mr Mitchel.

For his English enemies, the horrors which he and his country suffered were no more than a nuisance, an exaggeration springing from the minds of a voluble people who could not tell the truth to save their souls. Throwing money at them would, they felt, be a waste of time. Disraeli frowned at their claims; Peel smiled that smile which Mr O'Connell described as "like the silver plate on a coffin".

It was to the very den in Westminster inhabited by these enemies of O'Connell and of Ireland that he now travelled. The words he uttered were not those of the great orator but those of the panic-stricken sufferer of a softening brain who feared he might at any moment meet his Maker.

He sang them out hoarsely:

*Stabat mater dolorosa*
*Juxta crucem lacrimosa*
*Dum pendebat filius*

When he finished singing he wept again like a baby and whispered to me that he cried for the "sad calamity" which had befallen his country. All the work he had done, he sobbed, all the mass meetings, the stirring of pride within the people, his success in gaining entry to parliament for the Catholics, even his imprisonment and his victorious exit from it had been in vain. A mere fungus blown in on the wind from the Americas had undone it all.

He whimpered on at our arrival in London and had to be hurried to his carriage lest the city crowds of his Irish supporters see their great hero in his awful time of weakness. At his lodgings we washed him and put him to bed where he sobbed and trembled himself to sleep.

The auguries for the day when Mr O'Connell was due to plead for his country in the Commons were poor indeed. Our hope rested only in his previous unexpected recoveries from weakness and despair.

# CHAPTER THREE

## I Hear my Master in Parliament

Jones, the footman, told me he saw Mr Disraeli's carriage draw up outside our house in Jermyn Street and then move off very slowly as we were making ready to bring Mr O'Connell to parliament. Jones told the staff that Mr Disraeli sneered as he looked out at our preparations and that his eyes were full of hatred as he watched what was going on. I could see that he was doing this to agitate the rest of the servants who were already distressed by the arrival of Mr O'Connell in such poor health and spirits.

I was not sure, by the way, whether or not to believe our London footman. I had been told that in his time out from work he attended political meetings of an extremely radical nature and that he had lost his faith in our Lord Jesus Christ. And he truly hated Mr Disraeli who, he said, had given up his Jewish faith in order to advance himself in this world and gain entry to society. He felt Mr Disraeli was afraid of Mr O'Connell because he was opening up the possibilities of power to a much wider group of people than that which held sway at the time.

Not, mind you, that Jones had any great regard for Mr O'Connell himself. "The best of a bloody bad lot" he called him, accusing the Liberator of favouring Roman Catholic gentlemen over Roman Catholic peasants. At times he arrived late at night muttering about all religions being merely "a bundle of superstitions".

Our English servants were intent on informing the master of the footman's carryings-on, but were prevented from doing so by their Irish fellows who out of their own tradition refused to inform even on an Englishman, and even to Mr O'Connell himself. I had often remarked to myself in the past on the very different approaches to their positions of the English and Irish servants, particularly in the matter of informing the master.

But there was another reason why our master was not told. What use would it have been to tell the Liberator that our footman's bags, when discreetly searched, were found to contain the radical pamphlets of Mr Godwin and Ms Wollstonecraft? What use indeed, when all the writings of these radicals were to be found in Mr O'Connell's own library?

There is no doubt that the feelings between Mr Disraeli and Mr O'Connell were often fraught. The animosity began, I remember, when Mr O'Connell launched a fierce attack on Mr Disraeli in the Commons. There had been a famous battle between them in which Mr O'Connell had postulated the theory that Mr Disraeli had been descended from the unrepentant thief who was crucified with Christ. The words spoken at that debate were repeated so often at dinner parties in Merrion Square that I now know them by heart.

These and other sayings of Mr O'Connell, of his friends and of his enemies, I have kept in an old hatbox of the Liberator's. Some I jotted down myself and others I cut from the newspapers of the time, most especially the *Freeman's Journal* which always sided with Mr O'Connell.

The Jews were, Mr O'Connell said, "a great and oppressed nation" but like any other, there were "miscreants among them" and "it must have certainly have been from one of these that Disraeli is descended. He possesses just the qualities of the impenitent thief who died upon the cross – whose name, I verily believe, must have been Disraeli."

Bumpers of claret were invariably raised when those last words were repeated. Guffaws from the gentlemen and giggles from the ladies would be heard in the kitchen, the loudest laugh of all coming from the Liberator himself. Lord, what rude health he enjoyed in those days!

I sat with the other servants at Westminster at the time of that verbal duel and remember the tension that arose. The servants of Tories took the Tory side, the servants of the Whigs uttered Whig sentiments and the few servants of the radical and Irish members sided with Mr O'Connell. I remember asking myself then whether the people of our servant class had any opinions other than those of their masters.

As I have said, I do not know if Mr Disraeli passed our house on that day, but if he did he would have observed a scene of the utmost confusion. Mr O'Connell was in one of his most obstructive moods at first and after I had washed and dressed him he refused to move an inch, saying he abhorred the very thought of going to Westminster.

A "house of liars and thieves", he called it in terms utterly opposed to his truly expressed beliefs in democratic principles and methods against those of violence and the mob. Then he started to issue impatient orders to all and sundry. He demanded that lunch be served at half past eight in the morning. He called for musicians to play the national airs of Mr Moore. He insisted we all kneel down and pray for "Old Ireland" in her dreadful hour of need. Suddenly, I remember, upon the arrival of his Irish and English supporters he became quiet and almost seemed to have fallen asleep and, his previous frenzy having passed, he quietly asked to be taken to the House so that he could deliver his oration on behalf of his country. In the carriage he bucked himself up and sang Moore's "Avenging and bright falls the swift Sword of Erin," as if to muster up determination for what lay ahead.

We made our way slowly and circuitously through the bustling London streets, so similar in architecture to those streets near Mr O'Connell's Dublin house in Merrion Square. But those who swarmed in the centre of London, the sellers of materials and flowers and the myriad other products, even the beggars, looked so much healthier, so much more prosperous than the famished wretches we had left behind us in Dublin.

When we arrived at the House of Commons the lobby was all clamouring with people who had come to listen to Mr O'Connell. Some had dashed from their clubs and from the gaming houses, others from the dining places convenient to Westminster. They stood in groups discussing this matter and that, their servants standing a pace or so back from them as I did from Mr O'Connell and his party. The din of conversation was near to deafening, especially to us servants who were not allowed to speak inside the house itself.

In the chamber itself things were quieter, Mr John told us

afterwards. Some minor business was dealt with in the presence only of the speaker and a handful of Honourable Members. Mr O'Connell's entry was less than triumphant. He was almost carried to his seat by his few remaining allies, including his sons Mr John MP and Mr Dan MP.

But for all his weakness of mind and body his very presence brought energy to the House and within a quarter of an hour of his arrival the chamber was full and echoing to the rustle of silk as the members doffed their tall hats.

When Mr O'Connell rose to speak the eyes of the house were upon him. His eyes seemed fixed in a stare instead of darting from place to place, as was his usual practice. His cloak, which I had fixed perfectly upon him just a short while earlier, had slipped to the one side.

When he opened his mouth and uttered his first sentence there was an astonished gasp from the assembly. His mighty torso had been wasted since they had last seen him, but this did not prepare them for what was to come. What emerged from his barrel chest was the weakest of whispers that made every member strain to listen. His voice was fainter than I had heard it at any time since his illness began.

Those near him moved nearer. Those on the opposite benches, even Disraeli and Peel, were taken aback at the shambles of a man their mighty opponent had become. Snatches of his oration were picked up in the echoing chamber as he lowered himself for the first time in his career to beg on behalf of his people. The Irish beggarman he had so often been depicted as by *Punch* was now a reality. This was the feeling that overwhelmed me at the time. It made me feel ashamed, not of my master, but of myself for seeing even an iota of truth in the claims of his enemies.

His people, he told those who could hear him, were

"starving in shoals, in hundreds – aye in thousands and millions. Parliament is bound then to act not only liberally but generously – to find out the means of putting a stop to this terrible disaster". Ireland, he told those opposite him, was "in your hands, in your power. If you do not save her, she cannot save herself.

"I call on you solemnly to recollect that I predicted with the sincerest conviction that one fourth of her population would perish unless Parliament came to their relief."

Even Disraeli was touched, though by the plight of O'Connell rather than that of his people. It was, he wrote in a book that was later brought to my attention, "a strange and touching spectacle to those who remembered the form of colossal energy and the clear and thrilling tones that had once startled, disturbed and controlled Senates.

To the House generally it was a performance of dumb show, a feeble old man muttering before a table; but respect for the great parliamentary personage kept all as orderly as if the fortunes of a party hung upon his rhetoric".

"The fortunes of a party"! Does not that speak loudly of Mr Disraeli's view of the world? What was at stake was the survival of millions, but to the Tory leader it was as "orderly as if the fortunes of a party hung upon his rhetoric". These words rouse anger in me to this day.

It took some time for the members to collect their senses after Mr O'Connell's speech. On the Whig side there was a pathetic silence at the sight of a past hero become smitten by illness. The Tory benches hummed with chatter, the weakness of Mr O'Connell being a great item of news and intelligence to bring back to the shires.

Lord George Bentinck, after the members had calmed themselves somewhat, tried to help. He immediately proposed a bill to allow the government issue a loan of £16 million for the construction of railways in Ireland. Almost a million persons, he estimated would benefit from the employment given on the railway works and the Government would be paid back promptly. Mr O'Connell seemed heartened as he walked into the Aye lobby but his appearance took on a dejected look as member after member walked into the Nay lobby to oppose the bill with the Tories. He left the House, God help him, politically defeated, mentally crushed and physically broken. He whispered to himself in the carriage on the way back to Jermyn Street and asked for his bed to be readied as soon as he entered the door.

* * *

Indeed Mr O'Connell's appearance had been so frighteningly weak that within a day the rumour had spread through the entire city of London that he had died. Almost all the grandees of politics in the Lords and the Commons sent their messengers to Jermyn Street to inquire after his health. Even the Queen was interested enough to find out how he was. Her special messenger arrived with a note in her own writing inquiring as to his well-being. Mr John wrote in reply that Mr O'Connell was "somewhat indisposed", but not seriously unwell. The staff was instructed to answer other inquiries in precisely the same terms.

He was in fact gravely ill. His once robust constitution was weakened by constant bouts of diarrhoea, by the persistent bleeding, either by incision or with leeches, depending on the mood that prevailed among the doctors.

These medical men swarmed in Jermyn Street like midges of a summer's evening. They came and went, nodding seriously in conversation to Mr John or Mr Dan. Each one, I am sure, spoke in his club, over his port, on how he was in the process of saving the life of the Liberator. "Why save the demagogue?" I could imagine a ruddy-hued denizen of the Athenaeum ask in tones loud and indignant. I could picture the doctor too getting all moral and Hippocratic in his reply. "A demagogue he is, Sir, and a Papist demagogue to boot. But I am bound by my oath to save him."

My animosity towards those doctors began at that time and later it grew to far greater dimensions on almost every step of our fateful journey. It grew as our train moved through the south of England. It increased as we passed through the plains and mountains of France. It intensified with every knock of the steamboat's engine on the coast of Liguria and with every deathly toll of the bells of Genoa.

At that time in London, I did as much doctoring as any of the medical men. Frequently in the dead of night I had to dash from the house to the nearby hospital to fetch aid; by day I had to arrange for large wicker baskets of soiled bed linen to be carried off to the laundry.

Guests from Ireland arrived, their faces taut with anxiety. They left, their features loosened in resignation. Mr O'Connell himself was resigned to his imminent death.

He told everyone who called on him that he was about to pass away and wrote a series of "last letters" to his friends. He even attempted to settle his financial affairs before departing this life, something he had distinctly failed to do while in the full of his health.

But his doctors felt he could recover. Total rest, the abandonment of parliamentary and political business forever and a change of air and climate would, they insisted, prolong his life considerably. The Liberator impatiently agreed but was taking no chances with his soul, whatever about his body. He sent word to the Archbishop of Dublin that he wished to have Rev Father Miley of Marlborough Street at his side as his chaplain and confessor. Within forty-eight hours Father Miley arrived and Mr O'Connell's spirits rose a little.

Father Miley was then a man of forty-two years. He was an historian and knew almost everything that was to be known about the annals of every place in Ireland and Britain and the continent and beyond. He could talk and expound his great knowledge, it appeared to me, on every subject under the sun.

There was something uncanny about him too, something I cannot explain. I felt uneasy in his presence. His skin was strangely youthful, almost childish, for a man of his age. His hair was coal black and of an unnatural thickness. His face pallid and drawn and with large, dark, watery eyes above his small snub nose. His mouth was tiny and his lips, soft and bright red, gave the only dash of colour to his face. I often thought of him as a dead man come to life again. His complexion had something to do with it for he had that waxy look to him.

His hands, though, were the most frightening things.

Long fingers jutted out from his extremely narrow palms. His skin was so white I felt at times I could see through it all the way to the bones. He let his nails grow long, too long I felt to be respectable on a man. He had this habit too of forming those fingers into an arch at those times when he asserted his clerical authority over us. Every time I saw him do it, I felt the hairs on the back of my neck rising stiff and hard like the spines of a hedgehog.

Mr O'Connell liked Father Miley. The priest's talk seemed to enchant him. It was as a confessor, though, that he was most valued. To have a priest and the last sacrament near at hand meant a great deal to Mr O'Connell. It calmed him down for a while.

But the reports in the newspapers, all of which Mr O'Connell demanded be brought to him, depressed him once more. There was a tinge of condescension, he told me, in the attempts at compassion by those journalists who had opposed him vehemently in the past but who now went easy on him because they felt he was about to die. Even when the *Freeman's Journal* arrived from Dublin it was, though much more supportive of the Liberator, somewhat worried in its tone.

"My dear Duggan," he whispered to me in the morning-room, "we have had much better times in the House, have we not?"

# CHAPTER FOUR

## *I Remember Days of Glory*

There were other, better days indeed, when Mr O'Connell's voice was strong and his mind clear. There were days when the crowd of people that gathered around him was not a handful of members of parliament careful in their manners, circumscribed in their responses by the customs and unwritten laws of the House. In those other days crowds in their tens and even hundreds of thousands came together in the open in places where great historic events had taken place.

The first such event I went to with Mr O'Connell was at Athlone only four years before our final journey together. In this town, right in the centre of Ireland, a great battle had taken place in which the forces of King William led by General Ginkell had defeated those of King James, some eighty-five years before Mr O'Connell had been born. It had been a defeat for the Irish side but a defeat which had produced a hero in the form of Sergeant

Custume who had sprung from the stock of the ordinary people of Ireland.

The place set out for the meeting was about two miles from the town in a great meadow, and it being the middle of the month of June the weather was warm and the sun shone throughout the day. Mr O'Connell and his group had luncheon in a fine hotel in the town where he had stayed the previous night. I had ensured his clothes were cleaned and pressed and ready for the day. I lunched in the hotel's kitchen with the staff, on boiled mutton preceded by barley soup from the water in which the mutton was boiled, some good baked potatoes and green cabbage. The gentlemen had their mutton roasted and partook of a couple of glasses of claret each over the lunchtime.

After they had eaten, a line of carriages, a full forty of them, was drawn up outside the hotel door for the journey to the field. Some of the lesser members of Mr O'Connell's entourage were in the first carriages, followed by the more important of his friends such as Mr Tom Steele, and finally in the largest and best turned-out carriage of all was Mr O'Connell himself. Four grey geldings drew it, each of them almost white in colour and each of them so polished and pampered that his coat sparkled in the sunlight. The servants, myself included, followed in open cars.

It was a merry jaunt through the town. Many of those wishing to attend the great gathering were still making their way on foot in the direction of the meeting place. Most of them were of the poorest orders of society, badly clothed, kerchiefs tied over their heads against the strength of the sun. Some had a drink or two taken, some carried their food in cloth bags tied to stout staves which they placed over their shoulders in the manner in which soldiers place their muskets when on the march. The cheers and waves to Mr O'Connell came from all of them along the route to the meadow which was on high ground above the town. Because of this we did not catch a glimpse of the size of the assembly until we reached the crest of a hill just a few yards from where the crowd was gathered. Coming upon us so suddenly, the scene that lay before us was overwhelming in its size and in the emotion that carried from it to our carriages and jaunting-cars as we passed through.

At first we made reasonably good progress. But as we came closer to the vast wooden platform erected in the centre of the field, the crowd was so thick that we had to make our way inch by inch at a very slow pace. All the while the great "Hurrahs" rang out for Mr O'Connell. He acknowledged them as usual by nodding his head towards sections of the crowd, waving his cap in the direction of others and gesticulating with his hands towards others still. In this way, he used to confide to his friends over a glass of port, he could convey the impression to all those gathered at the great meetings that he had given personal recognition to everyone. Many, especially the more simple-minded and less educated ones, believed this to be the case and went back to their cabins and their villages with the tale that Mr O'Connell had nodded, or gesticulated or waved his cap directly at them. This gave them a tale to tell and a status of great importance among their neighbours.

The outer circle of people through which we passed was composed in the main of women and their children. Some sat in groups upon the grass sharing their food and talking in an animated manner. Upon our arrival many of them ran towards us, screaming Mr O'Connell's name, surging forward to catch a glimpse of him as he stood up in the box-seat of his carriage.

The next circle was composed of men on horseback, ranging from strong farmers to gentry. Each man displayed his rank by the type of headgear he wore: the gentry in their tall silk hats, the richer farmers in their conical soft hats belted and buckled at the front and the less prosperous but still comfortably-off farmers in their derbies and bowlers. These were exuberant in their reception of Mr O'Connell but they calmed as he came closer and gave quite a deferential air towards him, raising their hats and bowing as his car went slowly past.

Closer to the platform and entirely on foot were grown men and stout young lads in their shirtsleeves, crushed closely together and excited at Mr O'Connell's approach. *"Make way for Mr O'Connell! Clear a path for the Liberator!"* they shouted as they threw their caps in the air and formed a parting in the multitude to allow the carriages through. Finally at the platform itself, decorated in bunting and banners carrying patriotic slogans, the stoutest of the young men stood with staves in their hands ready to protect the Liberator should a member of the Orange faction or some of their paid accomplices attempt to do him an injury.

By now, we were told, a hundred and fifty thousand souls had gathered to support repeal of the Act of Union which had moved our parliament from College Green across the sea to London. The minor speakers took to the stage first with Mr O'Connell seated to the rear, shaded from the sun by a banner that his supporters held over his head.

At first the din of the huge crowd did not abate in the very slightest. As the inferior orators spoke a great hum of conversation came towards the platform from all directions without a single word being distinguishable until from time to time the crowd took up a chorus of *"Long live the Liberator!"* Gradually, the chants and choruses subsided as the other speakers made their points. They were heard only by those closest to the platform, but even those in the distance could see by the gesticulations made by those at the daïs, that a speech was in progress.

Special guests and visitors were brought to Mr O'Connell as others spoke. One man, obviously a foreigner by his attire, announced himself as a German who had never in his whole life seen such an assembly nor heard such praise for one single man. Mr O'Connell asked whence he had come and when told it was Cologne showed an especial appreciation of that city and its adherence to the Catholic faith.

Then suddenly there came the sound of cracking wood and the entire platform began to shudder under the weight of those who stood upon it. Mr O'Connell calmly rose to his feet and made to go around from one person to another to ask them to leave their places quietly.

But when he rose to his feet he was espied by the crowd and they all recognised his tall erect form and the sprightliness of his step and his proud head and his great mane of black hair.

A huge roar went up that drowned out the words he was uttering to those close by. It seemed to me like a great ocean wave crashing against the cliffy shores of Mr O'Connell's own Kerry coastline.

And yet this was followed by the most profound silence any of us had ever experienced as Mr O'Connell strode forward to where the other speakers had stood and raised his arms to indicate he was about to speak.

Strength, physical and moral, emanated from every pore

of his body at that moment just as weakness did on that day some years later in Westminster. His back was straight instead of bent, his voice a great resounding boom instead of the feeble echo. His head was covered in a shock of black hair and not the heavy wig of that same colour which his vanity later forced him to wear.

How well do I remember how he was on that day, his power, his sense almost of immortality, his belief he was leading his country and his fellow Irishmen to victory and to an end of rule from England. How often do I tend to compare those bright days with the dark ones when the Angel of Death appeared to follow us wherever we moved?

On that day he addressed not only the tens of thousands who came to that field outside Athlone. His words were aimed too at the Duke of Wellington, himself an Irishman, who ruled with less than welcome authority as Prime Minister of the United Kingdom of Great Britain and Ireland.

"This," Mr O'Connell told the multitude, "is the anniversary of the celebrated battle of Waterloo – a battle won by Irish valour; and the Duke of Wellington knows right well it is not the red coat that makes the soldier valiant and fearless in the field, but it is the innate courage of the Irish – as firm and unshaken beneath the grey frieze as it ever was in scarlet."

This brought a resounding cheer from the crowd, from those who heard what was said and from those so far away that they merely joined in the roar of approval because they had heard the roar and not the words.

Then he turned to the central topic of his address: the Repeal and who had supported it and who had not. He singled out Peel as the great villain who wished to deny

Ireland its rights of democracy; he pointed him out as a conniver and a teller of lies. He painted such a picture in words of this man whom I had not ever seen in my life, that by the end of the meeting I found my heart filled with bitterness and hatred towards this personage who was entirely unknown to me.

One man close to the front of the platform was so moved to hatred by Mr O'Connell's words on Peel that he shouted: "I wish a crow would come and pick Peel's eyes out!"

There was a smile on Mr O'Connell's face at this. But he did not like his speeches to be interrupted even by words that echoed his own. He pointed out the poor fellow with his cane walking-stick and admonished him by saying: "And I wish that a crow would come and stuff your mouth with potatoes."

Then he attacked the Arms Bill for allowing the police to search for arms with impunity. "The clauses in that bill are extreme. In reading some of them I had to lay down the bill and wipe my spectacles, thinking that my eyes deceived me, so extreme are the severities it proposes. By that bill the authorities could search even in the private apartments of a man's house. Oh, only think of their daring to enter the bedchamber of the pure and chaste!" There were loud cheers all over the field at this, again those nearer cheering at what he had said and those further away cheering because they heard the cheers.

He excoriated the initiator of the bill, the "sweet-tongued, ladylike Lord Elliott", and the people gasped at this insult. To them, and I should say also to me, until that moment it had been the custom to address the aristocracy with the greatest of respect even if their views on politics and religion differed totally to one's own.

So the crowd became more excited at every topic he raised. The House of Commons itself was subject to brutal irony. "What business have I there?" he asked, "Why, there is not an idle whipster that belongs to any club or gaming house that would not throw his dice-box aside and come down to the House of Commons and vote against me."

The crowd was halfway between being stunned at the near blasphemy that was being uttered and excited and furious at the harm that was being done to them in London, and Mr O'Connell sensed this and urged them on. "There are enough of you to take your enemies in your arms and fling them into the Shannon, if you thought it worth your while to begrime the waters with them. But that, you neither will nor wish to do. You will never again play into the hands of the Tories and if you continue in the path of peace and order, the rising of tomorrow's sun is not more certain than that the day of our freedom is near!"

These words were greeted with the most turbulent scenes I had ever witnessed. The explosion of shouting that greeted them was so tumultuous as to shake the earth beneath us and what followed was the most terrible sight I have seen in my entire life.

The great cheers and huzzahs caused a horse to bolt in that ring of men next to the outer circle of women and children. The crazed animal dashed wildly into the crowded assembly. People dodged out of its way. Other people dodged the people who dodged the horse.

Thousands were suddenly and urgently on the move in a huge wave of humanity and this wave spread with a ferocious intensity towards the fragile platform upon which Mr O'Connell was giving his address. The entire multitude was engulfed in terror and panic, the men roared, the women screamed and wildness and horror took over a scene which previously had been high-spirited and a good-humoured.

Some who had not seen the horse bolt thought a regiment of cavalry had been unleashed upon the people from the garrison in Athlone. They took flight in the direction of the platform where we sat behind Mr O'Connell. Our destiny it appeared was to be crushed by the violent onrush of humanity. And then the miracle happened. Aware that the convulsion had brought the crowd nearer him and therefore within better hearing of this voice, Mr O'Connell took in a very deep breath and held his ground. As those who remained of the platform group appeared ready to jump off and join the ranks of the confused and terrified he stood and composed himself.

He filled his lungs so that his chest enlarged to great proportions. I saw a button pop from his waistcoat and then in the most powerful voice I have ever heard he uttered the words: "*Stand still.*"

Those who had been consumed with panic obeyed the order as though it had been drilled into them for months by a sergeant on the parade ground. The surging mass in an instant became motionless as statues and they gazed at each other as if they had been frozen by a blast from the icy Arctic on this day of sweltering heat. As they stood there transfixed the most bizarre thing happened.

A man dashed from the crowd to Mr O'Connell and pressed something into his hand. The Liberator looked at it and smiled. He held it up for the stunned crowd to see. It was, of all things, a bright ripe peach. The Liberator took it in his hand and bit a piece from it and the spell was broken. He laughed and the crowd laughed. Another man ran up to give him an orange. He took it and squashed it symbolically making some reference to the Orange party which I could not hear but which excited the entire crowd to further laughter and merriment.

But he was not finished. He took to the platform again and spoke for another hour on the benefits the Repeal and the return of the Parliament to College Green would bring to us all.

That night a huge banquet was held on the very field in the open air that was especially warm for the time of year. Mr O'Connell and his party sat at a centre table from which other tables radiated like the spokes of a wheel. A special box was constructed for the ladies and a band of music played the patriotic airs composed by Mr Moore. At a short distance great bonfires were lit and cooks prepared the most sumptuous of meals. Great salmon from the Shannon nearby were poached in black cauldrons over the open fires; whole sides of beef were roasted and carved into portions by teams of cooks. Other bands of servants had peeled potatoes into buckets of water early in the day and these were now boiled for those people of quality who had been invited to intend the banquet.

Sheep too were roasted whole, and game birds had been brought from the estates of Mr O'Connell's landed supporters. There were pheasants from the woods close by, spike-beaked woodcock from the counties to the west where they are especially plentiful and partridges from the eastern counties and one large stag too, and the roasting, the boiling, the grilling and the basting continued for hours. Casks of claret and brandy from France had been delivered from the Liberator's own house in Darrynane.

The patriotic music faded away to be replaced by the romantic. The gentlemen and ladies danced into the night under the moon and warm sky upon a floor that had been improvised from the planks of the platform from which the speeches had been made.

I have seldom seen Mr O'Connell in better form and indeed he conveyed this to his friends and colleagues. "I have never," he told his friend O'Neill Daunt, "felt in more vigorous mental and bodily strength."

It is an awful exercise to compare Mr O'Connell at that time to the feeble wreck, mentally and physically, which presented itself to us just four years later as "The Liberator."

He may have felt himself to be in perfect shape at that time. But the mind and the body can flatter to deceive and can spur a man on to efforts which are so strenuous that in the end his entire frame will collapse underneath their weight.

But he kept going. He kept holding his "monster meetings" and the strain began to tell. As the numbers of his supporters increased, as the great meetings grew in size, imperceptibly at first Mr O'Connell's strength began to fail him. As the man closest to him in his everyday matters I noticed more than anyone else. It began one day in Darrynane with complaints of dull pains in his head; then his memory, which had been extraordinarily strong, began to fail slightly. Usually he could wake in the morning with his daily schedule of events clear in his mind down to the precise minute and second. But now he was asking me, not every day, but from time to time, what item was next on the agenda of his day's activities. He would place things in places most inappropriate for them. On one evening I found a salmon, given him earlier by a tenant, laid out incongruously on his writing-desk, a trickle of its blood from the gaff mark moving slowly over his correspondence of the day.

Occasionally too he would, at luncheon and dinner, spill food on his clothing. Gradually he grew absent-minded and lacking in memory about things which had happened minutes and hours beforehand while retaining the clearest of pictures in his mind of what had happened many years ago. These failings began to manifest themselves to a greater extent after his meeting at Tara, the Royal capital of Ireland. No accurate measure has been given of the crowd that came to Tara. Some of Mr O'Connell's guests have said that more than a million came to surround that low hill which symbolised Ireland's independent past. The cars and coaches that passed through the tollhouses on the roads north of Dublin numbered 1,400 by an early hour of that morning, and when the series of Masses that preceded Mr O'Connell's oration began, it was estimated that 700,000 had arrived upon the scene.

After a priest had preached the usual temperance sermon, Mr O'Connell addressed the people from the crest of the most historic hill in Ireland. "The overwhelming majesty of your multitude will be taken to England," he told them "and will have its effect there. The Duke of Wellington began by threatening us. He talked of civil war, but he does not say a single word about that now. He is now getting eyelet-holes made in the old barracks. And only think of an old general doing such a thing – just as if we were going to break our heads against stone walls. I am glad to find that a large quantity of brandy and biscuit has been lately imported and I hope the poor soldiers will get some of them.

"But the Duke of Wellington is now talking of attacking us and I am glad of it. But I tell him this – I mean no disrespect to the brave, the gallant, the well-conducted soldiers who compose the Queen's army and all that we have of them in this country are exceedingly well conducted.

"There is not one of you that has a single complaint to make against them. They are the bravest army in the world and therefore I do not mean to disparage them at all but I feel it to be a fact that Ireland, roused as she is at the present moment, would if they made war against us furnish women enough to beat the entire of the Queen's forces."

How well I remember the great burst of laughter that greeted this feat of oratory, the serious face with which Mr O'Connell had delivered its early parts and the huge grin of mischief he displayed while uttering the latter words.

Now he had the crowd in the palm of his hands like clay to the potter. "When on the second of January I ventured to call this the year of Repeal everyone laughed at me. Are they laughing now? It is our turn to laugh at present. Before twelve months are out, parliament will be at College Green!"

His great admiration, and that of the Irish people, for Queen Victoria was demonstrated when he placed her above the politicians of the day. He told the crowd she had the right to call a parliament wherever she wished and wherever her people were entitled to one. He attacked Peel as a liar for having said she was opposed in principle to the very idea of Ireland getting its parliament back.

"Let every man who, if we had an Irish parliament would rather die than allow the Union to pass, lift up his hands," he cried, and every hand to be seen was thrust in the sky. "Yes," he cried, "The Queen will call that parliament. You may say it is an act of the ministry if you please. To be sure it would be the act of her ministry, and the people of Ireland are entitled to have their friends appointed to the ministry.

The Irish parliament will then assemble; and I defy all the generals, old and young, and all the old women in pantaloons – nay I defy all the chivalry of the earth to take away that parliament from us again!

"Give me three millions of Repealers and I will soon have it. The next step is being taken and I announce to you from this spot that all the magistrates that have been deprived of the commission of the peace, shall be appointed to settle all the disputes and differences in their neighbourhoods.

"Keep out of the petty sessions courts and go not to them. On next Monday we shall submit a plan to choose persons to be arbitrators to settle the differences of the people without expense!"

It was hard to know at the time if he was being carried away with his own words but it seemed to me he was hinting that he would set up his own administration in Ireland.

The whole project of Repeal was now at its height and it was determined that the greatest of all monster meetings would be held on the eighth day of October at Clontarf, where King Brian Boru had routed the Danish overlords of Ireland in 1014. The preparations were meticulous. From Dublin the artisans were to march out of the city accompanied by cavalcades of horsemen carrying banners and wands, music was to fill the air from every brass and reed band in the city. The rural people were to march through Dublin on their way to the meeting.

But on the evening of October 7th, a proclamation signed by Lord de Grey and bearing the arms of her majesty Queen Victoria was pinned to gates of Dublin Castle proclaiming the meeting and forbidding attendance thereat. And peace-loving man as he was, Mr O'Connell called off the great meeting and gave the English their victory. But that was not enough for them. The city was filled with troops, their glistening bayonets fixed. Three men o' war sailed into Dublin Bay and trained their guns on the Clontarf Road and the big guns of the Pigeon House fort did likewise.

The Dublin people, ever eager for fun, followed the great regiments as they marched through the city, cheering them on with no little degree of irony in their voices. In the meantime a warrant for Mr O'Connell's arrest was issued on charges of conspiracy.

Many attempts have been made to put his deteriorating health down to his conviction and imprisonment but I am not one of them. First of all I heard him complain of the head pains long before he was imprisoned. I can tell you too that his spell in gaol did not impose any real hardship upon him. The Richmond Penitentiary in Dublin had dank and squalid cells to be sure but these were reserved for prisoners who had no influence in the outside world.

In Mr O'Connell's case a suite of apartments was at his disposal in which he received visitors daily, held dinners and lunches and lived, ate and slept as well as he ever did in Merrion Square.

His spirit grew stronger for a while after his release but soon his health began to fail once more. This time there was nothing gradual about it. His mind weakened, his voice grew quiet and his senses became dulled. The deterioration was rapid and dramatic and by the time he had spoken for the last time in parliament his doctors were despairing of conventional treatment.

## CHAPTER FIVE

# Our Pilgrimage is first Proposed

Doctor Ellmore and Doctor Chambers recommended a complete change of scene and climate. A change of air and a rest from political work were, they said, crucial to any hope of recovery. Mr O'Connell, as the fatigue incurred by his exertions in the Commons ebbed away, agreed after a great deal of pressure from his friends, that we should move to the seaside. I got to my duties of having all the bags and accoutrements ready for the journey by train to Hastings.

Our carriage pulled out from Jermyn Street at three o'clock on a sunny but very cold afternoon, the horses as usual in prime condition. Mr O'Connell may have been ill and the household in disarray, but appearances had to be kept up in front of an English populace, which would take pleasure in even the slightest lowering of standards. The Liberator was well wrapped up in his greatcoat, scarf and one of the Foxford blankets we had brought over with us from Ireland. He moved very slowly and had to be lifted into the carriage.

The station was crowded. Standing on one of Mr O'Connell's trunks I looked out over a sea of bobbing top hats to see our train pulling in to the platform just before four o'clock. The large group of servants present, myself included, set out to find the carriages reserved for our masters. Having found O'Connell's carriage, I had the luggage brought to it and stowed. I then escorted our party along the platform to the appointed place.

The passengers were mainly London gentlemen and merchants accompanied by their ladies and their servants, embarking on a short visit to the south coast to take the sea air. Almost all of them recognised Mr O'Connell and I constantly heard his name whispered in hostile sibilants as we moved down the platform. But the servants, many of them Irish, stood silently by, their faces betraying their shock and dismay at the condition in which they found their Liberator.

Some of them did not recognise him at all and pointed enthusiastically to young Mr Dan. In his thirty-second year, he was as tall and as handsome and as strong in his build as his father ever was. He had a thick shock of black curly hair and the O'Connell snub nose, and bore a very strong resemblance to many of the more flattering drawings of his father which the poorer Irish people had hung in places of honour in their homes.

I had known Mr Dan since he was a lad. He had been a quiet boy, very strongly attached to his mother. I always felt that as the youngest he had been Mrs O'Connell's favourite. When she died he was heartbroken. "A sensitive boy", she had always called him and I remember wondering as we set out on our journey if the choice of Mr Dan to accompany his father on such a trying voyage was the correct one. Perhaps

Mr John who was a good deal older and considerably tougher might have been better suited but as the engine got up steam and I busied myself with the luggage I realised there was little point in worrying about such matters.

The train departed perfectly at the appointed time. Mr O'Connell's stomach held up remarkably well on the journey. On the odd occasion when he was stricken with a real or imagined discomfiture, Mr Dan took him by the hand and consoled him. He addressed him always as "dear Papa," and the anxious concern he felt for his father was openly expressed on his face. Father Miley, who had donned his most elegant clerical attire for the journey, simply sat looking sternly out of the carriage window. Only once did he remove his silk top hat from his lap. This was when he handed it to me so that he could read his daily prayers from his breviary.

I could sense a tension between Father Miley and Mr Dan; perhaps a rivalry for Mr O'Connell's attention. This seemed to fade as we neared our destination. After three hours precisely we arrived at Hastings where the scent of the air and a lightening of the grey skies gave notice to us that the sea was not far away. The accommodation arranged for us was excellent. A fine house with a view of the English channel, it had good airy bedrooms, servants' quarters to be occupied by myself as well as a cook, housemaid and washerwoman, all of whom had been hired in for the duration of our visit. Most important and gratifying of all, we had a grand drawing-room in which to receive the many people of the district and those travelling from London who had sent their cards as an indication that they wished to visit Mr O'Connell.

While the great majority of English people were opposed

to Mr O'Connell – and indeed fiercely partisan in that opposition – there remained a considerable number, mainly English Catholics and liberals, who not only supported him but were dedicated in that support. Many of these were to come and see us and we were, of course, attended to by the local Catholic clergy and visited also by some ministers of the Church of England. The Mayor of Hastings, with great courtesy, took it upon himself as first citizen, to welcome us personally to his town.

Our time there was to be spent in a mixture of hope and despair as Mr O'Connell's condition varied from day to day and indeed, sometimes from hour to hour.

Doctors Ellmore and Chambers had appointed their friend and colleague Doctor Duke to attend to Mr O'Connell in Hastings. He did so with great assiduity, coming to the Liberator's bed twice a day: before breakfast each morning at half past seven and before supper in the evening also at half past seven.

No treatment was given, no leeches applied and no bleeding done. At the time I was quite surprised and even worried that Doctor Duke confined his attentions merely to observing Mr O'Connell's condition. I was later to wish that other doctors in the course of our long and tiring journey had adopted the same practice.

A robust and jolly man, Doctor Duke was confident that Mr O'Connell was about to make a full recovery. Mr O'Connell's spirits however were extremely low, not only due to his own weak condition but because the dreadful situation in Ireland continued to prey upon his mind. This latter was so much the case that he once woke in the middle of the night shouting out the words "hunger" and "pestilence".

It was in Hastings too that his preoccupation about being buried alive began to manifest itself. This obsession was to show itself at every stage of our journey, right up to the very hours before his expiry in Genoa.

I heard him speak to Father Miley of his fears. Ireland, he said, was about to lose half its people and therefore half its power. Its strength in relation to England would, he said, be diminished with every Irish death. Every Irish death meant one vote less in Ireland and a weakening of its representation in Westminster.

He was not, he said, mercenary in his views. He felt deeply for the people who were losing their fathers and mothers and brothers and sisters but he was simply pointing out that the famine would have consequences beyond those which were immediately visible.

As for his fear of being buried alive, he raised this question with me on occasions so numerous that it became a commonplace. "Duggan," he would say. "You are the only one I can trust. For God's sake make sure I am dead before they bury me."

His other great worry was that he would die unprepared, without the fortification supplied by the last rites of the Holy Mother Church. He became attached to Father Miley as an infant to its mother, never wanting the chaplain out of his sight lest there be a need to administer the sacrament of Extreme Unction. This might have led to some very embarrassing situations but for his remarkable ability to pull himself together before strangers. When a visitor arrived, for example, all Mr O'Connell's anxiety would dissipate, his manner would change from that of the fretting patient to that of the diligent and generous host. Conversation would turn from its previous concentration on his own health and his prospects of survival, to the ordinary topics of the day. The political manoeuvres of the Whigs and the Tories, the international relations between the great powers and, in smaller talk, the health and general situation of the visitor and his family would replace the previously morbid themes.

For some time we wondered which was the real Mr O'Connell. Was he indeed as ill as he appeared when he was alone with us? Was he indeed as well as he appeared when he had visitors?

As the one person who had to be almost permanently at his side, all the time reassuring him that Father Miley and the sacrament were near at hand, I felt that the good humour which came over him when others were present, was an affectation. It seemed to me that he summoned up all the strength in his body to appear as normal as possible when people from outside his immediate circle were present. I can in any event say with certainty that these performances were followed, upon the visitor's departure, by such an immediate collapse into exhaustion that I had barely time to wash and dress him for bed before he was asleep like a babe.

Next morning it would be back to despair. Mr O'Connell had taken to saying the rosary several times a day and one of my first duties after he had breakfasted in bed was to fetch him his beads and to sit by him uttering the responses to his prayers. It was he, always, who began the prayer and it was my duty, as his servant, to continue. He would start the *Pater Nosters*, *Ave Marias* and *Glorias* and halt at the appropriate moment for me to continue the prayers to their end.

The situation often infuriated me. Mr O'Connell had developed a tendency to believe that should his prayers not be uttered with absolute precision and perfection, the Lord would not hear them and the intercession of the Virgin Mary would have no effect. He would often, because of these scruples, lose his concentration and forget his count of the number of *Aves* he had said. "Duggan, was that nine or ten?" he would ask. I was quick to learn that I should tell my beads as accurately as he, but this too was of no avail for he never believed my count and called me for all the fools and knaves he had ever encountered in his life. Then he would realise he had committed the deadly sin of anger, burst into tears and apologise profusely to me.

The list of the Seven Deadly Sins would come to his mind and he would recite them: "*Pride, covetousness, lust, anger, gluttony, envy and sloth.*" He would examine his conscience on each one of them. "Pride," he would say. "I don't think I am a proud man. No, I am not proud."

I would reply, God forgive me, that of course he was not proud and all the while I would think of the huge triumphal coach he had had manufactured in Dublin so that he could parade through the streets like a monarch.

"Covetousness. Now that is possible; I have demanded money to support my luxurious life – it will damn me to hell, will it not?"

"It will not," I would reply, as of all his faults covetousness was the least evident in his character. His nature was generous to a fault and his financial difficulties stemmed from his giving away of money to others rather than coveting the possessions of those more prosperous than he.

"Lust? I have none left," he would laugh as he said this. "Anger? I still have some as I have just shown. I must curb my anger. Gluttony? No. my appetite has departed from me. Envy? Who is there to envy? Peel? Macaulay? Disraeli? No, not a one of them! My God, am I being proud, Duggan?"

I would answer, of course, that he was not, for after the first few of these litanies I had become aware that the climax was about to be reached.

"Sloth? Sloth! *Sloth!* Duggan, it is ten o'clock and I am still in my bed, why did you allow this? Get me up, get me washed, get me dressed!"

A reminder of his anger at this stage would serve only to repeat the process, so I would attend immediately to his needs. I would ring the bell for the chambermaid to collect his breakfast dishes and accompany him to the drawing-room where Father Miley would hear his confession and give him his spiritual advice.

On an average day he would, at the beginning of our visit, spend most of his time seated upon the couch at the drawing-room window looking out to sea and moping to himself that he was not at home in his beloved Darrynane. Mr Dan who had taken to rising at an even later hour than his father would occasionally come and sit by him to talk of Ireland and of Kerry and of Darrynane and most especially of its people. They seemed to know every member of every family in the district, their names, their nicknames, their habits, and their personal and family traits.

But even in his poor health Mr O'Connell could not dwell on trivial matters for long. By mid-morning the newspapers would arrive from London and he would read them meticulously, exclaiming frequently in anger in reaction to some biased article which had appeared, most often in *The Times* which was extremely hostile to Mr O'Connell, to Ireland and to the Roman Catholic religion. How I cursed that newspaper! The anger it caused in Mr O'Connell often started him away again on his scruples and on the litany of the Seven Deadly Sins. Then, when he had calmed himself, he would start to read *The Times* again and would get angry once more and the litany would begin yet another time.

I thanked God for the days when the *Freeman's Journal* would arrive from Dublin. Its tones of adulation would please him. He would sit at the window seat, smiling. He would soak in the flattery and never once accuse himself of the sin of pride.

By lunch-time he might on some days be able to complete his meal but on others would not even start it, turning up his nose either at the dishes themselves or the manner in which they had been cooked or served.

Then in the afternoon when visitors arrived, the great change would occur. His energy would return, his anger and his fear of death would disappear, a smile would creep across his face and he would, consummate politician as he was, dredge up from the back of his mind the most incredibly detailed knowledge about the visitor's life. He would remember the last time they had met. He would recall the gentleman's wife's name and inquire after her health. He would even remember the children's names and ages and if their birthdays were coming near.

The visit over, he would collapse from exhaustion and be taken to bed where he would fall into a state of self-pity and fear of imminent death. In order to keep him sustained, therefore, we began to arrange visits so that they would include supper otherwise he would have fasted from lunchtime until next morning's light breakfast of porridge and milk.

It was in the course of one of these dinners that the idea of the pilgrimage to Rome was raised. We had with us that evening: Lord Dunboyne, Mr O'Connell's great friend Mr

Patrick Vincent Fitzpatrick, and Doctor Michael McCabe of Hastings, a brother of the author Mr William McCabe. Mr Christopher FitzSimon, the husband of Mr O'Connell's eldest daughter Ellen, came out from London and arrived at the same time as Doctor Duke. The famous Dublin lawyer Sir Philip Crampton was travelling to Brussels and had left his card that morning. He was immediately invited to join the guests.

It was to be the grandest occasion of our stay in Hastings and extra help was brought in to meet demands for additional work in the kitchen and the dining-room. Mr O'Connell's condition had been improving steadily for the previous three days. He had been on his feet most of the time during his waking hours and instead of reclining on his couch had taken to pacing the drawing-room. I might add that while he was doing that he was pestering me with questions about whether or not he had given into temptation and committed any of the Seven Deadly Sins.

He had also taken upon himself a series of earthly scruples to pile upon his spiritual ones. These mainly concerned the possibility of intruders appearing in the house from outside. It was not robbers or burglars that he worried about but he feared strangers seeing him in a condition of physical and mental weakness. Three, four and five times each day he would set off around the house checking that all the doors were locked, that the latches were fast upon all the windows. Then in case Peel or Disraeli or some other enemy might, through a telescope, peer into his rooms, he began to insist that all the blinds be drawn.

This, not surprisingly, caused pandemonium in the town. The populace, seeing every blind in the house pulled down, believed that Mr O'Connell had died. A considerable number of his English supporters gathered, clamouring for news and information on the Liberator. They were dispersed only when, on one of his better days, we brought Mr O'Connell out onto the front balcony. There he waved and smiled and nodded as in the old days. He even gave a short exhortation in favour of the Repeal, which they cheered.

# CHAPTER SIX

## *I Learn a Terrible Secret*

As I have said, occasionally all the symptoms of illness in the mind and body would disappear or would be subdued by the efforts of Mr O'Connell. So it was on the evening of the grand dinner. Father Miley best described the improvement in a letter he gave me on the day of the dinner, to post to Mr Morgan O'Connell in Dublin. This was to become part of a controversy later in the week in Dublin, when Mr Morgan had it published in the *Freeman's Journal* to contradict reports which suggested that Mr O'Connell was on the verge of death.

I and others most certainly did not share the optimistic opinions held by Father Miley, Doctor Duke and Sir Philip Crampton.

"My Dear Sir," Father Miley wrote, "*It delights me to inform you that the rapidity with which your illustrious father's constitution has rallied since our arrival in this place offers us the most decisive and cheering proof that when the physicians promise such great things from change of scene and climate, they are beyond question right.*" He continued to describe the scene in Hastings and the improvement in Mr O'Connell's condition, saying that he had a sound and placid sleep from which he rose much refreshed. "*As he paced our delightful drawing-room, looking out on the sparkling waters of the sea, you would hardly believe he was the same man. He breakfasted well, ate a hearty dinner. His spirits were warm and cheerful and the doctors here had entirely coincided with the London Physicians as to his soundness of constitution and the certainty of his recovery.*"

I can vouch that his sleep was neither sound nor placid. He woke several times in the night and spoke of his fear of being buried alive. This great fear began at home in Ireland where, at the time of his departure, the famine and disease raged at the greatest intensity imaginable. The sad calamity which afflicted our homeland had, since its inception, weighed most heavily upon his spirits. This manifested itself at first in his determination to put matters right for the Irish people. When that failed he worked to ensure that his own peasants were safe and when failure met him here too, he became overcome by the horror of it all.

At that time, most particularly in the poorest regions of Munster, the people were dying in such great numbers that a peculiar method of burial had been devised. So many died by the side of the road that they were buried where they fell.

In those days when fever and starvation raged through the land, nothing could be taken for granted. The world was turned upside-down. Babes suckled not sustenance but doom from the breasts of their mothers. The embrace of a friend could convey the typhus. Young children, girls and boys, grew a profusion of hair on their faces. Grown women went bald.

It is difficult to explain all this in these better times.

In time the very compassion one human being had for another in distress, was replaced by a rapaciousness and a complete lack of feeling. The coffin men were paid for each burial they performed regardless of whether the victim was dead or half-dead.

Others were taken to common burial pits and given the semblance of a funeral. Special coffins with hinged bottoms were designed. They could be opened by means of a small lever. So after the funeral of one unfortunate wretch had taken place and the mourners had departed, the lever would be pulled, the bottom of the coffin would open and the wretch would be left naked in the earth. The coffin would then be removed and used for the burial of other unfortunates who had starved to death.

Hunger and pestilence raged throughout Ireland. The stench of the dead was everywhere. The burial teams worked hard and worked in a hurry. Stories abounded of "corpses" shouting from these hinged coffins on their way to the burial pits, of bodies twitching to life as they lay waiting for the earth to cover them .

It was certainly true that the men hired to bury the dead were less than cautious. They picked up bodies on the side of the road and did not take time to examine them properly. If they were not already dead, the reasoning went, they soon would be. Mr O'Connell had heard these stories prior to his departure and this had caused in him a morbid fear of being entombed alive. He would sometimes awake in the night screaming aloud, calling to tell me he had been scratching at the lid of his coffin. Thomas a' Kempis, the author of the great religious work *The Imitation of Christ* had been exhumed from his grave, he told me, by those who wished him to be canonised as a saint. They had hoped his body might be intact after its years in the earth and that this would be seen as sign of his sanctity.

Instead they found the marks of his nails tearing at the lid and the sides of his coffin. The Church had appointed an *Advocatus Diaboli*, a devil's advocate, at the hearings on this holy man's canonisation. He declared that the scratch marks meant that he was buried alive and could therefore have been guilty of the sin of despair as he lay there under the earth using up the final and minute particles of air which had been trapped in his coffin. This evidence had destroyed all the good works he had done when alive and wiped out his chances of being declared a saint.

When Mr O'Connell got the *Freeman's Journal* a few days later he simply grunted, tore up the paper and told me that the letter was rubbish and that Father Miley was simply trying to comfort Morgan who was a very temperamental young man. "I will not live much longer. I must make peace with my Maker," he told me, and off he went into the whole business of the Seven Deadly Sins once more.

On the night of the dinner Mr O'Connell had pulled himself together remarkably well. He, Mr Dan and Father Miley received their guests with great grace. I served champagne that had arrived from France that very morning and before dinner was served Father Miley entertained the guests with the playing of some national airs on the piano.

At dinner itself I acted as butler. Staging such an evening without a full establishment was, you should appreciate, very taxing. I had not only to serve the champagne and other wines at dinner but earlier had taken part in the preparation of the meal and the lighting of the chandeliers throughout the house. All this was done after a difficult day with Mr

O'Connell and when the dinner ended there was more work to do.

As butler I could hear all the conversations which passed between our guests. The champagne had produced a great conviviality and by the end of the evening every one of the gentlemen, including Mr O'Connell, was in good spirits and swore that the idea of a change of scene, climate and occupation had produced a remarkably beneficial effect.

Sir Philip's voyage which was to take place on the next evening raised the idea of a continental tour, with the south of France (where many invalids from England had taken up residence) suggested as the main venue followed if possible by a visit to Rome to see the Pope. Mr O'Connell, however, had long harboured bad memories of France, having been schooled there during the revolution and also having sent his family to live there at one time when he was in financial difficulties.

Paris, he said, was a "beautiful but filthy capital," the French themselves were untrustworthy and he even included the Comte de Montalembert, his best friend and greatest supporter in France, in this category of people. It had always amazed me that England, in which Mr O'Connell was generally held in great contempt, seemed much dearer to his heart than France where he was lionised as perhaps the greatest political figure of his day.

Indeed he then went into a rambling attack on the French and their "filthy habits" of eating frogs and snails, not washing frequently enough, being bombastic in their speech and generally behaving in an obnoxious manner. One could have taken him for a man born and bred in Hastings rather than in the south-west of the county Kerry.

It had been more than twenty years since he had been outside the United Kingdom. His body and soul were weak, and the idea of a journey through France was almost an anathema to him. In London he had at first rejected the idea of travelling even to Hastings.

When the matter was raised again he went silent, contemplating his reply, and had to be prompted by most of the gentlemen present. The climate would be much warmer if he continued the journey to Italy, Father Miley suggested. A visit to the Holy Father would be widely reported in Ireland and would be of great benefit amongst the electorate, said Mr John. Sir Philip stressed the benefits of the climate change. Doctor McCabe said nothing. Mr Dan called for his third large brandy of the evening. Finally Mr O'Connell announced that he would consider the proposal and give his answer within three days. He stated that he was fatigued and wished to retire. The guests drank up and prepared themselves for departure.

It was my duty to see them to the door and in doing so I overheard a conversation between Doctor McCabe and Mr John. Being a servant is a strange business. Gentlemen seem to have the impression that one is either deaf or dumb or invisible, or perhaps all three. They will hold the most important conversations in one's presence without seeming even to notice that one has ears.

They were discussing Mr O'Connell's health and Mr John asked Doctor McCabe, who had paid a number of visits to Mr O'Connell in the course of his stay in Hastings, what his opinion was of the Liberator's condition.

Swearing him not to tell another human being, the doctor said: "My conviction is that he has not sufficient strength to reach Rome; that if he does reach it, it will be but to be entombed there in the city of the Scipios but my firm belief is that he never will live to see it."

Mr John simply answered with the words "I see", and as far as I was aware never brought up the matter either with his brother or Father Miley.

I gave them their cloaks, bade them good night, got Mr O'Connell to bed and found it difficult to get more than a fitful sleep that night. I now knew a secret. For the first time I had heard a doctor say that Mr O'Connell's health was in such a state that his life was endangered. Not only that but Doctor McCabe seemed to hold the view that the proposed voyage to Rome could indeed shorten rather than prolong Mr O'Connell's life. But to recount this conversation to others would indicate that I had been listening to it in the first place, something that I was not, under any circumstances, permitted to do.

Doctor McCabe, I argued with myself, had not visited Mr O'Connell in his professional capacity, but as a friend. He had made no detailed medical examinations, he had just sat in the drawing-room or, if the weather was not too cold, on the verandah and talked to Mr O'Connell who had long been a friend of the McCabe family.

At one stage on that night of feverish thought I felt that I had a real inspiration. I would, I thought, ask Father Miley to hear my confession and then inform him of Doctor McCabe's opinion. He would then be bound by the secret of the confessional not to reveal that it was I who told him. But then I thought of confession as the Sacrament of Penance ordained by the Lord for a particular purpose; to use it for something other than the remission of sins for which God had ordained it, seemed sacrilegious. I was, therefore, trapped within my secret, bound to hold it to myself and to allow the plans for the journey to go ahead.

Next morning Mr O'Connell was worse than ever. He had moved from the Seven Deadly Sins to the Ten Commandments, reciting them to himself as I shaved him.

*"First: I am the Lord thy God and thou shalt not have strange Gods before me,"* he declared, and then went into a long rambling monologue about his youth in London and something called Deism and being a follower of Godwin.

*"Second: Thou shalt not take the name of the Lord thy God in vain."* This produced a mixed fit of whimpering like a child and giggling like a little girl, which ended with a repetition of the words "only venial, only venial."

*"Third: Remember to keep holy the Sabbath Day."* Response calm with the words "nothing to worry about."

*"Fourth: Honour thy father and thy mother"* brought a flood of tears, for they were both long since dead and he had had little to do with them in their lifetimes having been fostered out as a child and then adopted by his uncle.

*"Fifth: Thou shalt not kill."* He grabbed his right hand tightly and shouted, in full, the name of John Norcot D'Esterre, a captain of the Royal Marines, whose life he had ended in a duel in a bleak field in the County of Kildare thirty-two years previously.

This he had regarded as the most heinous sin he had committed in his entire life, though many have told me that he was goaded without cease by Mr D'Esterre to defend his honour. Mr O'Connell was now very upset indeed and asked me to scour the house for the black glove with which, popular belief insisted, he had covered his right hand at all times after he had taken Mr D'Esterre's life.

He had never worn such a glove and to be asked so

demandingly for an item which had never existed confused me at first. Only my quick thinking in retiring from the room and asking Father Miley to lend one of his black gloves prevented a serious deterioration of the situation.

By the time I returned to Mr O'Connell's room he had resorted to the Seven Deadly Sins again, punctuated by disconnected verses from the *De Profundis*. I dressed him and he donned his new glove which helped him calm down again, but he spent most of the day in a dreadful condition, sitting on his couch sobbing to himself, fondling the black glove and repeatedly muttering "my dear Mary". This I took to be a reference to his late wife.

Mr O'Connell refused to eat lunch or supper that day and was so distressed that he retired early in a state of absolute exhaustion. He did, however, sleep exceptionally soundly and woke the next day refreshed, sharp in mind and happy in spirit as though the unfortunate interlude had never taken place.

Reminded by Father Miley that he should make his decision on the journey to Rome, he sighed and called Mr Dan to join himself and the priest. I was asked to arrange for coffee to be served and I did so. As I left, I heard Mr O'Connell say that he felt he did not have the strength to travel such a distance and that even setting foot in France would make his illness worse. When I returned with the coffee, Father Miley was telling Mr O'Connell that the journey through France would be made as quickly as possible.

There were, he told him, railways all the way from Boulogne, through Paris to Orleans. At that stage they would be half-way through France. But this did not seem to impress Mr O'Connell who replied that French trains would certainly be as unreliable and fickle as the people of that country.

Mr Dan spoke of the southerly places where the weather would be warm and the air balmy. The climate would, he said, be conducive to a recovery if only they could get as far south as possible by the quickest means available.

I then sat in the corner of the room at a table with the *Freeman's Journal* and waited to be of service. I could hear the conversation of the three men quite clearly although from time to time Mr O'Connell's whispering tones became very difficult to pick up.

Mr Dan mentioned that he had never seen Italy and that such a journey would provide him an opportunity to do so. This caused me some excitement for I too had harboured a wish to see that country.

Mr O'Connell kept his own counsel. He nodded, not in agreement, but to indicate that he understood the points being made. It was when Father Miley raised the question of the Pope, however, that the decision was forced. I should stress once more that vanity was an important weakness in Mr O'Connell's character and it was to this weakness that Father Miley played.

The Holy Father Pius IX, *"Pio Nono"* Father Miley called him, joining the tips of his soft fingers to make a delicate arch, "would welcome us with great pomp. We would be included among the élite of the church for the duration of our visit and perhaps for some time afterwards."

His Holiness had been very supportive of Mr O'Connell and it was well known that they had admired each other from a distance for some time. At first Mr O'Connell shook his head. Then he thought a while and hummed a little to himself. Then he asked Father Miley if he thought the doctors believed his health was up to it. Father Miley immediately said that they had not only said his health was good enough but that their important recommendation was that his health would be bettered by the journey.

At this Mr O'Connell said: "Well. I'll go to Rome. I'll go to see the Pope. I might not make it back to Ireland but I'll go to Rome. I admire Pio Nono. We have similar views. If my visit can help him pursue his liberal course then it will be worthwhile."

Father Miley dismantled the little arch he had made with his hands. He now rubbed them vigorously together in satisfaction and proposed an immediate discussion on the details of the journey. I was sent for more coffee.

Mr O'Connell sat for most of the afternoon with Father Miley and Mr Dan as they planned his journey to Rome. The early part was simple enough. We would travel by carriage to Folkestone, thence to Boulogne where we would stay at the Hotel des Bains which Father Miley, having visited France recently, highly recommended. The journey would continue in short stages through Montreuil to Abbéville and Amiens before arriving in Paris where we would spend several days.

"Write to Montalembert immediately," Mr O'Connell instructed, and this was his only contribution to the travel plans at any stage.

No one seemed to have any idea how we should travel onwards from Paris, as the main railway lines were still being constructed in that country. So Mr Dan and Father Miley went together to the railway office in Hastings to determine which route should be taken. On their return they sketched out a further map of the journey, with Mr O'Connell looking silently over their shoulders. The railways would bring us only as far as Orleans. From there we should face the most difficult part of our journey by carriage and diligence though remote countryside, some of it amongst high mountains, staying in the towns of Gien, Nevry, Lachorite, Nevers, Lapalisse, Roannes and Pain Bouchain before arriving in Lyons, the second city of France. From Lyons we would move southward by steamer on the River Rhone through Valence, Avignon and Arles to Marseilles whence we would take a steamer to Genoa, Livorno and Civitavecchia, which was a six-hour carriage-run to Rome.

Even to this day the names of these cities and towns conjure up romantic visions for me but on that day in Hastings the excitement was overwhelming. For a person in my position I had travelled well. I had been to London, Birmingham and Hastings in England, and Dublin and Kerry in Ireland, but the thought of a continental visit, the idea of being on the Grand Tour would put me in a category above the servants of all but the most exalted members of the nobility. I had met, in servant's halls of some of the great houses of England, just a dozen or so who had been permitted to travel through France and Italy with their masters. Now I was to join the cream of the servant classes and I must say that although this was not to be the type of pleasure trip enjoyed by the others I had met, I looked forward intensely to the experience.

It took some days before the reply from the Comte de Montalembert arrived, detailing the names of the hotels we should use on our journey. He advised us to set out on March 22nd, reaching Paris on the 26th. While he advised us to pay in advance for the rest of the journey, he suggested that no dates should yet be fixed as he wished to organise a number of meetings with Mr O'Connell in the French capital. The

Cardinal Archbishop of Paris and the nobility and gentry of that city would, he wrote, need to be informed in advance of Mr O'Connell's proposed visit.

All this was agreed without demur from Mr O'Connell who appeared not to be listening as Mr Dan somewhat listlessly read out the Comte de Montalembert's letter. He cordially expressed his disgust and annoyance at the name of every French town and city along the route, calming down only at the mention of Genoa, Livorno, Civitavecchia and Roma. The names of these cities he repeated in what he fancied to be an Italian voice, trilling the Rs like a warbling bird and chuckling to himself as he clutched his black glove for reassurance.

Overwhelmed by the excitement of it I silently agreed to their plans and day-dreamed of the great places I was to visit. The dreams turned to nightmare after I had put Mr O'Connell to bed and was left in the dark with my secret. I was, I realised, personally destined to usher Daniel O'Connell MP, the Liberator of Ireland, to his death.

# CHAPTER SEVEN

## The Great Journey Begins

The two men, master and servant, faced each other in the morning light. The master stood tall but corpulent, a vacant look in his eyes. He wore only his underwear and the wig which his vanity and political considerations insisted he wear.

The servant, a good deal smaller in stature, was already washed, dressed, brushed-up and breakfasted. His back was stooped to an angle of subservience, bent from a hundred thousand obsequious bows in the course of his lifetime. The stoop made him look considerably older than his forty-two years; so too did his attire. He was dressed almost entirely in black, in clothes which should have been replaced a year back. The seat of his pants shone almost as brilliantly as his shoes but his white shirt had dulled from age. He was a moon-faced man, slightly jowly, and his pink skin with hardly a wrinkle compensated for the aged look given to him by his stoop.

He held his master by the hand and led him to the washstand where a tall jug of steaming water stood in the centre of a large bowl. Duggan sat O'Connell down beside the wash-stand and poured the hot water from the jug into the large bowl. From a smaller jug he added cold water until he was satisfied that the correct temperature had been reached. Deftly, Duggan removed the wig. O'Connell shuddered as he gazed blankly in the mirror. He recognised his own face under the shining bald crown that only he, his servant, his doctors and his late wife had ever seen. Not even his sons were allowed to witness him thus. "A plucked turkey" was the way he described himself.

Duggan dipped a towel in the water and with it massaged the cheeks and jowls of the Liberator, softening the grey hairs of a beard that was weak in its growth. He conjured up a cloud of foam from a stick of shaving soap, a brush and the swiftness of his hands. He applied the cloud gently to the soft face in front of him. Then he worked the razor on its strap to ensure its perfect sharpness.

At the first touch of the razor, O'Connell cried out. "I feel the cold steel. The guillotine, the guillotine!"

"Now, now, Mr O'Connell we are just shaving you for the journey. You're off to Folkestone today. Your admirers are already downstairs. You wouldn't want them to see you like this, would you?"

"I am heartily sorry," the master replied.

"There, there. Nothing to be sorry about," said Duggan, removing the first stray hairs from the chin. He was moving quickly and expertly and now moved on to the Liberator's downy cheeks.

"For having offended thee," insisted O'Connell, as his servant took a scissors and clipped the hair at the back of his neck.

Duggan worked on the Liberator's locks to the words: "I detest my sins above every other evil."

"Dear, dear, Mr O'Connell! Please don't agitate yourself," Duggan droned softly as he tilted his master's head back to deal with the tricky operation of shaving round the Adam's Apple.

"Because they displease thee my God," O'Connell replied.

Just the intricate work of the moustache was needed now and for this he needed his master's lips to cease their movement.

" . . . who art so deserving of all my love," O'Connell murmured.

"Keep your mouth closed tightly, Sir. I shan't be a moment," said Duggan going for the strap to sharpen up again.

O'Connell took a deep breath and then gushed out the words: "And I firmly resolve never more to offend thee, but to amend my life. Amen."

As the "Amen" rang to its conclusion and O'Connell's mouth closed, Duggan applied the steel and in a matter of seconds the work was done.

"Perfect," Duggan said with a gasp of satisfaction.

"Perfect," said O'Connell, "a perfect Act of Contrition. I can die today if the Lord wants to take me. Let's meet the gentlemen visitors before we go a' beagling."

Duggan held out O'Connell's right arm and slid the sleeve of a silk shirt up to the armpit. Expertly he brought the shirt round the back and dropped the left arm downwards and into the other sleeve. Now the front was to be buttoned up and the collar tightened under the tender, newly-shaved skin. Duggan's hands and fingers moved up along the front seam plucking the buttons through their fastening holes with a swift and nimble movement for all the world like that of a harpist coaxing a melody from his strings.

Then came the britches and the boots and the frock-coat and the topcoat and all was ready for the carriage.

O'Connell's mind dwelled elsewhere. "I am," he exclaimed as he reached the staircase, "the only fellow who knows how to hunt rationally." He moved slowly downwards as though making his way gingerly down the bed of a rocky Kerry stream. When he reached the drawing-room and saw the group of men waiting upon his arrival, O'Connell tautened. The empty gaze vanished and, with a great effort, he brought himself back to the here and now.

* * *

The Mayor of Hastings and the entire compliment of Roman Catholic clergy of the town were in attendance for O'Connell's departure. Each one of the well-wishers shook his hand. He had a word for each of them before boarding his carriage. The journey of twenty-five miles, it was estimated by the English coachman hired for the occasion, would take four hours as the road was a good one, skirting the coast of the English Channel for almost its entire length.

O'Connell, who hadn't been outside the house for several weeks, was seated in the centre of the main seat, facing the front. To his right sat his son Dan. Father Miley was on his left, close to his good ear should words of spiritual consolation be needed. Duggan placed himself in the fly-seat, his back to the horses and looking directly into O'Connell's eye. Of late the Liberator had felt the need to see his manservant at all times. In the small space of the carriage the four men were close enough to feel each other's breath. They coughed together from the dust that rose from the green leather upholstery as they sat down and moved themselves into the positions they felt most comfortable.

Although he was wrapped up in his travelling rugs the hood of O'Connell's carriage was drawn over in case of rain. The only ventilation came from a slit at the front of the carriage space through which they could communicate with the coachman. Father Miley gave the command and they left to a brave and hopeful cheer from the small group of the town's Irish inhabitants who had come to see their hero off. At street corners, in little knots, people pointed to the carriage as it passed. Many of them crossed themselves to show their religion and nationality. Then, quickly, the town was left behind. The sea air which seeped into the carriage through its cracks and crevices and the rocking of the carriage springs made O'Connell drowsy.

To the right, as the horses quickened their pace in the open country, stood the English Channel and to the left the rolling hills of Sussex. The road ran just a few feet above the level of the shore with good views to either side.

Back in that drowsy state, which he now inhabited for a large part of his waking hours, the landscape, for O'Connell, took on new shapes. The flat stretch of the channel became the great expanse of the Atlantic Ocean. The meek waves that surrendered themselves to the gently-sloping beaches changed to mighty grey-green breakers attacking the giant stacks and cliffs of Kerry. To the left the modest hillsides, clad in green pastures, donned heather and furze and trebled in height and steepness. Meandering English streams turned to foaming Irish torrents. The ordered streets and houses of Winchelsea and Rye with their neat shops and tidy footpaths suddenly transformed themselves to Cahirciveen and Waterville where sheep in phantom flocks scurried their way to market.

Fortunately, all four men were inside the coach and separated from the driver who sat outside and in front of them. No stranger was present to hear the Liberator of Ireland mistake Dungeness for Doulus Head. No enemy saw him point out the immense stacks of the Skelligs where, in truth, the seascape was entirely featureless.

Then, a fierce *"View Halloo-ooo"* erupted from the great man's mouth. His face was flushed with the excitement of the chase. "Old Drummer's got the scent," he cried. He stared, and the scarlet of the huntsmen came into focus. Dawn broke on the hills above Darrynane and his beagles surged into action after a mountain hare. He was young now, charging on foot over terrain no horse could cope with, clearing a stone wall with ease. His senses were aroused to the point where the coats of the beaglers shone like crimson fire; the hillsides turned from misty indistinction to a sharpness of focus that took the breath away.

The yelping of the hounds, once distant in the ear now became like the beating of the voodoo drums young Morgan had spoken of in his tales of the Caribs of the Americas. The smell of every wild flower, every blade of grass and sod of turf shot to his nose. It was as if through some miraculous transfer the senses of the hounds had been installed in his human frame.

Now the hare would dart uphill with hounds almost on her tail. Now she would stop in her tracks to make the dogs collide against each other. She would force them to turn a full circle and career downhill. She would make for the shelter of the yellow furze, which for an instant blazed into flame as the sun emerged from the clouds.

Greener slopes soon replaced the high mountainside. The rock-strewn cascades of peat-brown water gave way to the blue expanse of the ocean below. There on the shore, nestling in a copse, stood the limewashed walls of Darrynane House.

Young Dan and Father Miley and Duggan heard O'Connell's shouts of encouragement in English and Irish to his fellow hunters. "Go on there, my lovely hounds. *Ar aghaidh, ar aghaidh libh go tapaidh!*" He let out little whoops of savage delight as the spectral hounds finally trapped the shrieking hare and tore its life away, as a brutal highwayman would snatch a lady's purse.

Then silence. But he was still on that Kerry mountainside, dining now and joking with his friends while the postman arrived to the stone wall where the hunters quaffed their cider and ate their pies. Letters from Bolivar, the other Liberator in South America; the newspapers from Dublin, London and Paris, all briefly perused.

A grin spread across O'Connell's face while, in his horrid reverie, he recounted one of his *bons mots*. He always liked to recount them, for he was vain about the sharpness of his wit. His mind brought him back to the day when verbal swords were crossed with Tadhg a' Bhata (Ted of The Staff), a wild mountainy man. Tadhg was renowned for using his stout wooden staff to great effect at faction fights at the fairs of Cahirciveen, and fancied himself as a great breeder of beagles.

"Liberator, I have a murdering new beagle now, the killingest slaughteringest dog that ever followed a hare in Uíbh Ráthach. I wish you could see him now but you won't let any dogs but your own hunt with you," said Tadhg.

"And what name do you give this killing dog of yours?" asked O'Connell.

"I have two names for him," said Tadhg a' Bhata, "Savage and Cannibal."

"Oh, ho! Tadhg!" said O'Connell, "Are you not the extravagant one in these bad days to have two names for one dog? Could you not have kept one of those names for yourself?"

And then the sound of the beaters driving another hare from the heather and a great *"Hallooo"* again from O'Connell, so loud this time the coachman heard, and had to hold the horses back from bolting.

And the Liberator of Ireland, travelling between Littleton-on-sea and Dymchurch, was running through the hills of south-west Kerry once again. Another hare was there to be caught, visitors from Britain and the Continent to be entertained and local poachers and mountain men to be put in their place.

After the hunt it was to Darrynane and his big lead-lined bath, the stove-heated water melting the salts into foam to dissolve the aches and pains of hours in the field. It had been a great show by his hounds, the best without doubt in the two kingdoms and he boomed a sudden and mighty:

*"Tantum ergo Sacramentum, veneremur cernui*

*Et antiquum documentum, novo cedat ritui."*

And all that young Dan and Father Miley and Duggan could do was laugh aloud with embarrassment. The laughter brought the Liberator to his drawing-room, refreshed from his bath and in form for an Armagnac brought into Darrynane's own cove in the darkness of the previous night, almost under the noses of the excise men. The sight of his rambling house satisfied him. A fine drawing-room with windows on three sides of the first floor the better to appreciate the stunning views. The dining-room was directly below on the ground floor, furnished with good sofas bought at the auction of the estate of Lord Clare, that same Black Jack Fitzgibbon, architect of the Act of Union, whose funeral car had been pelted with dead cats by the citizenry of Dublin. These sofas had seen high Orange rites, he often mused, as he set about to undo the Union in the final years of his life.

The hunt and the early supper which invariably followed, with decent claret and a selection of smuggled brandies, had always relaxed O'Connell and eased his cares.

* * *

O'Connell woke refreshed next morning, his thoughts rational, his mind firmly in the present. He said his prayers methodically and his appetite returned. He remembered nothing of his journey to the past on the previous day; his companions thanked God his insanity appeared to have gone. The sea journey would be short: two and a half-hours on the *Prince Ernest* to Boulogne and a suite of rooms there in the Hotel des Bains. At the quayside, where his many friends and colleagues from London had come to bid him farewell, O'Connell's mind was sharp.

He brushed aside all those whose adieus showed the slightest touch of sentiment and with Father Miley, young Dan and Duggan, boarded the steamer in time for a copious lunch washed down with good English cider.

By the time the meal had finished the *Prince Ernest* was at sea, the chalk cliffs of England fading in the distance, their French counterparts not yet visible. On deck the sea air seemed to invigorate him further. There he met Mr Gully, the former Member for Pontefract, and they spent some time in conversation until the faint outline of the French coast came into view.

The vague form on the horizon made him feel uneasy. It had been more than twenty years since he had visited France and the very thought of the country bothered him. France brought too many uncomfortable memories. There was that visit to his uncle General Count Daniel O'Connell, in his Paris quarters. The old man, mutilated in mind and body by his military exploits, was a firm and staunch believer in the divine right of kings. He had tried to convince O'Connell to drop his democratic notions. It would be better, he argued, to concentrate on gaining as much income as possible. The old man had laid down the law on these matters, clutching his wounds almost absently from time to time. O'Connell was forced to listen, for he needed money.

The General had scratched what remained of his right ear, the victim of an English bullet at the siege of Gibraltar. O'Connell had simply sat without speaking and with no intention of doing as he was told.

They were so different, so mercenary, that earlier generation of O'Connells. Uncle Maurice had earned himself the nickname "Hunting Cap," for his refusal to pay the tax on gentlemen's hats. He would turn up, even for important social occasions, grinning from under the peak of his velvet cap. He had a shrewd head for business, and gathered his rents with efficiency. He smuggled in good claret and brandy from Bordeaux that helped him make not only money but influential friends as well. He even kept a special eye to the shore for flotsam and jetsam that might help him turn a penny or two.

Maurice extended the house at Darrynane, making it

large and comfortable if not architecturally elegant. He was in such deadly earnest about accounting for every farthing spent or gained that when he died in 1820 he had £50,000 pounds cash in hand and was perhaps the richest man in the county.

It was Uncle Maurice's French money which gave O'Connell a comfortable life, though. The old man died childless at ninety-seven. He left Daniel the house and lands in Darrynane and about £15,000. O'Connell, thanks to the "brandy money" was, for a short time at least, free from the debts which had dogged him for most of his life.

The old General too had a head for business. For a small fee he would arrange commissions in the French and Austrian services for the young Catholic gentlemen of Cork and Kerry. The English authorities ignored this, for the young men might otherwise have been a threat to society with their high spirits unharnessed. And, for the General, money was more important than rank. He dropped his status of General in France for that of Colonel in Britain where the pay was better. Not much of this ability to spy out financial opportunities, to earn and save and prosper, seemed to have been passed on to the next generation.

France too had been the place of O'Connell's schooling and he gained no solace when thoughts brought him back to St Omer where he learned the classics and where the principal, Doctor Stapleton, had singled him out as one "destined to make a remarkable figure in society."

Douai, where he later moved, was worse still. The educational standards were higher there but the quality and, more importantly for a young man, the quantity of the food barely enough for survival. He had been a young lad out from Kerry, where visits to Tralee had been the main experience of urban life, and found himself overwhelmed by the size of the French towns. His very being had cried out for the solitude of his mountains and the hunting of his hares.

There had been bloodshed in those days of revolution. From Douai the artillery fire at the battle of Jemappes could be clearly heard. And the local populace had a pent-up hatred for the staff and pupils of the "English School". O'Connell and his classmates were soon assaulted verbally on the streets as "young Jesuit pups."

His entire upbringing had placed him on the Royalist side against the revolutionaries. He was not as firm a monarchist as the General, of course, but some of it had rubbed off on him. Most certainly a strong Catholic, his faith, for him, meant not only the means by which he would reach the Kingdom of Heaven but also the mark which distinguished him and his people from their oppressors. That the French could regard his church as an oppressor itself astonished him. Those who jeered and teased and threatened the Douai students he regarded simply as a beastly mob.

In those revolutionary days he and his brother Maurice had been forced to flee the country, wearing for their own protection large tricolour cockades. The cockades marked them out as revolutionaries but they threw them into the sea as soon as their ship had lifted its anchor at Calais. On that ship he was disgusted to hear two young Irishmen support the revolution. They had even paid money, they boasted, to bribe members of the mob to allow them gain a front-row place for the execution of the King. A crowd gathered around them to hear their vivid description of the bloody events and one of the young men took a piece of white cloth from his pocket, which had been stained by the King's blood. It was, he said laughingly, his "holy relic".

Less than ten years later O'Connell, then a young barrister, saw these lads, John and Henry Sheares, themselves taken to the scaffold in Dublin as republicans and traitors to the King. He felt no sympathy for them.

He was rescued from yet another French disaster more than a quarter of a century later by his inheritance from Hunting Cap.

Almost ruined by debt and financial miscalculations he had decided – wrongly as in all his dealings with money – that the cost of living in France would be considerably lower than in Ireland. So he shipped his family off to live in Pau and followed the legal circuit as a barrister at home. He planned to rent out his mansion in Merrion Square to balance the books, once and for all.

It didn't work, of course. All that France gave him then was a dreadful wrench to his heart. He pined for his dear wife Mary, the sole font of common sense in the O'Connell household. He sorely missed his children. He became a most dreadful bore in the presence of his fellow attorneys. On the bibulous Munster Circuit the maudlin outpourings of a sentimental father bewailing his misfortunes were not appreciated.

He had written to Mary almost every single day during her absence, inquiring after each of the children by name, especially for his "saucy Kate" and his poor little "spoiled Daniel", the youngest of the brood. He had written too, of course, to any relative he could touch for money. But the funds were running dry and he was even reproached by his brother James for his plans to move the family from France to England.

"*In the course of a few months,*" James wrote, "*they move from Dublin to Pau, from that to Tours, now they are in the most expensive part of Paris and will wind up by fixing their residence in England, the dearest country in Europe to live in."*

All the while Hunting Cap, from whom he knew he would inherit Darrynane and a portion of the estate, tenaciously clung to life before expiring three years short of his hundredth birthday. The death and the inheritance came just in time to save O'Connell from bankruptcy.

In the meantime he had to put up with the wagging finger of the General. The old man had sat in his Paris apartment with the Creole widow he had brought back from the West Indies, and lectured him on extravagance.

He disliked the French also because of what he thought of as their bombast, their false promises and their vanity; qualities with which, his critics would say, he himself was endowed in abundance.

When he thought of his French "supporters" he was enraged. Every decent and intelligent Frenchman like Montalembert was more than cancelled out by inflated, long-winded and pompous blockheads. Well-intended French aid was annulled by those whose support for Repeal stemmed from a hatred of England's financial dominance of Europe. It was hindered by those who did not care a whit for Ireland or its people, even now as they starved to death in their tens of thousands.

Above all there was Ledru Rollin and his interminable dinners where he spoke for Ireland's cause.

"Gentlemen," he would say as the Muscadet was poured to accompany the Varennes oysters, "drink to Ireland, a country where in the most melancholy manner the miseries of a protectorate are personified. We drink to that land which nature has made so fair and so fruitful, but which despotism has laid hold of for the advantage of a privileged few – to Ireland, so admirable for its resignation and manly energy – sacrificed as it has been to foreign interests!"

And when the Sancerre came with the turtle soup, he would be off with: "We drink to the freedom of its oppressed religion – to the blood of its martyrs from which, thank God, a race of patriots has arisen. We drink to the people who suffer with her and for her and to that cause which is in our estimation holy!"

With the Meursault and the salmon of the Loire he would agitate himself and his guests with: "Yes, gentlemen, we drink to Ireland at whose name the secret sympathies of all nations are excited. Hear you not now the noble accents, which have just been uttered at the other side of the sea? They are the accents of republicanism in another hemisphere, which the American-Irish address to the generosity of France. They invoke her glorious history – her impassioned vows in favour of heroic Poland – Greece liberated by her arms – the liberty of the New World established by her courageous efforts."

And the claret with the goose or truffled turkey would warm his oratory further. "Let England know that if she attempts to overcome legitimate rights by violent and coercive measures, France is ready to lend to an oppressed people in their decisive struggle experienced heads, valiant hearts and sturdy arms. Let her remember that such causes led to the independence of the New World and that the simple citizens, the courageous volunteers of America, won at the sword's point that liberty which they maintain and which I trust they will maintain to the world's end!"

By the time the Burgundy came to add savour to the array of cheeses, Roquefort always at their head, passions would be further aroused. The attendance of deputies, electors, officers of the national guard, artists and writers, lawyers and men of science were on their feet demanding that Ledru Rollin lead an army of Frenchmen to end the coercion of the Irish peasantry by the British aristocracy.

After the coffee had worn away some of the wine's effects it would be proposed and seconded and voted upon unanimously to send Ledru Rollin to visit Ireland and take up common cause with O'Connell. The next morning when a calm breakfast had dissipated the ardour of the night before, the rallying to the Irish cause from Paris would finally consist of a letter of support from Ledru Rollin addressed to O'Connell in Darrynane. In it he would hint that should all peaceful efforts fail, he could count on the might of France.

To his dinner guests at Darrynane after he had read the letter aloud to them O'Connell remarked: "Some fellows have such an enormous deal of balderdashical vanity about them, that it is not unlikely he only meant to get a little notoriety."

To Ledru Rollin himself, O'Connell replied: "You indeed allude to another contingency in which you may be disposed to be more active in our support. But that is a contingency which we decline to discuss, because we deem it impossible that it should arise, the British government having retracted every menace of illegal force and unjust violence and confining its resistance to our claims – if it shall continue to resist those claims – within ordinary channels of legalised administration."

* * *

Immersed in exasperating memories of France and the French, O'Connell was being bathed in the spray thrown up by the cutting wind and the speed of the steamship knifing its way through the grey-cold waters of the channel.

Young Dan, Father Miley and Duggan each in his turn attempted to draw him away from the rails and indoors to more comfortable surroundings.

Each in his turn was told brusquely to stay away and as the ship entered the harbour at Boulogne the dark figure of the Liberator of Ireland stood at its prow gazing forward. His eyes were fixed on nothing in particular. His three companions stood dutifully about five paces behind him, intent on getting to the warmth of the Hotel Des Bains where they could dry out his sodden clothes and warm him with brandy and bath-water. Only when the gangway was drawn and the large crowd, led by a group of the local Abbés and Curés, approached it on the dock, did O'Connell straighten his black wig under his top hat and move away from the rails. And his thoughts dwelled on what he had called "rascally France".

## CHAPTER EIGHT

# All Paris Turns Out to Meet Us

I was not prepared for Paris. All through our journey in the wretched towns of the north the innkeepers had treated us dismally. Our baggage had been searched as though we were criminals. Readying a bath took hours, so stingy were the innkeepers with heating the water. At Montreuil the beds were damp, at Amiens the food, though palatable, was served with an inexcusable gruffness.

But Paris was different. I have never heard so much noise as I heard at the railway station there. The hissing and puffing of the steam engine was much louder than our engines at home. The people were chattering away on the platform waiting for their friends to arrive and the passengers were pushing through the corridor with their valises, talking and even shouting all the while. The tumult was almost unbearable.

Father Miley said we should wait until things quietened down, but the place got no calmer. The people on the platform, it turned out, were waiting for us.

I saw one man carry a newspaper with the words: *"M. O'Connell à Paris"*, and then the servants of the Count Montalembert arrived and helped us down from the railway carriage, which was much higher from the ground than we are used to in Ireland or England. And the police arrived too and pushed and shoved to force a passage for us to the station's entrance. I could not believe that Mr O'Connell was so popular or so renowned in this country, especially after the reception he had received in the paltry little towns to the north. In those places his scorn for France seemed to be returned even by innkeepers who should have been respectful to a man of his rank. But here in Paris the men and women of quality (I judged them by their dress for want of a knowledge as to their personages) heaved and pushed like beggars or hawkers on a Dublin street, all to get a glance at Mr O'Connell or a word in his ear. All the while he was being helped down the platform, Mr Dan holding him up on one side and Father Miley on the other, they still heaved and shoved in their excitement.

Count Montalembert's servants helped me take care of the baggage. It took the best part of a quarter of an hour to reach the end of the platform, so thick was the crowd which moved along with us and so slow and weak was Mr O'Connell's gait. At the station's entrance stood our carriage, a wonderful affair if ever there was one. The leathers polished to a spanking shine, the brasses of the doors resplendent against the jet black of the carriage work, the Count's coat of arms emblazoned on the side, the four horses perfectly groomed, their muscles straining as they tensed themselves for the coachman's command.

As we readied Mr O'Connell for the lift to the carriage steps a woman of quality broke through the crowd to greet him. I do not know what she said. What struck me, though, was Mr O'Connell's response.

He had always been courteous and attentive to ladies, even to the ladies of his enemies in London. This woman, dressed in the highest fashion of the day, was surely trying to show her friendship. But he looked through her as though he did not see her. His eyes were empty of recognition and his lips bore no greeting. He just stared blankly into the distance.

Mr O'Connell was on the verge, I knew then, of taking one of his turns. We got him on board quickly. Mr Dan apologised to the lady, saying his father was tired from the journey. Father Miley opened the door, the Montalembert servants helped me hoist him up the steps and onto the seat.

My God, the smell was awful. I can remember it to this day. He had dirtied himself again and we closed the door before he started to sing:

"*Dies irae, Dies illa,*
*Solvet saeclum in favilla . . .*
*Tuba mirum spargens sonum*
*In sepulchra regionum.*"

It was the hymn of the dead, of the Day of Judgment, the song of the last trumpet. The sound and the stench had us disquieted completely, especially myself as I was the one who, once more, would have to clean him when the hotel was reached.

It seemed hours before the coachman cracked his whip and we were away. As we moved off other carriages started too, scores of them, all fine equipages worthy of the high status of their owners. They filed in behind ours, maybe fifty of them and, God forgive me, all I could think of was that it was Mr O'Connell's funeral and him still alive. His oft-repeated command rang once again in my ears: "Duggan," he had said, "you are the only one I can trust. Listen to me carefully, Duggan. Make sure they do not bury me until I am dead."

I looked him in the face but he did not see me. He just stared ahead, the smile of a simpleton on the face of a man whose mind was once the greatest, the most admired, in the Kingdoms of Ireland and England and, as I saw for the first time, the Kingdom of France as well.

He smiled his simple smile and sang his song of doom. His once-great voice was a cracked whisper now, but it carried the tune right enough. The O'Connells always had music in them. They were known for that in all of Kerry.

The streets in Paris are broader than in London with fine buildings on either side and straight as an arrow allowing for a quickness of travel most necessary in a city of such great size. We reached a huge square, completely paved and without as much as a tree to adorn it. There was a large Egyptian obelisk in its middle and Father Miley blessed himself and us all as we passed it. He told me it was here that the King and the priests and bishops had their heads severed from their bodies not fifty years ago by the revolutionaries.

Close by the square was the Rue de Rivoli, a wondrous street where the Hotel Windsor was situated. Along one side was a great public garden: the Tuileries, Father Miley told us it was called. Along the entire length of the other side, the first floors of all the buildings extended over the footpath supported by strong stone pillars to form a long arcade. Thus, even on the rainiest of days one could walk for almost a mile without the least risk of being drenched. We pulled up at the Windsor to find the entire staff of the hotel ranged out across the entrance hall. The maids were in their white lace and black dresses, the butlers in long frock coats trimmed with green velvet, the footmen in shining high boots. In front of the receiving line stood the proprietor and the manager who immediately stepped out across the marble floor to greet us. Under no circumstances, we were told, would there be a search of the baggage of such an illustrious personage and his entourage. The best suite of rooms had been readied at no extra cost and an extra-large drawing-room had been made available in which to receive the large numbers of people who had left their visiting cards.

Mr O'Connell fortunately had quieted down and the simpleton look had gone from his face. He shook the proprietor's hand but said nothing. Father Miley gave a short address in the French, saying that the Liberator was exhausted from his travels and unable to thank them or to wish them well but that his feelings were of gratitude and of benevolence towards them.

We were taken up a broad staircase which, like the hall, was of mottled marble, with great pillars at either side. Our rooms were as comfortable and as impressive as had been described to us and upon our arrival a team of porters arrived with great vessels of steaming water, salts, soap and unguents to bring Mr O'Connell around from the tiredness of his journeying.

With the help of the hotel servants, I placed Mr O'Connell in the bath and washed and oiled him as best I could. I am not a man of medicine of course, but I have noticed before and noticed again on this occasion, that the warmth of the water transferred to the flesh and bone brought about a resuscitation of Mr O'Connell's spirits. The coldness of the day when working its way to the bone brought about an altogether opposite result.

He called for luncheon to be served and this was brought to us in our own suite of rooms very quickly indeed. For the first time in many years I was given the same meal as those I served, not below in the kitchens but in our own suite of rooms.

I did, of course, dine separately from Mr O'Connell, Mr Dan and Father Miley, at a separate table and in a separate corner. The hotel servants even brought me a small carafe of wine and one of water to accompany a meal of five full courses. I cast my mind back to the starvation that was destroying Ireland and weighing so heavily upon the mind and the sensibilities of Mr O'Connell. He slept most of the afternoon while Father Miley and Mr Dan dealt with the visiting cards of all those who wished to pay their respects. It was decided that no visits would be taken today and that tomorrow would be a day of relaxation. After Father Miley had said Mass on Sunday in the main room, a particular privilege granted expressly by His Holiness, we would take luncheon and then receive Count Montalembert and the members of the French Catholic committee at two o'clock in the afternoon. An invitation to dine with the British Ambassador was declined due to the weakness of Mr O'Connell's constitution.

I was sent to the entrance hall as Mr O'Connell's man to meet the men of those who had sent him their compliments. I explained to them his illness and his inability to receive gentlemen individually but of his intent to meet as many of the prominent people as could attend on Sunday.

Father Miley took all these decisions. He studied each visiting card personally, joined his hands in an arch under his chin as he made his decision on whether or not to exclude this Vicomte or that Baron from the presence of the

Liberator. He did all this with a complete lack of expression, grimacing only when Mr Dan's stomach rumbled. He did not say a word to Mr Dan, mind you, but the look he gave him indicated that had he the choice, he would exclude even the Liberator's son from the list of those invited.

We all slept well that night, helped no doubt by the length of our journey and the genuine excitement of the fullest and most occupied day of our travels so far.

On Saturday morning there was a large number of people in the courtyard, perhaps a hundred, and policemen kept them from entering the hotel or from blocking the doorway. I went out to take the air down the long arcades of the Rue de Rivoli. There the nobility and gentry of the city promenaded with great formality. The gentlemen were dressed in what they perceived to be the English style, in top hats and tailed coats. The ladies, with their parasols and their lap-dogs, strolled a pace behind while the servants lagged several paces further behind. It drizzled but because of the arcades no rainwear was needed. The thought struck me that the arcaded street had been constructed not as an example of the most advanced architecture but in order to allow the people of quality desport themselves in their best attire and thus to make great impressions upon each other.

My reverie was interrupted by the call of my name. I heard a refined woman's voice ask "Why, it is surely Duggan, Mr O'Connell's man, is it not?" There, on the Rue de Rivoli, so far away from home, were the Misses Conyngham who had frequently attended evenings at Merrion Square and were a great support during the period after the untimely death of Mrs O'Connell.

They inquired after Mr O'Connell and asked to see him. I explained that people were being kept away but that I was sure they would be received as friends and moreover as Irish people, for our party had not seen anyone from Ireland since we had departed from Folkestone five days earlier. We went back to the hotel together and at my bidding they were given entry, a fact which made me feel an importance above my station. I bade them to remain in the anteroom of our suite until I ascertained when Mr O'Connell would be available to receive them.

I opened the door of the suite a little and the first thing I noticed was a flash of scarlet in the corner of the room. Mr O'Connell was seated at table in black; Mr Dan sat in black too, as did Father Miley and four strange priests attired in the French style. In their midst sat a man clad from head to toe in brilliant crimson. I allowed the Misses Conyngham to peek in. They recognised him instantly and informed me that he was His Eminence Cardinal Affret, the Archbishop of Paris, the primate of France, the chief prelate of that country known throughout the World as "The Daughter of the Church."

I had not seen a cardinal before, as no archbishop in Ireland had yet attained that rank. Mr O'Connell, I am sure, had met many cardinals in his day but there was no doubt that the honour of this visit brightened his spirits. The company of important people had always, I had noticed, increased his own sense of importance and put him in excellent humour. But in these latter times the good humour lasted only as long as his constitution could bear it.

The Misses Conyngham and I removed to the foyer of the hotel until we saw Cardinal Affret depart to his carriage. I then ventured to bring them to Mr O'Connell. When they arrived, an effusion of good spirits and warmth of feeling overcame him. He sat talking with them for quite some time after I retired into the background. He smiled frequently, even laughed on occasion, his face showing an agitation and a liveliness that I had not seen for a year at least. When the ladies departed Father Miley called me aside and chided me most severely for having brought them to Mr O'Connell without asking permission.

I can see the tips of his fingers touching each other as he searched for the most precisely demeaning words with which to chide me. He seemed intent on showing me that it was he, and no one else, who was in charge of this venture to Rome. In that he succeeded most clearly.

Mr Dan tried to come to my aid. "He meant well," he told Father Miley, "and didn't their visit cheer my father up a great deal? I haven't seen him so happy in weeks."

"The care of your father's body and of his immortal soul has been placed in my hands," Father Miley said as he formed that arch once more with his fingers. "It would be remiss of me if I were not to take my duties in the most serious manner possible. You are a young man, Mr Dan, and you have grown up with Duggan. That may have led you to a familiarity that is unpardonable.

"You must remember, you must remember always, that he is a servant and you are his master. You should remember too that you are Mr O'Connell's youngest son, and that I, as his adviser, will make the proper decisions in the course of his journey to Rome."

Father Miley and Mr Dan dined in silence but the visitors had brought life and vitality to Mr O'Connell. He ate well enough and drank even a glass of red wine before the arrival of Doctor Chomel, the physician to the King, and his colleague Doctor Oliffe.

It was my duty to prepare Mr O'Connell for their

examination. I brought in the lavatory equipment as they waited for his bowels to move and for him to pass water. I then cleaned him and washed him. I brought him his best poplin dressing-gown and dressed him in it and helped him to the bed and announced to the doctors that the Liberator was ready for inspection.

The French physicians behaved in almost precisely the same manner as their English colleagues. They minutely examined the stools and the water Mr O'Connell had passed. They investigated them and poked through them with their little batons as though Mr O'Connell's waste contained great and important secrets. They sniffed and swirled at the effluence of a man greater than they and made notes in their little pads now and then in the Latin tongue for fear someone not of their lodge might understand their meaning.

Doctor Chomel placed a leech to the Liberator's temple, for a doctor without a leech would make little mark on those who watched. Doctor Oliffe felt the pulse and observed the breathing and touched and watched the different parts of Mr O'Connell's body.

Mr O'Connell, for his part, made remarks across the room to me. It was always his wont to mock the physicians who attended him.

"I prefer the small leeches to the big ones, for they suck one's blood and do nothing else. Most assuredly they do not talk nor give their opinions nor send their bills as the big leeches do." He said this to me in what was meant to be a shout but it emanated as the broken whisper to which we had all become accustomed.

When all the sniffing and the swirling and the watching and the feeling had been done, the King's doctors emerged to announce their verdict to Mr Dan and Father Miley. Mr

O'Connell, the main personage of the entire affair, was not informed and neither, directly, was I. But I was able to move to the drawing-room, there to listen discreetly from a distance. It was my intention to return to tell my master, who had requested me to keep him informed. He was after all the person to whom I was most obliged.

Doctor Chomel and Doctor Oliffe approached Mr Dan and Father Miley and placed on the table of the drawing-room a tiny phial of blood from the leech, a small bottle of urine and a little cake of excrement, to emphasise the scientific nature of their profession.

His English being better than his colleague's, Doctor Chomel pronounced the verdict. He was convinced of the certainty of Mr O'Connell's recovery. Not only would he live for a number of years more but he would be capable of returning to the political leadership of his nation and continue his struggle for Repeal. All that would be needed, they said, was to ensure that the diarrhoea, which constantly weakened his constitution, be kept under control.

I felt distinctly that much of what the doctors said was mentioned in order to show off their knowledge of Mr O'Connell's political activities rather than in any assuredness in their predictions.

The consultation over, I retired to his bedroom and as instructed informed him of the prognosis, at which he at once laughed and sighed. At the same time he expressed anger and mirth, good humour and despair. "Charlatans the lot of them with their bleedings and their pisspots. What comes out of a man interests them more than what happens inside him and when they are incapable of knowing what will happen they invariably try to please."

"Mr O'Connell," and here he made a whining accent to

portray the subservience of the doctors, "will survive for many a long year and will once again lead his country and will bring them their own parliament to College Green once more." And then in his own broken voice though in a deeper whisper than usual: "A parliament is not what they need now, but the fill of their bellies. I might get them a parliament but no one alive to sit in it." And then a whisper: Doctor McCabe in Hastings was the honest one. He warned me of my lack of strength and told me to prepare myself spiritually for my end. He did tell me this truly and he did not tell anyone else and I entreat you in particular not to mention a single word of this to Mr Dan. But I want you to know that I myself know that the end of my days is near."

The agitation tired him and he fell asleep, his countenance still bearing a trace of his anger and frustration. But he slept and I was glad of it for it permitted me to sleep too and sleep was needed for the important day to come. And it was a relief to me to know that what I had believed to be my darkest secret was, all the while, shared by my master.

\* \* \*

On Sunday morning Father Miley said Mass. Mr Dan and I were the servers. Mr O'Connell watched but barely listened. He occasionally picked up a response, usually the most morbid. *"Dona eis requiem"* and *"Domine non sum dignus"* and above all chanting the *"Stabat Mater Dolorosa"* at odd and inappropriate times to the embarrassment of us all.

He appeared to lose the run of himself mainly when those he knew well were around him. The presence of a stranger for some reason helped him keep a rein on the excesses of temper which his illness forced upon him.

Luncheon was remarkable in quality and quantity. To begin, there were raw vegetables and pressed meats and olives. Then a broth, light but delicious in its flavour, and a small dish of perch, the taste of which I had not experienced before. There was then turkey studded with truffles, and potatoes cooked with cream and onions, which brought tears to all our eyes; to my eyes in my corner of the room and to the eyes of Mr O'Connell and Mr Dan and Father Miley at the main table. The potatoes were perfect in their firmness and without blemish in their colour and they were sprinkled with green herbs, like the grass of our own land under which no sound potatoes now grew. And I felt the guilt of eating well while others starved and I felt grateful that I ate well and did not starve with them.

The Mass and luncheon over, we waited for the great event of the day, the arrival of the members and supporters of the Catholic Committee. The hotel servants and those of the Count Montalembert began their work. Mr O'Connell was placed at a table at the end of the drawing-room, chairs were ranged about in lines for the guests. A young man with a great booming voice took up his position at the door to announce the notables as they arrived.

A frail gentleman redolent of great wealth and nobility arrived at the double doors and Count Montalambert's servant announced him as "Monsieur le Marquis de Barthelemy", then a darker, younger and perhaps even wealthier man judging by his attire, was called out as "Monsieur le Vicomte de Falloux." After that it was the Count Beutrebarbes, Deputy Chappier and Deputy de Rozier and the Marquis de Dampierre. Then came the Messieurs Lenormant and Mauvais of the Institut Francais, Baron de Montigny, a judge of the Royal Court; Vicomte de Bonneuil of the Petition committee, Monsieur Decous and Monsieur Oueillot, editors and proprietors of the newspaper *L'Univers*. Each one as he was called walked up the room, bowed to Mr O'Connell, shook his hand, turned on his heel, walked to a chair and sat down.

Then the Count Montalembert – a man who, I was told, was regarded with equal displeasure by the Church and the state although he belonged to both – began his oration. The church disliked him for he argued against its interference in the State's affairs and the State abhorred him because he spoke against its interference in the affairs of the Church. In this he attracted, in my view, as much displeasure in France as Mr O'Connell did in England.

Mr Dan kept notes of the proceedings which he left in my keeping and which I now use to describe what happened, for he has never asked for his notes to be returned to him.

Here, according to his record, is an account of how Montalembert addressed Mr O'Connell, according him the greatest of tributes and on more than one occasion placing him second only to the Almighty.

"Sir and illustrious friend," he began. "When I had the pleasure of seeing you for the first time sixteen years ago in your castle at Darrynane, the Revolution of July had just taken place and your solicitude was already ardently directed towards the future stability of religion in France."

He had, he said, learned a lot from the Liberator, especially how important it was so keep religion and politics apart and he had brought with him those Frenchmen who had accepted that doctrine. It was quite impressive to hear the Count describe those great men who came gathered in our hotel as Mr O'Connell's pupils and children and to say that the Liberator was their master and their model and their "glorious preceptor." I had not realised the esteem in which he was held by the French and it made me all the more puzzled as to why his esteem for them was so low. Usually he was a man who had a high regard for those who flattered him.

And the count was a great flatterer. Mr O'Connell, he said, was "the man of the age," and that, after God himself, he had done most for the dignity and liberty of mankind and for the freedom of Catholic people and Catholic nations.

And he called Mr O'Connell "the man of all Christendom," and said that when people strove for their religious freedom it was to Mr O'Connell "after God" they were indebted.

"May that thought fortify you," he said. "May it revive you in your infirmities and console you in the affliction with which your patriotic heart is now overwhelmed."

It was clear to me that Mr O'Connell had not taken everything in. He appeared to doze off at times, indeed the length of the speech and the lack of air in the crowded room had almost caused me to doze off myself but for the surprise I felt at the terms used by the speaker. To compare a man, even one of Mr O'Connell's stature, to Our Lord seemed to me to be close to blasphemy.

It was not unusual, I should explain, for Mr O'Connell to appear to be sleeping when he was instead concentrating every fibre of his brain on the subject under discussion. I had seen him in court appear to snooze and the same in parliament but all the while taking everything into his mind.

Rather, on this occasion, it was his demeanour when his eyes were open which betrayed his lack of comprehension. The faintest trace of that simpleton look crossed his visage from time to time; but when the oration, all of it in the

English, and accented perfectly by the Count, was ended Mr O'Connell had gathered his wits about him sufficiently enough to say: "Gentleman, sickness and emotion close my mouth. I would require the eloquence of your president to express to you all my gratitude. But it is impossible for me to say what I feel. Know simply that I regard this demonstration on your part as one of the most significant events of my life."

This Mr O'Connell accompanied with a wave of the hand, a mere flick, but it was as though all his physical strength had been gathered to dismiss the company. I noticed something small falling to the ground as he did so.

The French notables recognised his weakness and they left, whispering their concern for his health to each other as they did so. I went to him and saw on the floor Father Miley's black glove, sodden with Mr O'Connell's perspiration.

He spent the rest of the day on his couch, morosely staring out to the street and the Tuileries gardens until it was time for supper: a light broth and some bread so as not to disturb his stomach again. If Doctor Chomel and Doctor Oliffe were right about anything it was that his stomach was not to be disturbed. This brought weakness upon him and affected the rest of his constitution, his heart and his lungs and most especially his brain, the congestion of which was the main cause of his infirmity. Almost all the doctors had agreed on this.

That evening he slept as well as he had done at any time since the head pains began to afflict him in Darrynane almost a year back.

On Monday Father Miley and Mr Dan decided to allow Mr O'Connell rest for most of the day. They fed him little in order to heal the diarrhoea so that by the time we were ready to depart to the train station for Orleans his bowels would not be loose and no embarrassment would be caused to those who came to bid him adieu.

By early in the afternoon a very large crowd had come together in the courtyard of the Hotel, perhaps three hundred or so, all of them from the higher orders of society. Count de Montalembert had once again made his coach and his servants ready for us. The proprietor and manager came up to pay their respects to Mr O'Connell and we proceeded through the crowded courtyard to our coach. Mr O'Connell did not appear to notice the crowd but seemed to recognise Monsieur Berryer whose hand he clutched weakly and into whose face he gazed blankly. M Berryer spoke to him briefly in French before Mr O'Connell's hand fell from that of his admirer's and we approached the street.

The coach was done up very smartly again but what struck me this time was the number of beautiful young ladies, exceptionally well-dressed in the latest and most expensive fashions for which this city is noted. Each one had a tear in her eye for Mr O'Connell.

For his part, he straightened himself to his full height, raised his cap, was helped into the carriage and we were gone.

# CHAPTER NINE

## O'Connell's Way with Women

Are you weeping yet for the mighty O'Connell? Have you fallen into a state of uncontrollable grief at the fate of the Liberator, the great saviour of Ireland? Does it distress you to see a great man reduced to a babbling idiot?

I can tell you it doesn't distress me in the slightest. I want you to hear my story, to know how he ruined my life and the life of our son. I want you to see what an evil swine he is and I don't care if I destroy what's left of my own reputation in doing so. Daniel O'Connell was a depraved brute. You all know that he was a cheat and a liar as far as his money, and other people's money, was concerned. You know that he sponged first on his relatives, then on his friends and finally on the near-destitute people of Ireland.

You have heard of his behaviour with women. Yes, yes, of course you have heard, the whole world has heard that a stone could not be thrown in Dublin without hitting one of his bastards. And still you admire him to the point of adoration? Well, I hope to God my story will change your mind.

You might believe poor Duggan, another of his dupes, when he says that Daniel O'Connell had a "way with women"? He had his way with me so he did, and he didn't give a damn about the consequences. I had to look after our son on my own, apart from the odd pittance he threw my way to keep me quiet. I hope to God the poxy bastard suffered on that journey from Paris. I hope to Jesus he died roaring. I hope his pain was unbearable. If it was, he deserved every bit of it. Those fine ladies who went to see him off from Paris should have spoken to me.

My name is Ellen Courtenay. Daniel O'Connell raped me in his own home in Merrion Square. He is the father of my son Henry O'Connell, but won't admit it. His status as a gentleman and a great politician, if you don't mind, wouldn't allow him to tell the truth. It wouldn't permit him to say that he took advantage of a young girl of fifteen just come up to Dublin from the provinces. And an orphan girl at that. He couldn't have found a weaker victim.

Listen to what I have to say and you'll see another side of the "Great Liberator of Ireland". He might have believed in freedom for "old Ireland" and a "parliament on College Green", but as for freedom for myself and for Henry, he simply didn't care. He simply lied and left us to scratch out our own living.

Only for his political enemies we would have starved. Mr Peel and his friends encouraged me to publish a pamphlet denouncing O'Connell for the cowardly liar he was. And yes, I did accept money from the Tories. How else was I to feed and clothe Henry and myself? I make no excuses at all for taking the money and I don't see why I should. If a "great man" left you in poverty would you not take money from his enemies?

Revenge is sweet, that's what they say, isn't it? I can tell you that there has been little sweetness in my life – other than my son – and the revenge I have had against his father.

O'Connell destroyed my life. I lived in poverty. I did time in the Fleet Prison in London for debt. I worked as an actress in London and Paris. I taught in a school. I would have done anything – short of whoring – in order to keep Henry from starving. But O'Connell's gang called me a whore anyway. "Patriots" they called themselves, God bless the mark.

I was just fifteen when O'Connell raped me. I came to Dublin in that fateful year of 1817, I saw him the way most Irish people did. I believed all the talk of his greatness and of his wonderful powers of persuasion in the courts and his legal battles for the poor and those badly done by. That's why I went to his house. He was my last hope. I left Cork to seek out O'Connell after my uncle and his family had challenged my father's will. I was sure that O'Connell was the one man in Ireland who could see that I would rightly gain my inheritance.

And I have a letter here that proves I am not the loose woman O'Connell's crew would have you believe. It is a testimonial from the Bishop of Cork himself. *The bearer, Miss E Courtenay, of the North Parish in the City of Cork, has always conducted herself in an edifying manner. I feel a pleasure in being able to bear testimony to the excellence of her moral character.* It is signed *John Murphy, RC Bishop, March, 1817.*

Now I'll tell you something about Daniel O'Connell's moral character.

When I came from Cork to seek his help I first went to

the Law Library in the Four Courts. Every one of the hundreds of people there seemed to be looking for O'Connell. I simply could not even get a note to him to ask for his help.

Then I set out to wait upon him at his mansion at Number 30 Merrion Square, where there were none of his agents and clerks to deter me from meeting him.

After a day or two I managed to be at Merrion Square when he arrived from the courts. I stopped him on the footpath, I was that desperate. I explained my legal problems to him and he expressed his sympathy for my plight. He was kind and courteous and explained that he would need more information before he could proceed on my behalf.

I set out to gather as much information as I could. When a new detail was discovered I would go to Merrion Square to inform him. He had a small office there, in a room on the first floor, in which he met his clients.

At first he was helpful. Then came the flattery. I was, he said, a very pretty young woman. This, all right, I will admit, impressed me at the time. I had never been called a woman before. I had always been regarded as a girl, as someone not grown. It was some time before I noticed his eyes, at each of our meetings, were fixed on my body all the time. Then one day he moved his chair out to my side of his desk to be able, he said, to hear me more clearly against the rattle of the carriages on the street. He sat beside me from the start each time we met after that.

From time to time his leg would press against mine and then he would move it away in an embarrassed manner. Frequently he would stand up – he was a very tall man – and look down at me with the most penetrating of stares.

Then in the summer of 1817, I received a letter from him, couched in the most urgent terms, asking me to come to see him about my case. I went to his house without a worry about what might happen there.

This proved to be the greatest mistake of my life. He took me into his study and it was there that he removed his false veil of nobility and high character.

There was no "my dear Ellen," no "my sweet little woman", this time. He held his hands out as he usually did when meeting me but there was no kiss on the cheek. Instead he overpowered me with his great strength, stripped me of my clothes, forced me to the floor and violently raped me.

Not a word did he speak during this vile act. The only sounds which came from him were snorts and grunts that might just as well have come from a pig. My screams and cries for help went unheard.

After he had spent himself I was left in a stunned condition. I could neither speak nor move. I just lay there on the floor of his study not truly realising what had happened to me. When I came to my senses again and understood what he had done to me I screamed again and again. He just stood above me hitching up his britches, as I lay there mad with pain and horror.

As you will know he was a very big and strong man, a huge man by anyone's standards. I was very much afraid of him. He made me swear that I would see him again, see him again regularly. But he told me that day I would never have to worry about money. His rich Uncle Morgan in Kerry was near ninety, and there would be tens of thousands in his will. I would be "looked after", he said.

I came to his house several times over the next months and each time he used my body for his lust and it was horrible for me to think that he was doing this in his own house, his Dublin mansion where lived his wife and his sons and his young daughters. I beseeched him to advance me a small amount of money, which would pay for my fare by boat and coach to London. There at least my ruination would not be known. After much difficulty and delay he gave me a trifling sum and I set out from Dublin for London in the belief that I was freeing myself from an evil which had imposed itself upon my young life.

In London I found a job with a good Irish and Catholic family who were very kind to me but I was not long there when I discovered that I was carrying the child of Daniel O'Connell. My condition could bring nothing but dishonour on the family I was living with, so I felt then it was imperative upon me to return to Ireland.

I had my baby boy in Dublin, at a midwife's house in Dominick Street. I tried again and again to get him to come and see Henry but he did not even bother to answer my notes. So I went back to London with my child.

I have humiliated myself for my son's sake. I have confronted Mr O'Connell openly in order to discredit him and bring attention to my plight. Each Sunday as he walked from his house on Langham Place to the Spanish Chapel for Mass, I followed him and I heckled him and I brought our son with me in order to cause him the greatest possible shame in front of the people of London. I admit before God that it brought me true pleasure to shame him in his Sunday finery, dressed up like a peacock on his hypocritical way to church in one of the city's most fashionable districts. Heads turned, all right, and stared at the big Irishman who was, in any event, cordially despised by the honest Protestant gentry of our sister island.

*The Times* took up my case, and, I am very glad to say, caused further embarrassment and harm to the Kerry twister.

O'Connell had had the nerve and impudence once to impute immorality to the private life of Lord Lyndhurst. *The Times* put a stop to that and put him firmly into his place. It declared that if he dared invade the privacy of Lord Lyndhurst, "or of any other man, woman or child, that may happen by themselves or their relations to be opposed to him in politics, so surely will we carry the war into his own domiciles at Darrynane and Dublin, and show up the whole brood of O'Connells, young and old."

I really enjoyed reading that article. It shut O'Connell up too, for I read no more of his attacks on Lord Lyndhurst, and I knew that my own actions in decrying him as a scoundrel had played a good part in the game.

That's my story in short. You will agree that it takes the shine off our great hero, won't you?

Finally, may I take this opportunity to solicit from you any monies you can spare to help me in my plight. Although my son is now nearing thirty, the money I have expended upon him over the years has left me in dire straits. Please send what you can to me care of the Editor of *The Satirist* on the Strand in London from whom you can also receive in print a much fuller account of the indignities forced upon me by the member for Kerry, for the price of two shillings and sixpence.

\* \* \*

I am Nell FitzSimon, the wife of Christopher FitzSimon, Barrister, of the City of Dublin and eldest daughter of Daniel O'Connell MP of 30 Merrion Square. This is my honest testament on the despicable allegations made against my father by the London actress Miss Ellen Courtenay. I know my father far better than she does, the sum total of her acquaintance with him being her acts of harassment upon him on the streets of Dublin and London.

Firstly my father was a loving man to me, to my sisters Betsy and Kate and most of all to my mother whose death was, I am sure, hastened by the theatrical performances of Miss Courtenay. Her story is simply full of holes. My father had no "Uncle Morgan" to leave him a fortune. Indeed the Morgan O'Connell of that generation was my father's father; his uncle was Maurice O'Connell of Darrynane, the famous Muiris a' Chaipín who always wore a hunting cap to avoid paying the tax on silk top hats. He was a wealthy man and he did leave my father a lot of money but under no circumstances could my father have spoken of an "Uncle Morgan".

And this very story of his raping her in our house on Merrion Square in the middle of the afternoon is complete nonsense. I can tell you that our house was indeed a substantial one, but not so large that a scream from my father's study would not be heard in every single room from the top-floor bedrooms to the servants' quarters below stairs.

I would have been twelve years old at the time of the alleged incident, my sister Kate ten and my brother Maurice fourteen. We had, as my mother described it, "the run of the house" at that time. We were spirited children, inquisitive to the point of impertinence. "Forward" was the word my father used to describe us and he was not at all being complimentary.

In our chasing through the house we often blundered into his little study. It was on the second floor and not the first as Miss Courtenay claims. We often vexed my father's clients by bursting in unannounced. I remember many of them. But I cannot recall anyone called Courtenay or anyone fitting the description Miss Courtenay gives of herself.

And another point I would like to make: in a pamphlet she published at Mr Peel's instigation, she refers to her baby as "my male child." I am now a mother with my own young children. Some of you who listen to me now will also be mothers. I ask would any of you, as Miss Courtenay did, refer to a son as "my male child"? Could a mother refer to her son in such a clinical way? Of course she could not. Everything I have said so far points to the inevitable conclusion that Miss Courtenay is lying and doing so for money. She admits Mr Peel's involvement but we, in our family, know of others in this shoddy conspiracy. I can tell you too that we know who was behind the attack launched by Miss Courtenay. It was no surprise to us to hear that among her backers was the abominable Mr Henry Hunt, the Member for Preston who worked diligently throughout his parliamentary career to defame my father.

In the tracts published in her name Miss Courtenay goes out of her way to be kind to the worthy, intelligent and excellent gentleman, as she calls him, The Knight of Kerry, Mr Maurice FitzGerald, who ardently supported the Union with Great Britain, which my late father fought so strenuously to repeal. We believe that Mr Peel, Mr Hunt and Mr Maurice FitzGerald were the ones behind these scurrilous accusations.

To our family my father's character is of the utmost importance. He was steadfastly loyal, indeed completely in love with my mother from the time they eloped with each other as a young couple. They were thoroughly devoted to each other, as can be witnessed from their letters to each other.

The Ellen Courtenay affair was a *cause célèbre* at the time. My mother knew about it and her response was to accompany my father on a tour of the midlands of England where she showed him, despite her terribly failing health, every possible affection and poured absolute and total scorn on Miss Courtenay's horrible tale.

Yet the rumours and the tales persisted mainly because the religious, and more especially the political, atmosphere of the time was one of unabated sectarianism. My father's name was not the only one dragged through the mud for political reasons and the imputation of fatherhood to famous and wealthy men was a mere commonplace at that time. Almost invariably these stories were false. Some, I will state, are true. It is sad to relate that my brother Maurice did the family name no good by fathering numerous bastards. The adage about a person not being able to throw a stone in Dublin without "striking a child of O'Connell's" applied as truly to him as it did falsely to my father.

I have here a sheaf of letters written by my mother to my father in and about the time when our house was supposed to have resounded to the screams of the ravished Miss Courtenay.

*On July 14th 1817 she wrote: "I don't think there is such a husband and father as you are and always have been. I think it quite impossible there could, and if the truest and tenderest affection can repay you, believe me that I feel and bear it for you. In truth, my own Dan, I am always at a loss for words to convey to you how I love and doat on you. Many and many a time I exclaim to myself: 'What a happy creature am I! How grateful*

*should I be to Providence for bestowing on me such a husband!'
and so indeed I am."*

He and my mother were deeply in love until her sad and
most untimely death at the age of fifty-eight years having
borne a large and devoted family. I know they loved each
other because I could feel it in their presence, by their
attitude to each other, by the way they unashamedly
hugged and kissed each other in our presence, seeing no
embarrassment in expressing their affection.

And my father was devoted to his children, especially to
his daughters whom he dearly loved and to whom he showed
the strongest and deepest paternal affections. When my
sister Betsy fell prey to the most awful scruples of religion it
was my father who coaxed her out of the mental torment to
which she returned every time he left the country.

I myself and my other sister Kate could raise so many
matters in which our father has been of most important
assistance to us that you would either be reduced to boredom
or simply regard our testimony as that of daughters who find
it necessary to defend their father for the sake of
appearances.

And when we were forced due to financial stress to go
and live in France and he to stay at home, he wrote to us
almost every day during our separation. Would a heartless
man like that depicted by Miss Courtenay be capable of such
a thing?

Those accusations put forward by Miss Courtenay not only
caused great difficulties for our family and for my father as far
as his public image was concerned, but they also helped spawn
a virtual industry of false stories about his unfaithfulness and
sexual promiscuity. It might be thought that a lady such
as myself, Daniel O'Connell's eldest daughter, might be

protected from hearing about such scurrilous talk but I am a grown woman. I know what is going on, I have my informants from the highest echelons of society to the lowest. There is perhaps nothing strange in the difference between the attitudes of those of high and low station, for their very cultures are at odds with each other and their respective aims in attributing the fathering of bastards to my late father, are on the one hand, to denigrate him in the eyes of his peers and, on the other, to make him into a hero of the lower orders.

So while *The Times* and Henry Hunt and Lord Lyndhurst spread lies about my father's infidelity in order to harm him, the peasants of Ireland told stories of his illegitimate progeny as a matter of adulation. I have heard these stories myself from the country people around our family estate in Darrynane in Count Kerry. The poor people there and in other parts of Ireland live in a world of heroes and villains and their greatest hero of all is my father.

Most of these tales refer to his confounding the villains of his time in the courts of law as Counsellor O'Connell, the clever, astute almost infallible defender of the rights of the dispossessed. Raised to the status of a Gaelic hero it was necessary for him to take on all the characteristics of such and one of the more important traits was a superhuman ability to sire children.

Such stories were of so remarkable a character that one could only laugh at them. My father, it would appear, would have sired a child in every town and village in Ireland save that of Rathkeale in West Limerick. That town was then cursed in the stories as inhospitable for its lack of an O'Connell bastard.

I once spoke about this to an old woman, an O'Sullivan,

of Caherdaniel, asking her in jest did she not feel ashamed that my father was by all accounts a most awful man. "*Níl ionnta ach scéalta,*" she replied; they're only stories. She made it very clear by her speech that these stories, though a necessary part of building up a great reputation, were of course not necessarily true. As far as the Rathkeale story was concerned she grinned toothlessly and told me of a minor Gaelic poet from Kerry who started that rumour because an innkeeper of that town refused him drink.

It is true there was talk of wild oats sown by him as a young man of nineteen, a student of Lincoln's Inn in London. I even heard that he almost fought a duel with the son of the owner of a porter brewery over the attentions of a young lady. But that was in the last century, in the 1790s. It seems more like my father to turn away, as he did, from the attentions of a married lady who acted the inammorata towards him at that time, describing her in his own diary as a "most debauched woman".

He was, of course, a most attractive man, even in his latter years. As a woman I could see that for myself and indeed I even noticed it as a young girl, a subject on which my mother often teased me.

Once she even wrote to my father while he was away on the circuit about an occasion when a certain gentleman was commented upon as a handsome man and a good father: "*Nell and Kate look with such anxiety for my answer to their question, 'Mamma, sure he is not half so handsome or so good as my father?' My reply is just what they wish, and it speaks the real sentiments of my heart.*"

\* \* \*

I would be avoiding the most uncomfortable of truths if I did not admit there was an episode, late in his life, of which we were all ashamed and which perturbed our entire family. It was one of those things which, I am told, frequently happens to a man who, when advancing in years, imagines himself to be back in his prime. When he was almost seventy, my father became infatuated with a young women of twenty-three. I was so thoroughly and completely enraged at the time that I refused even to speak to him.

In latter years I have come to understand that the awful weakness of his brain which later reduced him to such horrible feebleness of mind and spirit had already begun to manifest itself at this time. It was heartbreaking to discover that my forgiveness and understanding, when I expressed it to him, had come too late for him to comprehend.

My mother had been dead for eight years and my father was most definitely a lonely man. He was a man who liked women, who liked being in the company of women and who spoke to women not as inferiors but with due regard to their mental capabilities. He was in prison in the Richmond Penitentiary at the time but was allowed all the visitors he wished and some visitors he did not.

Indeed, it appeared that any person of quality was permitted to enter the Richmond to see my father as though he were an exhibit in a zoo. Some came because they supported him and to give him encouragement, others came because they opposed him bitterly and relished seeing him in such circumstances.

The young woman with whom he became so infatuated was attached to the latter category. Her name was Rose McDowell. She was not only young enough to be his granddaughter but was a Protestant from Belfast, where her father was a merchant and supporter of the Union. She, through her father, had contacts with our family through Margaret O'Mara the half-sister of my husband.

When the subject of his possible marriage to her arose, my brothers and sisters and I were united in our determination to prevent it. This was unusual for us. We were a large family of strong-willed young people. We took issue with each other over almost everything from the running of the house to the main political questions of the day. But the arrival at Merrion Square of a slip of a girl as its mistress was inimical to all of us, even to Maurice who, no doubt, would have thought of wooing her for himself.

My father, however, persistently contacted Margaret O'Mara to bring Rose McDowell to see him in prison describing her as "one of the most superior women I have ever met with intellect, sound judgment and fascinating sweetness." Fortunately he was right about her sound judgment and due to this our family need never have worried. The young Miss McDowell tenaciously rejected my father's courtship and refused all his requests to marry.

There had been, apparently, a large correspondence between them which he ordered our friend and his legal colleague PV Fitzpatrick to destroy. There was nothing untoward, let alone lewd, in the letters Fitzpatrick told me afterwards. They simply contained my father's fanciful proposals of marriage and her adamant refusals.

I am of course glad that no marriage took place and that Rose McDowell turned out to be such a sensible young woman; there were many of her young age who would have been so overcome by the flattery derived from the attentions of a man so important as my father that they would have answered "yes" to his very first proposal. All public discomfiture was therefore saved by Miss McDowell's common sense on the one had and by our own pressure on our father on the other.

The private shame remains. You cannot fully appreciate how I and my sisters felt about our father as we grew up. Here was one of the greatest men of his time, admired by the better people of Ireland and England and despised by the baser elements in both countries. He was lionised in France and other countries on the continent of Europe to the extent that once there was a move to make him King of the Belgians. He was famous from the wastes of Canada through the entire United States of America and down all the way to those Spanish colonies liberated by his friend and admirer General Bolivar.

And this great man of his time was none other than our dearest father! It made us feel so proud, so romantic to be part of his family.

And when my great father in his latter years turned out to be a besotted old man like so many of his generation, it left me with a feeling of the most awful sadness. It was through this episode in his life that I foresaw that his spirit was waning and that he would soon die.

He had his faults and I knew them. But I knew too that he did not posses the faults Miss Eleanor Courtenay accused him of having.

## CHAPTER TEN

# I am Deceived by my Master

Our journey was a dreadful one until we reached Lyons. As far as Orleans we went by the train, fast and comfortable but for the smuts which flew into our carriage when we opened the windows to give Mr O'Connell an airing. After Orleans we travelled by road in a rented carriage with decent horses to start with but these being replaced by horses of decreasing quality at every inn on the way.

In Orleans Mr O'Connell had rested well but from there onwards until Easter Sunday, the going was terrible. It snowed unseasonably almost without respite. The prescription of the London doctors that he should proceed southwards so the warmth of the sun should comfort him and heal his weariness was completely unfulfilled.

Easter Day was spent at Nevers where Mass was said in the hotel through the kind indulgence of the Holy Father, given in advance of our journey. Mr O'Connell was now convinced his recovery was impossible and his state of agitation almost permanent.

We travelled on through the sleet, the hail and the snow, the wind howling louder and the ground rising further into the mountains with each mile of our journey. I have noted the towns in my journal: Bissay, Varennes, Lapalisse, Roannes, St Symphorien, Tarare. My memories of these places are as slim and as bereft of importance as the towns themselves, for Mr O'Connell's state of health was so poor that my time was taken up entirely with my duties. I do remember that he had a terrible panic in Lapalisse, a town in which some French people of the Protestant faith dwelled at that time, for there was a church of the Huguenots as well as one of the Catholics on the main street.

Mr O'Connell had seemed rested and Father Miley, in the interests of his own health, determined to walk some distance around the town and its environs as the evening light faded and the mountain air freshened. Mr Dan, who by now felt as irritable in the chaplain's presence as I did, was pleased at Father Miley's departure. He called for a bottle of the local red wine, which he said, would help him relax. Father Miley had gone perhaps half an hour when Mr O'Connell noted his absence. He flew into a tumult of panic lest he pass from this life without his priest at his bedside. His attempts to make his Act of Contrition failed after a few words each time he tried.

In these last days his mind had filled itself with scruples. Each word of this prayer, he had resolved to himself, had to be pronounced perfectly in a particular tone of entreaty to the Lord God, and if he was not satisfied that this special note had been achieved he would start all over again. His frustration caused him to cry loudly and roar out the name of Father Miley, cursing his priest for the betrayal of his leaving him to die without the last sacraments and to journey to the next life prepared only for the fires of hell.

The keeper of the inn, a stout, slovenly woman came to the room and made it clear to Mr Dan in the French that however illustrious her guest might be, she would be forced to expel him from her hostelry if he continued to behave in so disturbing a manner.

But when she saw the tears streaming from the eyes of Mr Dan her heart softened and she backed down the stairs quietly, holding her frock up slightly lest she trip. Mr Dan was indeed distressed. Perhaps the wine had loosened his control over his emotions, for he trembled and said to me that he felt he could not continue on this "journey to hell".

He knelt by his father's bed and tried desperately to comfort him. "The priest" is what he called Father Miley. "The priest will be back soon," he told his father. This was a small place and he would be found in no time at all. And he impressed upon his father, too, that death was far away and that he should try to think of other things. But it was all to no avail. Mr O'Connell moaned and cried and repeated Father Miley's name and began to pray aloud in Latin and in English.

Mr Dan and I stayed with him and two porters from the inn set out in search of Father Miley. The hunt was not a long one for from the front door they saw Father Miley making his way back. I heard the commotion as the porters ran towards him and he ran towards them and I put my head out the window.

Father Miley seemed as agitated as Mr O'Connell himself. "Is he gone?" he shouted towards me. "No Father, not yet," I shouted towards him. I ran to meet him on the stairs. Mr O'Connell was not, I told him, near death, his strength had not yet fallen to that state, but he was terribly agitated and feared being without his priest.

Father Miley's arrival in the room brought about a remarkable transformation. By the light of the candles I could see a tightness which had been present in Mr O'Connell's entire body loosen itself throughout. When the wave of relaxation finally reached his face, its mien changed from that of utmost terror to a sweet and childish smile. His eyelids dropped and he slid into the deepest of sleeps. Though the sacrament had not been administered he seemed content that his confessor was at his side.

\* \* \*

Next morning, April 8th, it was decided to rest a further day at Lapalisse to allow Mr O'Connell recover further from the exertions of that awful evening. On April 9th we set out for Roannes, through Droitunieres, St Martin, La Pacaudiere and St Germain, hill towns which remain but a blur in my memory.

At Roannes Mr O'Connell slept, I can remember that all right, for it brought me the comfort of sleep as well.

On Saturday, April 10th, we moved through St Symphorien and Pain Bouchain to Tarare where we spent the night. Next morning at seven o'clock Mass Mr O'Connell raged at being charged five centimes for a chair in the church of Tarare. He muttered and fumed under his breath for the entire liturgy, not, I felt, because of the money he had been charged, but at the insult he conceived had been offered to his dignity by the Curé's recognising neither his person nor his importance.

When we left the church Father Miley calmed him and forgave him his sin of vanity before the Lord's Holy Sacrifice. In the carriage I heard Father Miley whisper to Mr

Dan while Mr O'Connell slept: "Our patient could be on the mend. His bad temper at least has returned to him. On this morning indeed you appear sicklier than he."

That day we first of all wound our way up through a desolate mountain district, the highest pass being 3,000 feet above the level of the sea, as high as the highest mountains in Mr O'Connell's county of Kerry. Luckily he slept through all of this and we were spared the anguish of his hallucinations bringing him home again to his mountains, of his exclamations of false recognition of a landmark, a rock, a mountain stream or a remote hamlet. Certainly had he seen the people he would have known that he was in a foreign place. Their attire was far from the raggedness of the unfortunate peasants of Kerry and farther still from the sturdily-clothed English farm labourer with which we had become familiar. Here the people seemed to come from the Bible times: the villagers swaddled in robes, the shepherds on the hills tending their flocks and hauling in stray new-born lambs by the crook of their sticks.

Father Miley told us they were not only backward in their dress but in their civilisation and that they showed hostility to strangers. Their world was encompassed entirely by the great walls of their mountain valleys.

We did not stop to experience their lack of kindness but pressed on until finally the narrow road wound downwards and a great plain through which a broad river flowed could be seen in the distance. The snow became thinner on the ground as we descended and eventually disappeared altogether. It was almost nightfall when we entered the handsome town of Lyons, the second city of France. There we put up at the Hotel de l'Univers, which was comfortably appointed and had helpful and kindly servants and maids.

We spent eleven whole days in Lyons and knew the city quite well after a while. Though hardly as big as Dublin, Lyons was impressive and presented an infinitely more prosperous aspect. Two great rivers, the Rhône and the Saône, met in the town's very centre, and grand houses, many as big as those on Merrion Square, fronted the quaysides. Their style was more modern though, with plastered walls painted in bright colours instead of the mellow brick of Dublin. Away from the rivers one part of Lyons resembled Paris with wide streets and large paved squares and inhabited by the gentry and the merchants. Another part was full of rambling little lanes in which the artisans, notably the weavers of silk, had their workshops. In no place was there the poverty or the squalor that so often met the eyes and the nostrils in Dublin at that time.

Our first days in Lyons were fraught with the frost and the snow, which had followed us down from those strange mountains with their even stranger people. In these days Mr O'Connell was, at certain times of the day, strangely calm, his bowels steadied themselves and thus the amount of time and attention I had to spend on cleaning him was lessened. But he displayed some other, more menacing symptoms of illness, which suggested a return of the congestion of the brain that the English doctors had told us about. He complained consistently of vague pains in the head. Some of them, he told me, were of extremely short duration and sharp, as though a needle had been pushed right through his skull. Others lasted for minutes on end but were dull, rather like the beginning of a toothache. Sometimes when he thought about the nature of the pain it would suddenly disappear, he would tell me with a puzzled look.

The Liberator had always suffered from an habitual

catarrh but here, confined to his room by the weather, it deteriorated into a racking cough which rasped on the nerves of those attending to his well-being and indeed, upon his own nerves which became more brittle by the hour. After a day or two he also developed a trembling and weakness in his right arm which became considerably weaker than his left one. He did not, all the same, loosen his grip on the black glove. Since the day I had given it to him it had become his habit to hold tightly on to it at times he perceived danger to be near. At meal after meal the knife would fall from his fingers, which he seemed incapable of pressing firmly against the handle while holding the glove at the same time. Worst of all the sorrow of his mind made him prey to the saddest of preoccupations, the most frequent of which was, once again, his fear of being buried alive.

It was a great relief to me in the midst of this morbid speculation by my master to be fortunate enough to spend some time in the company of the two women who owned the hotel. They behaved to me in an open and friendly manner, unlike other innkeepers whose attitude to servants generally had been one of complete disdain.

I was soon to learn they had been servants themselves. Miss Glover was once housekeeper to an English noblewoman who had moved to the vicinity for the sake of her health and Mademoiselle Vuffruoy had served the family of a wealthy local merchant. They had met, many years back, below stairs at a great house on the quays where the Saône meets the Rhone and vowed to save their francs and their centimes to start the great venture which would bring them out of service for the rest of their lives.

We sat and talked about this by the fireside in their private quarters, for it was a topic in which I had an abiding interest. It was, at that time, my greatest hope that some day I would leave the service of Mr O'Connell, decent master and all that he was, and be my own man in some way or other. I did not for one moment think that escape from service would lead me to the horrors which I endure to this day.

When Mr O'Connell would finally sleep, I dreamed of my freedom as a small hotelier in Dublin, catering for the needs of the less-than-wealthy, the not-so-fashionable castes of society; the commercial travellers with their account books, the minor government officials, the farmers and their wives. I would work with people I could look in the eye as fellow human beings, as equals on this earth.

As though he had been reading my thoughts Mr O'Connell, later in that week, proceeded to destroy my hopes completely.

His health had deteriorated once more and the local medical men, Doctor Viricel and Doctor Bonnet, had become concerned at his weakness. They paid particular attention to what they described as an "obstinate attack of dysentery". This, they felt at first, might have resulted from a contamination in his food but later admitted that they were entirely ignorant of its cause.

I have my own view on this and one with which no doubt Mr O'Connell would concur were he alive to recall these events. Mr O'Connell's bowels, as I said earlier, had settled but the doctors demanded his stools and he was unable to comply. In order that they could perform their rites of investigating the excrescences of the great man, they performed upon him an enema. It was hard to know which was worse: the violence of the act committed upon his body or the assault they conducted on the dignity of so great a man. It was Viricel, I think, who held Mr O'Connell down as Bonnet forced the long tube into his unwilling body. My master pleaded with them to stop but their invasion continued unabated until he had voided himself completely and his very blood began to exude from him.

From that moment onwards his condition deteriorated considerably. He became lamentably weak. He spent his entire days reclining on a sofa in his room. He recited his prayers and was seemingly not content until he had driven his spirits to the lowest point of depression, morbidity and a horrifying fear of death.

This took the form of a strange apprehension that his expiry would lead him not to the great happiness of heaven nor to the burning tortures of hell nor even to the temporary discomfort of purgatory. He would die, he thought, and then spend all eternity in Limbo, the place where the unbaptised dead children are sent. He feared, he told me, that he would spend countless thousands of years in which he would not exist. He would be condemned, he felt, to be truly dead forever and to be unable to think or to feel or to have any communication with any being whatsoever.

But at least this deepest depression put him off his food temporarily and gradually his looseness, with which I was the one who had constantly to deal, began to ease.

Each morning a report on his health was written in the French by Father Miley, and handed by me, on his instructions, to the representative of the *Gazette de Lyons*. It showed a welcome improvement, Father Miley told me. And the weather improved too moving from winter to summer with only an hour or two of spring in between. Each morning the sound of the bells came in on the warm air as Masses were said in every church in this great city for the recovery of Mr O'Connell.

Then, when the clamour of the bells died out, the sound of the birds singing, almost imperceptibly at first, entered into our room. It is strange, is it not, how that sound, when first heard after the silence of winter, can raise one's spirits and one's hopes?

A single blackbird in a budding poplar outside our window did far more good to the four of us, most of all to Mr O'Connell himself, than all the doctors of France could have hoped to do.

Soon, very quickly indeed, Mr O'Connell's improvement became remarkable. His looseness ceased completely, thank God. He slept better and he ate full and decent meals consisting mainly of a soup, some portions of the Lyons sausage with potatoes and a green vegetable, not spinach but not unlike it. Miss Glover told me its name at the time but I cannot remember it now.

Mr O'Connell's mental agility improved as his strength slowly built up and on the 19th day of the month he was in such good spirits that we decided to take him out in the carriage for an airing. The hotel was situated on the main promenade of the town on which the young gentlemen and ladies strolled daily in the sunshine. Mr O'Connell's presence being the main interest in the city, many of the strollers gathered outside the Hotel de l'Univers out of curiosity. Some had been turned away because of the earlier state of Mr O'Connell's health. Some of them had come to the Hotel de l'Univers thrice daily to enquire after his condition, to present their cards, to wish him well and to assure Mr Dan and Father Miley they would remember Mr O'Connell daily in their prayers.

That was a great day, the 19th. Out into the streets we went together. A cheer rose from those in front of the hotel when they saw Mr O'Connell. The horses pranced, the carriage, open to the warm air, was comfortable and some little colour began to return to Mr O'Connell's face. Along the banks of the rivers we drove, right out into the open country and everywhere the people seemed to know who we were and waved us their greetings and wished us well and they shouted a "hurrah" for "Monsieur O'Connell".

Our spirits were up and our hearts beat lighter and I was happy for Mr Dan in particular. To see such a good-natured young man, of such an easy personality having to suffer so much by the health, the frustration and I might add the sheer stubbornness of his great father, had saddened me. Mr Dan would most certainly have felt more comfortable at a grand ball, receiving and returning the attentions of the young ladies, than seated daily and nightly at the bedside of his cantankerous though illustrious father.

I had become worried too that the strain imposed upon him by the journey had provoked him to drink more than his measure. On several occasions I had removed empty wine and brandy bottles from his room in the early morning as he slept. I particularly did not wish Father Miley to be aware of his predicament.

On the 20th matters improved even further and Mr O'Connell was deemed capable of setting out on foot into the streets of the city. This was a mistake, though not a grave one. At first he was in great form entirely. There may not have been a spring in his step, but he walked the broad streets of our side of the town with a confidence and agility we had not seen for a long time.

All the while, a large crowd of local people followed him. Some were anxious to wish him well. Others were merely curious as to how he looked. This was, after all, the man who had been painted to them as the evil genius of the age in the pages of the conservative journals, and the great hero of his time in the liberal sheets.

By the time we had crossed the river to the old artisan quarter, his strength had diminished considerably. Though he managed to clasp the hands of some of his well-wishers, his gaze became vacant and he seemed incapable of uttering a single word to satisfy their interest. He began also to complain of a shortness of breath which was bringing him to the point of collapse.

We put him down in an eating-house, where he remained with Father Miley and Mr Dan, while I walked back to the Hotel de l'Univers to arrange for the carriage to be brought out to retrieve him. Once back there he slept soundly and next day he recovered further. On the 21st day of the month I wrote in my diary that it was my confident opinion that the crisis in my master's health had passed.

\* \* \*

Every one of us, Mr O'Connell included, was now in high good humour. Even Doctor Bonnet and Doctor Viricel, men of unusually grim countenance, began to look cheerful. Mr O'Connell would undoubtedly recover his strength, they told us. He would not only be able to live a normal life for a man of his three-score and twelve years but would be capable of resuming his career in politics. Not completely, but at least to the extent of being able to guide and direct others to the political goal of Repeal which he had set himself.

They insisted, however, that their young colleague Doctor Lacour should accompany our party to Rome, he being, according to their account, a young man of the brightest intelligence who promised a brilliant medical career. It was decided therefore that on April 22nd, 1847, we should embark upon a steamer for the town of Valence on the first stage of our journey down the Rhone to the port of Marseilles. Thence we would proceed by ship to Genoa, onwards to Livorno, and on to the port of Civitavecchia, which is but six hours' carriage ride to the Eternal City. Father Miley planned out the journey himself. We should arrive in Rome, he said, by Low Sunday. The Pontiff, he was sure, would arrange a great welcome for the Liberator and his party. He then wrote a note to the Cardinal Secretary of State to inform him of the approximate date of our arrival. I took it to the post house where the master of the mails was very much impressed and scrutinised the address a number of times before accepting my payment.

It was with some regret that we left the city, its kind people and its beneficial climate which so greatly contributed to the improvement in my master's health. Our departure was recorded in the *Gazette de Lyons*. I asked Mr Dan to tell me what it said and he obligingly wrote it out in English for me. I have kept it since in my diary because the correspondent described the scene with far greater fluency than I could ever hope to:

*"A steamboat running from Lyons to Valence took Mr O'Connell and his suite (his son Mr Dan O'Connell MP and his chaplain Rev Father John Miley DD) along with his physician and valet, on board at 11.00 am. It has been arranged that he shall stay in the south of France until his health recovers and hence continues his journey to Rome. We saw Mr O'Connell descend from the carriage that conveyed him to the steamboat and an indefinable feeling of sadness ("un sentiment indefinable de tristesse" – these words underlined by Mr Dan for me) came over us.*

"How, said we to ourselves, is this the man who has filled the world with the thunder of his name, and made England tremble to her centre. Animation seems to have fled from the face, once so expressive, of the Liberator. He advanced slowly, sustained by his physician and chaplain, not taking the slightest notice of those persons who bowed before him in token of respect or who had come to bid a last adieu to the members of his suite. Doctor Bonnet and Doctor Viricel having insisted that Mr O'Connell be accompanied by Doctor Lacour, it is then to a Lyonese physician that will henceforth be confided the precious life of Daniel O'Connell."

These words shocked Mr Dan and myself for we had felt Mr O'Connell to have recovered considerably. I still believe that he really had improved but perhaps only to a stage at which he still looked very ill to those seeing him for the first time. The newspaper report was a sharp reminder to us that we had overestimated the betterment in his condition.

As things turned out Mr O'Connell and Doctor Lacour had personalities which did not complement each other. Indeed towards the end they had become bitter enemies.

Mr O'Connell made enemies easily, mind you. He had them everywhere; in the parliament, with the Young Irelanders, among his fellow landlords, with a small number of disaffected peasants around Derrynanebeg whom he had allowed to squat and throw up their hovels or botháns on his land, but who still demanded more of him. He even had enemies in his own Catholic Association and, I fear, had my temperament not been blunted by the necessary servility of my occupation, he might have made an enemy even of me that very morning before we set out for the steamer.

With great fussiness and pretension he called myself and Mr Dan and Father Miley to his room. He made us all sit at a table as though he were engaged as a counsellor once more and were taking a brief from us in the Library of the Four Courts. The bustle and excitement of that place was missing, though, and, I must say despite his obvious recovery, the intensity of expression he used to bear on such occasions was absent.

"Duggan," he said. "I have called you before me to say something to you of the greatest importance to your future life. I have called my son Daniel, a Member of Parliament, and Father John Miley, a Doctor of Divinity and one of the most promising young clergymen of his church and of his nation, to bear witness of what I have to tell you."

He threw back his head with its great mane of a wig, and he tucked a thumb into either side of his waistcoat just as he used to do in court to signify that a telling, a very decisive, statement on behalf of his client was about to be made.

"Duggan," he said, "you have been a completely trustworthy servant to me over the years. When I was impecunious you went a week or two without your pay at times. When I was under attack from all sides you remained loyal and faithful to your master. You gained the friendship of my sons, Mr Maurice, Mr Morgan, Mr John and Mr Dan here. They trust you and admire your qualities as a good servant.

"But I have felt for some time that servitude has been a burden thrust upon you by the circumstances of your birth, a means by which you can be fed and clothed and survive, rather than a way of life which can also nurture your spirit and your soul.

"Servitude is but one step above slavery, that great abomination of our age. You have, yourself, heard me tell those who have invited me to visit their country, the United States of North America, that I should refuse to do so until the day that evil has been abolished and uprooted from that land.

"Slavery binds a man to his master forever, it allows that master to sell his slave, as a chattel, to another master and that other master to yet another. A servant is a free man. He is free to leave his master upon tendering him appropriate notice, but the theory of that freedom does not match its practice and for all his rights before the law, a servant, in spirit if not in body, can be no better off than a slave."

His voice was weakening now. I had noticed recently that early in the day his energy was as strong as it had been some years past, but it left him quickly if he became involved in any lengthy exertion either of the body or of the mind. The thumbs began to slip down the sides of his good mustard-coloured waistcoat, his face grew paler and head fell forward showing how sunken his cheeks had become. And then he became agitated.

Mr Dan and Father Miley were, I remember, already clearly bored by what they regarded as his pompous speech, for while some of his orations have been considered wonders of their art, others were tawdry works, of pathos and often of sheer bombast. The two men had lost interest and were impatient to make arrangements for the day's journey ahead.

I, as a servant of course, was bound to pay Mr O'Connell my undivided attention and this I did to the very best of my ability. I clenched my teeth to give my face an expression of seriousness and intense concentration – a trick I had learned from my seniors in the apprenticeship to this trade.

"Mr Daniel!" my master roared in anger. "Father John!" he called in a more respectful tone. "I am about to make a statement of some importance. I demand that you pay me some attention." It was as though he had read their wandering minds and they both stiffened like soldiers coming to attention.

"Duggan, as I have said earlier, has been a trusted servant to me. A man who has known many of my secrets and someone who has kept those secrets, thanks be to God. I have, as I have said earlier, determined that it is not his wish to remain in servitude for his entire life. I have therefore decided that if I should emerge from this illness and from this journey with my health restored to half of what it was, I will mark my gratitude to him in a way he little thinks or least expects.

"I am an old man now, in the seventy-third year of my existence in this world. I have been a spendthrift in my time but I have some wealth still at my disposal. My will and testament has been made and I wish you all to know that it is my intention and my wish that Duggan shall be provided for in a manner in which he shall be forever independent of servitude.

"Mr Daniel and Father John I wish you to witness that I now solemnly bind myself to this promise. Mr Duggan, you may go now."

I went with some sorrow but with a great anger in my heart. I had heard his enemies call him a charlatan and a mountebank and a liar and a big beggarman. But how could he lie so openly to me, his own servant? To me, his Duggan, who had signed his will and who had signed the codicil too, and who knew, of course, that they excluded me in participation of any benefits arising from them.

We heard the horses neighing in the yard and we walked out into the courtyard to make our short journey to the steamboat. And my heart was so bitter that I wished that the angel of death, which now appeared to have lagged behind us on our journey, should now put on such a spurt as to catch us up.

# CHAPTER ELEVEN

## O'Connell's Knavery

Allow me to introduce myself. My name is Alexander Raphael. I am the Member of Parliament for St Alban's and I can tell you a thing or two about Mr O'Connell's dishonesty. The man, without doubt, is a charlatan and a knave. I have learned this to my cost. As Mr Robert Peel MP can confirm, I was one of many aspiring, ambitious and naïve politicians cheated by Mr O'Connell.

First I should tell you a little more about myself and correct some misconceptions, for I have been described variously as an Armenian, a Jew and an Indian. I was indeed born in India and I have, I believe, some Armenian blood. People of that nationality have been noted for their travelling to live in every corner of the earth. As for Judaism, that was the religion into which I was born but I am now a practising Roman Catholic and therefore have no reason to be antagonistic to Mr O'Connell on account of religious persuasion.

I am by profession a broker in the City of London and, I am ready to admit, a man of some wealth. My association with Mr O'Connell began in the summer of 1835 following the Carlow by-election. Colonel Bruen and Mr Kavenagh were elected but unseated following a petition by their opponents. The election was declared void due to the discovery that large numbers of those who voted had been in serious arrears of payment of their rates.

It had been my great ambition for quite some time to enter parliament and I felt that membership of such a body would be, for me, a very great honour. There is something you should understand here. Westminster has been described as the most exclusive club in the United Kingdom. This description has always had an attraction for me. You must put yourself in my shoes. I am a Jew of Armenian extraction, born in India. My family was, and is wealthy, having accrued a large fortune in that British colony. We were merchants, importers of those stuffs that the English people who found themselves in India felt they needed.

Goods from home were the main demands. The Raphaels supplied everything from cricket bats, wickets and balls from Hampshire, golf balls and clubs from St Andrews in Scotland and biscuits and whiskey from Dublin. Reliability was our watchword. Our stores always had good supplies of everything that was needed. It was indeed my father's policy to overstock in case of delays in deliveries. The slogan "You will always find it at Raphael's" became a by-word, first in Calcutta, then in Bombay and later in Delhi. Ships from Liverpool and Southampton were laded with plywood boxes with the name of Raphael francoed to their sides. Our family firm allowed the British abroad to remain as British as possible under the circumstances which prevailed. The only thing my father could not do for them was to change the climate.

In time our family, despite its origins, came to regard itself as British too. I was sent to Harrow as a boy, my parents having conceded me to the Anglican Church in order to secure my future. Thence I went to Oxford for my Bachelorship in Arts and then it was on to London to take charge of the English side of the family business. I extended my interests by becoming involved in the stock exchange.

But my increasing wealth and status within the business community was never fully accepted by those established in money and power. My entire life depended upon making contacts with English merchants and men of commerce. Few problems arose in my days at Harrow where I made valuable acquaintances and visited the families of my school friends during the long vacation in summer.

I was also lighter in hair and in countenance than many people of Jewish or Armenian descent. I could easily have passed for English but for two things. Firstly there were many in business in the City of London who knew from their families in India that my origins were not British. Secondly, when in Oxford I had become involved with those intellectual Anglicans who had joined the Roman Catholic Church. When it came to entering important gentlemen's clubs in London after I had come down from Oxford I discovered that my former friends and colleagues who were of the Established Church gained admission without difficulty while I received cautious letters explaining that my application had been refused. Englishness and Anglicanism appeared to be the keys to entry to these places.

It struck me that membership of "the most exclusive

club" would be easier to achieve. It might also shame the gentlemen's clubs to accept me.

These demands, by the way, were not on my part directed at being completely accepted as an Englishman. I was not born in this country and despite my English manners and speech, I recognise that my background precludes me from being totally accepted in this country. But I have sons and daughters who themselves now have children and who are truly British by birth and culture. The only things that set them apart is their religion as Roman Catholics and their Jewish origins. Because of this they are precluded from high office.

This is something I can understand. Religious discrimination has been part of our country's fabric for centuries. By the year 2000 even, I would not expect Roman Catholics, let alone Jews, be allowed marry members of the Royal Family, or be permitted to become Lord Chancellor or hold other important posts.

I do, all the same, believe that membership of clubs, so essential to maintain business relationships, should be open to all those wealthy enough to pay the membership fees.

I embarked on a parliamentary career, therefore, to pursue my ambitions to serve my adopted country and to become prominent enough a personage to be admitted fully into English society. It is hardly surprising that in this context the name of Mr O'Connell became prominent in my life. I knew him from his reputation for efficiency in political matters and I knew he was capable of having any person he recommended elected for certain constituencies in Ireland. I had written to him, putting myself forward as a possible Member for an Irish constituency some considerable time before the successful petition against Colonel Bruen and Mr Kavenagh.

Shortly after the news reached London of the success of that petition, Mr O'Connell called to my London house and pressed me to stand for Carlow. He was a striking man, tall and straight, his topcoat finished off by a flamboyant cape and, when he removed his silk hat, a shock of black hair uncommon for a man who had passed sixty. He was very insistent and told me that all I stood to lose in the event of putting my name forward was £1,000. This was to cover expenses, etcetera, and such a fee appeared no greater than those demanded by either the Whigs or the Tories at the time.

I asked Mr O'Connell for twenty-four hours to consider the proposal and he immediately agreed, suggesting that I call round to his house in Clargess Street on the following day with my decision. Having thought things over, I decided to accept the nomination and duly called to his house. There a ghastly Irish servant type called Duggan met me. He bowed and scraped and whimpered to me in his obsequious brogue that his master was out for the day. No matter how hard I questioned him this Duggan would not tell me when his master was due to return. The moonfaced blockhead simply kept repeating that his master was away. I left, ordering the silly servant to brush the dandruff away from the shoulders of his jacket.

That evening, however, I received a note from Mr O'Connell suggesting a meeting on May 31st. We met on that date and agreed on terms for my candidacy. Just as my father had always done in matters of importance I submitted the agreement to paper and am in a position to quote you verbatim Mr O'Connell's letter to me of the following day.

*9 Clargess Street*
*St June 1st*

My Dear Sir,

*You having acceded to the terms proposed to you for the election of the County of Carlow – viz you are to pay £1,000 – say one thousand pounds and a like sum after being returned – the first to be paid absolutely and entirely for being nominated, the second only to be paid in the event of your being returned. I hereby undertake to guarantee and save you harmless from any other expense whatsoever, whether of agents, carriages, counsel, petition against the return or of any other description and I make this guarantee in the fullest sense of the honourable engagement that you should not possibly be required to pay one shilling more in any event or upon any contingency whatsoever.*

*Daniel O'Connell.*

The first difference between us arose over the payment of the first £1,000. I lodged the sum with my solicitor, Mr Hamilton, but Mr O'Connell wished the money to be paid to his account at Messrs Wright and Company in the City of London.

Consequently he subjected me to a barrage of letters. On June 4th he wrote: *Who is the Mr Hamilton with whom you have deposited the £1,000. I do not know any person of that name in London.*

Four days later, on June 8th he wrote a long letter to tell me that he had written and sent off a letter to the electors of Carlow asking them to support me and saying that in his view my victory was all but assured. *I doubt whether there will be more than the show of a contest,* he wrote. He enclosed a cutting in my favour from a Carlow newspaper and a draft of his full address to the electors in my support for perusal and corrections. His letter concluded: *I also send you a sealed letter for Mr Vigors. I beg of you to return the address as near to four o'clock this day as you can, that I may transmit it to the Dublin Pilot for publication on Wednesday next. All the good men of Carlow see that paper. Let me know who the Mr Hamilton is with whom you deposited the £1,000. I expected you would have lodged it at Wrights. It is time this were done. Faithfully yours, Daniel O'Connell.*

I should stress that I am telling you all this to show how inordinately keen Mr O'Connell was to get his hands on the money. But the matter was finally settled on June 10th when Mr John O'Connell called on Mr Hamilton with the following note:

*Sir, I beg you will hand my son, Mr John O'Connell, the £1,000 placed with you by Mr Raphael for my use. My Son will give you a voucher at foot. I have the honour to be Sir, Your obedient servant,*
*Daniel O'Connell.*

Mr John O'Connell then wrote the voucher: *I acknowledge to have received £1,000 by draught on Wright and Co. June 10th 1835, John O'Connell.*

You can see therefore that there is no question but that I fulfilled the first part of the bargain. In any case, I did not hear from Mr O'Connell again until June 21st and his letter of that date was an exuberant one:

*My dear Sir, Glorious news! Raphael and Vigors returned on Thursday. I do not know the exact majority but I know the fact. My communication is from a cabinet minister but this is private. You can take your seat tomorrow.*
*Ever yours faithfully,*
*Daniel O'Connell.*

I took my seat on the morrow. This was a very great mistake. Before I left my house for Westminster the following note was delivered, addressed to Alexander Raphael MP: *Ultimate majority is 56. You are entitled to get your letters free this day.*

*D O'C.*

He had written the word "FREE" in capital letters which I remember at that time considering as not only as vulgar but indicative of his inherent greed.

By giving in to my eagerness to attend at the Commons on that day, it has since been argued, I was accepting that I had been returned and was therefore liable to pay the second moiety of £1,000. Not surprisingly the Tory candidates raised a petition against the election of Mr Vigors and myself. Almost every election in those days was contested.

But Mr O'Connell's demand for the second £1,000 arrived in haste on July 17th.

*My dear sir," he wrote, Send to Mr Baker (my agent) the particulars he wants of your qualification. I will stand between you and him for all expenses. I promised you, and repeat distinctly my promise, that upon payment of the second £1,000, to which you are at all events engaged, no demand shall be made upon you for an additional sixpence. Do then at once pay the other £1,000 into Messrs Wrights to my credit. Confer with Mr Baker as to his defence as much as he chooses. I am bound to indemnify you from all expenses beyond that £1,000 (this latter word greedy capitals once more) – that is the second sum. Believe me to be,*
*Very faithfully yours,*
*Daniel O'Connell.*

Eleven whole days passed without a missive from Mr O'Connell demanding the money and then on the 28th he wrote: *You did not say to whom I was to apply for the second sum of £1,000 according to our arrangement. It is necessary – absolutely necessary – it should be paid this day. Let me know at once who is to give it to me. I have a note from Vigors to whom I am pledged.*

And then he wrote accusing me of shrinking from my pledge. I wrote back denying this and then in order to make things absolutely clear to the world that Mr O'Connell was the offending party I agreed, under protest of course, to pay the £1,000 and I did this promptly. And when I further complained of his haste in demanding money he wrote hinting that he could get me a baronetcy. He held out the title of Sir Alexander Raphael Baronet, and in the subtlest of language insinuated that such an honour could be mine and that my heirs could inherit this honour.

Surprisingly this offer was not accompanied with an invoice for his possible expenses in gaining me the title. And what do you think happened next? Well, I was left to pay the costs of the petition out of my own funds. His promise that I would not have to pay sixpence was fulfilled. I had to pay thousands instead. I had to pay every single cost of lawyers, carriages & Co.

I was not the only one to be betrayed in this way by Mr O'Connell. You will realise that Mr Peel has consistently been Mr O'Connell's political opponent. But his famous address at Tamworth was a true and honest one and brought to light a further impropriety on the part of Mr O'Connell against a man who had, hitherto, been one of his best friends and supporters. On Edward Ruthven's own written evidence, disclosed by Mr Peel, Mr O'Connell asked Mr Ruthven to call on him.

I present now what happened to Mr Ruthven in order to show that I was not the only political candidate to be cheated by Mr O'Connell.

When Ruthven met Mr O'Connell he was told that Kildare was "settled." Poor Ruthven took this to mean that he would be returned without opposition but he was quickly made aware of his mistaken impression.

Lord Mulgrave, Mr O'Connell told him, wished to have young Lawless (Lord Cloncurry's son) returned as soon as he came of age. He would be of age in a few months and it had been determined that Ruthven would hold Kildare as his *locum tenens*.

Being an honest man Ruthven replied that he most certainly would not. "If the people of Kildare return me I will never desert them as you would have me do, never," he cried.

Mr O'Connell paused a moment. He then offered Ruthven £1,000 and the first worthwhile colonial situation that become available if he should promise to stay quiet until polling day and then retire when asked. Not surprisingly Ruthven refused to be part of this deceitful scheme. This infuriated Mr O'Connell who threatened to "make things hot" for Ruthven on the hustings and even hinted that he could arrange for the Bishop of Kildare and Leighlin, the celebrated Doctor Doyle, speak out against him.

Ruthven challenged the "Liberator," the "incorruptible patriot," the "Friend of Ireland", to deny if he dared that this event had taken place. O'Connell never denied this but set out to destroy his one-time ally. This was his manner, the way he worked. Ask anyone in politics in any of the three kingdoms and they will vouch for the fact that he was a ruthless and uncompromising man.

I know his supporters often reveled in the nasty tricks he played upon his opponents. I am aware they were simply indulging in revenge against those who had treated them badly in the past either in fact or in their own imagination. But Mr O'Connell could repay those foul deeds with interest.

He addressed the electors of Kildare, accusing Ruthven of the most disgraceful behaviour. Lord Howth, Colonel Westenra and Mr John Maher had, O'Connell alleged in the address, accused Mr Ruthven of unfair practices in horse racing.

It should be remembered that to the electors of Kildare more than any other constituency in Ireland the racing of thoroughbreds was of the most extreme importance.

The exact allegations were that Mr Ruthven had frequently substituted and disguised one racehorse for another in order to confuse the bookmakers and make a financial killing at the racecourses of the Curragh and Punchestown in the county of Kildare. Mr O'Connell was careful not to make these allegations himself. He ensured the claims came from other gentlemen. The method was simple. All he had to do was pass the word along the servants' network. Mr O'Connell's footman would drop a hint to Lord Howth's butler and soon the entire racing fraternity would be talking.

Mr O'Connell also accused Mr Ruthven of the type of duplicity of which only he himself was capable and appealed to the voters in the following words:

"Above all do not disgrace yourselves by listening one moment to a man whose canvass, as a candidate for your county, is directly and obviously calculated to injure the honest candidates, Archbold and O'Ferrall, and to aid the interests of the Orange Faction, the unmitigated enemies of the religion and the liberties of the people of Ireland. This is the sincere advice and cordial entreaty of a man whose every energy is devoted to the prosperity and Glory of Old Ireland."

This, I point out to you was the man who called for "purity" in politics. He was the man who on the one hand described Mr Ruthven as unfit for public office in the United Kingdom of Great Britain and Ireland, but fit to be bribed with the promise of public office in the colonies. It was all due, in my view, to an insatiable desire for money. Why, he accepted the miserable pennies of his own starving peasantry to allow him dwell in a mansion in Merrion Square in Dublin. It is a house which, in its elegance and spaciousness exceeds that of my own London residence, paid for by my honest financial dealings in the City. Even his own brother, nothing greater in his wealth than a strong Kerry farmer, was subjected to letter after letter demanding funds to help satisfy O'Connell's appetite for cash. In the case in which I was involved, a parliamentary inquiry was set up to investigate allegations from several quarters that Mr O'Connell was involved in selling parliamentary seats. He was able, however, to produce receipts which showed that the monies procured from me were used in the expenses of my running mate Mr Vigors and on that account he was acquitted and saved from the fate of being permanently barred from the House. The Committee of Inquiry did find him guilty of being "intemperate" in his demands. To me that part of the verdict seemed to understate the case in the extreme.

My bitterness towards Mr O'Connell has remained even though I have been successful in most of my ambitions. My wealth has increased. I hold a safe seat for the Whigs in St Alban's, thanks to political magnates who are more scrupulous than O'Connell.

I am a member too of the Reform Club – of which Mr O'Connell is a founder – and of a number of other clubs in Piccadilly in which I can pursue my business through those of a similar mind who are also members. My wealth has enabled me to set up members of my family for the future. My daughters have married well; my sons have proved to be invaluable assets. One of them pursues the family interests in India, the other works with me in the stock exchange.

I feel, indeed I know, that had I continued to depend on Mr O'Connell for support I should have been ruined. I warn all of you against him and his duplicitous ways.

# CHAPTER TWELVE

## *My Master Recovers Miraculously*

We proceeded on the steamer in journeys of six hours every day along the river Rhône, an expanse of water that appeared to get broader and broader with every mile of our travels. In parts the water was dark and menacing and in other places a friendly green. In other spots it was so perfectly transparent that we could see the perch and the pike on their wriggling journeys, always it seemed, in the opposite direction to ours. In some parts it was so deep that great river steamers could ply, and in others it was shallow enough for a heron to stand in wait for fish to spike with its beak. But what was common to all places through which the river travelled was its great width, and the deeper channel through which we moved was marked by large mounds of stone painted white to catch the eye of the navigator.

On the first day Mr O'Connell slept when he was not being examined by Doctor Lacour, the young Frenchman who had accompanied us from Lyons. Lacour was meticulous in his inspections. He was a man of very low stature, five feet tall at the most though broad-shouldered. His low height and exceptional breadth gave the rather amusing impression of his being a perfectly square person.

His eyes were an unusually dark brown and above them stood black eyebrows of exceptional thickness. His skin was almost the colour of a new penny and the hollowness of his cheeks was exaggerated by the large, hooked nose which dominated his countenance. The space between those eyebrows and his copious growth of black hair was so narrow as to give the impression that his forehead was almost non-existent. This combination of features gave Doctor Lacour the appearance of a man with a short and vicious temper.

This impression was an accurate one. He would storm out of the room at what he might imagine to be a slight to himself personally, to his profession or to his nationality and there were many of the latter from Mr O'Connell.

On the positive side, his presence appeared to be good for Mr Dan. They were close to each other in age and appeared to get on well together and to have similar interests. I often found them together deep in conversation, laughing and joking with each other. It was good to see some of the gloom lifted from Mr Dan who had been obviously down at heart for most of the journey until now.

There was little doubt that Doctor Lacour was dedicated to his task and was particularly assiduous in the examination of Mr O'Connell's stools and most especially in the placing of leeches. He kept a veritable little farm of them in a series of black leather boxes with solid silver clasps. In one of his rare conversational moments, he told Father Miley his mother had bought the boxes as a present to celebrate his qualification as a medical doctor. Lacour treated his leeches as though they were pets, like dogs or cats. Though they all looked the same he seemed to be able to distinguish between one and another and called some of the larger and fatter ones by name. He would put them to Mr O'Connell's temples on one day, to the anus on another and the backs of the ears on another, all to relieve the congestions of blood which had afflicted our master.

Mr O'Connell, though, had always been a stubborn man and his dislike of being continuously told what to do, combined with his lack of trust in the French people began develop into an active hatred of the young doctor and I am sure I detected that Doctor Lacour was beginning to develop similar feelings towards Mr O'Connell.

Mr O'Connell's tiredness had kept him from conflict with the doctor as we arrived at Valence, a town on the left side of the river which appeared to be prosperous with solid buildings painted in light colours and with tiles rather than slates on the roofs. The Bishop was in waiting at our arrival and Mr O'Connell appeared reasonably well able to understand what was going on. An offer to stay at the Bishop's palace was politely but very firmly refused by Father Miley. He bowed, just slightly enough to accept the authority of the Bishop in whose diocese he found himself. The little obeisance completed, he arched his fingers together in an indication that he would not be deterred from moving on. There was a firmness in his voice too, I remember noting at the time, which showed he regarded himself at least as the Bishop's equal. The decision to move on, inspired as it might have been by Father Miley's ungodly haste, spared us the embarrassment Mr O'Connell's incontinence would have presented in the home of a senior member of the clergy.

We rested well that night and on Saturday we sailed

another six hours to Avignon where it was decided we should spend five days in the Hotel de l'Europe. This was a wonderful old building turned into a family hotel and counted as the best place to stay in the city. As usual Mr O'Connell's bowels caused our first problems but after the first night he began to feel better and to gain in strength.

These signs of slight improvement allowed me some time to myself, being relieved as I was from full-time attendance upon him. At least the diarrhoea had ended and with this the most painstaking, time-consuming and unpleasant of my duties.

On the Wednesday I accompanied Mr Dan to view the palace of the Popes – Clement V to Gregory XI – who had lived here, according to our guide, from 1309 to 1377. The place was a huge ensemble of buildings surrounded by the highest walls I have ever seen. Long corridors with marble floors led from one huge chamber to another. Great oil paintings of the Popes draped in their white robes, their triple crowns on their heads, their right hands raised in blessing, hung on the walls.

There were also men called anti-Popes who lived here until 1424. Mr Dan joked that he thought the anti-Popes had lived in Belfast but our guide seemed not to understand.

* * *

Thursday, April 29th 1847:
I marked this day down specially in my diary for our hearts were raised by the most remarkable of miracles. From this morning Mr O'Connell appeared to have effected a complete and total recovery. The first signs were far from pleasant. I was awakened at six o'clock to a great

commotion. Mr O'Connell was already on his feet shouting orders to me, demanding that I rise immediately and prepare him for his journey on the steamer to Arles. A "lazy lout" is what he called me but there was a smile full of mischief on his face as he said it. Mr O'Connell himself was clearly surprised by the strength he had gained and was determined to show it off to everyone. "My God, I feel great," he told me as he slapped me on the back. "I'm ready for Rome and the Italians and for the Pope himself. I'm right ready for the wine of Falerno and the best roasted songbirds they can provide. Rouse the lazy birds from their beds and let's get on our way. The eternal city awaits." He declaimed all this as an actor would·from the stage, gesticulating all the time, bowing at his mention of the Pope and making signs of eating, drinking and wiping the sweat from his brow in an imaginary Italian sunshine.

The noise, the shouting and finally the laughter aroused Mr Dan and Father Miley, who were truly amazed by the sudden arrival to Mr O'Connell of his full strength and humour. Doctor Lacour, whose room was on a different floor from our suite, was last to find out about the great and unexpected recovery, but he was apprised of the news in the most remarkable fashion.

"Where's that French pup," Mr O'Connell demanded and he was not even fully dressed when he descended to the next floor, rapped on Doctor Lacour's door with his walking stick and demanded he rise without delay.

It was like the old days. Mr O'Connell completely in charge, orders being given out, demands being made not only on myself as his valet but upon everyone with whom he came in contact.

He marched through the hotel's great hall like a storm,

grabbed the lapels of a hall porter who addressed him as an Englishman and lectured him on the history of the English in Ireland. The poor porter could barely understand half of what he had said until Mr O'Connell switched to speaking the French.

His next victim was the coachman whom he berated on the state of his brasses and upholstery. By the time our bags were loaded, Mr O'Connell had, as though in court, launched into a comparison between our humble coach – which was simply taking us the short journey to the steamer – and the triumphal coach he had constructed in Dublin to allow him drive through the city like a Roman emperor, with the sweeps and tradesmen rushing before him menacing the Unionist gentlemen, and the Trinity students with their cries of *"Hats off for Mr O'Connell!"*

\* \* \*

His banter brought to my mind the scenes of less than two years earlier, September of 1844, when Mr O'Connell was released from prison and mounted the topmost level of the triumphal coach. It was an improbably high contraption.

Below him sat a blind harper representing the nation and playing patriotic tunes while the bottom tier was large enough to hold all of Mr O'Connell's grandchildren, who were rigged out in green velvet costumes and hats with white feathers. Tumultuous crowds were with us at every street of the journey, their cheers blotting out all conversation on the coach.

On that glorious day six dapple-grey horses pulled the carriage through the streets, the ships in the river flew messages of joy in their buntings. The Lord Mayor and the aldermen wore their crimson robes in a carriage which preceded the Liberator's. At the Old House in College Green all he had to do was point silently at its portals and the citizenry cried out as one for Repeal of the Union.

Then at his house on Merrion Square he addressed the people standing high above them as the wind whipped at his cape and made his figure more dashing than before. "There must be no illumination this night," he said, exhorting against the triumphal practice of lighting up the city to celebrate a victory. "Tell that to everybody you meet and say it is my advice, aye, and say it is my command. Conciliation is what we want, Protestants, Catholics, Dissenters, Irishmen of all classes, let us combine them all." And he spoke from the top of his carriage of his time in prison in the Richmond Penitentiary: "Yes, I am glad," he said, "that I was permitted to suffer for Ireland. I rejoice that I was permitted to dwell in prison for your sake. The Liberator wanted to be liberated himself after three long months."

And I grinned to think about it at the time and I still do when I read it from time to time in the copy of the *Freeman's Journal* in my collection. This was Mr O'Connell in his most artful mood. He had, he said, suffered for Ireland in prison but I knew that he had lived a privileged life there holding grand receptions in the governor's gardens, receiving visitors from Ireland and abroad, living and eating well, drinking fine claret and burgundy and, on the eve of his release, some particularly renowned champagne specially imported from France for the occasion.

It was on these events that my mind had settled when we departed in the coach with Mr O'Connell at his most energetic once again. But my reverie of those happier times was, I remember, interrupted suddenly by a massive breaking of the Liberator's wind. To our anxious glances he replied with a wicked grin: "I held it in, though, I held it back. No diarrhoea." He smiled broadly, his countenance beaming happiness and affection first at Mr Dan, next at Father Miley and finally at myself before putting on his darkest and most menacing look for Doctor Lacour.

Then he burst into song. He had become once more, as he had so been spoken of in the past, a "holy terror."

*"Lauda Jerusalem Dominum,*
*Lauda Deum Tuum Sion,*
*Hosanna, Hosanna, Hosanna!*
*Filio David!"*

What a change from the *Dies Irae* and the *Stabat Mater* of earlier journeys, what a remarkable turnabout after his despair of ever recovering. For the first time since we left Hastings we were united, Mr O'Connell included, in the belief that a real chance of recovery was possible.

On reaching the steamer, his ebullient mood persisted. An hour passed from the scheduled time of departure and the nobility, gentry and clergy of the town of Avignon were treated to his berating the captain and crew, in their own language, of their inefficiency in being unable to depart in accordance with their timetable.

After we had set off he calmed down somewhat and ate a decent luncheon of veal and mushrooms cooked in a sauce of thick cream. He then took me for a walk around the decks, so much had his energy increased in the last day. He was still full of talk as we pulled in to stop at the town of Tarascon and he told me that this place was once inhabited by a great monster called the Tarasque. I can't remember if he said it was a dragon or some other creature. But I seem to recall he said it had three heads. This beast had ravaged the countryside all around only a hundred years after the crucifixion of our Lord and was finally defeated by the arrival of St Martha, whose church stood below the castle which overlooked the entire area from a huge rock above the town.

We did not leave the steamer but instead stood, our arms resting on the ship's guardrails, looking at the comings and goings on the dock and waving at the crowd of people who had come, just as in every town we had passed on the banks of the Rhone, to catch a glimpse of Mr O'Connell. He was still in his mischievous mood, waving happily at his admirers but cursing them under his breath. The French did not admire him for his own sake or for the successes he had achieved for the Catholics of Ireland, he said. They liked him simply, he said, because he had embarrassed and harmed the English. He ordered Burgundy and had Father Miley and Mr Dan raise their glasses to Queen Victoria while those on shore presumed he was toasting their presence.

When the gangway was taken on board and we set off again Mr O'Connell was full of impish good humour, bowing and smiling to the ladies on the deck and uttering insulting phrases in Irish to the gentlemen who, on seeing his smiling countenance, took them to be remarks of a complimentary rather than disparaging nature. He promised us that at our next stop, the town of Arles, he would be our guide on a tour of the town which, he told us, was known throughout the world for its ruins dating from the time of the ancient Romans.

At Arles we disembarked in time for supper at the Hotel du Nord and retired, promising Mr O'Connell we would rise at six o'clock to accompany him on his tour of the Roman amphitheatre and ancient cemetery.

*   *   *

We retired early but secretly I was in dread that the
wonderful improvement in Mr O'Connell's health might
prove illusory. Since the head pains had begun in Darrynane,
there had been a clear pattern. Improvement would usually
be followed by an appalling deterioration. On this occasion
the recovery had been so immense and so dramatic in its
onset that I feared an equally immense and dramatic
collapse.

But on the next day he was again well and energetic as
ever. He declared to all who would listen that his enhanced
condition was due to a lack of intervention on the part
Doctor Lacour whom he now described as "a bloody
charlatan" and a "French liar". His first orders of the day
were to Father Miley to pray for his further recovery, then to
Mr Dan to prepare for a further stage in his education, to
Doctor Lacour to stay at the hotel during our day's outing
and to myself to shave him and make him presentable again.
His pallor was receding, he declared, and he wished to take
the opportunity of cutting a fine figure in front of the French
wretches.

The carriage supplied by the hotel was a good one, well
turned out and with a wicker basket containing a picnic
luncheon presented by the hotel management on account of
Mr O'Connell's notoriety in the district. In the carriage the
Liberator read to us from a small red book printed in the
French tongue and given him by the proprietor of the hotel.
This small volume gave details of the monuments and
principal places in the town of Arles. Mr O'Connell was able
to read the descriptions in the French and speak them out to

us in the English language, a feat which indicated at least to me, his humble servant, that as well as his body having recovered its strength, his brain had regained its previous agility.

By reading from the book and by showing us the places marked out in it Mr O'Connell had, for the first time since we left Hastings, taken control of the party. It was he now who was in charge. Father Miley hardly uttered a word. It was as though he were annoyed to lose his position as leader of the group. He kept his respect for Mr O'Connell, mind you, perhaps out of his duty or perhaps he too knew the secret of Doctor McCabe and was content to play the inferior until Mr O'Connell took ill again.

"*In Hoc Signo Vinces* – In this sign thou shalt conquer," Mr O'Connell declared and went on to tell a tale of the Emperor Constantine the Great, his vision of the holy cross, his victory over his enemies and his conversion from the pagan gods of Rome to his belief in Our Lord Jesus Christ Our Saviour.

We were, the Liberator told us, following in Constantine's footsteps. The Emperor had been several times to Arles which in the Roman times was inhabited by 100,000 souls, more than four times its population of today.

Our hotel in the Place du Forum was quite close to the main sights Mr O'Connell wished us to see: the Arenas, the ancient theatre and the Roman cemetery of St Trophime.

The Arena was a giant stadium where gladiators fought to the death. There was a special bridge, an aqueduct, which carried a canal of water into the stadium in order to flood it so that mock naval battles could be staged, each ship's crew fighting to the death. Though now partly in ruins and, of course, not used for such savage purposes, Mr O'Connell brought it to life for me. His gift of oratory too had returned.

The ancient theatre was in ruins too, and Mr O'Connell pointed out the sculptures and the types of pillars on the front of the building, asking Father Miley for confirmation of his statements, and all the while trying to impress upon Mr Dan the cultural importance of the place.

For myself I did not find any great culture in the idea of human beings fighting wild beasts, or fighting each under unto the death for the entertainment of the onlookers. But the construction of such imposing monuments and buildings did impress me and I was interested too in the seating of the Arena. Mr O'Connell explained to me that the front rows were reserved for the people of noble birth, the next rows for the plebeians, or people who were not of the nobility, and the back rows for the slaves. I imagined myself seated in the back rows, my hand shielding my eyes from the setting sun and, as a slave, cursing the very idea of the games and their subjection of an entire class of people. I pictured Mr O'Connell seated at the front opposed completely in theory to what was going on but partial to the use of animals for sport and enjoying the fights between lions and tigers if objecting to the use of humans for similar purposes.

We walked on to the cemetery, a place of burial from the Roman times and later enjoying such a reputation that people from distant lands had their bodies brought here for burial. This was so much the case, Mr O'Connell told Mr Dan, that the poet Dante mentioned the cemetery as a gateway to Hell. But what we saw were simply ruins, graves broke open, bones of ancient men and women exposed for the sun to bleach and the visitor to see. All amongst them played scores upon scores of green lizards, more of them than

I have ever seen in any other place. They lay still at times absorbing the heat of the sun into their bodies, then they would dart about and crawl into the graves, leaving upon me an impression of horror that those who have died so long ago were being so badly disturbed when a team of decent labourers could, in a week, close up the graves and repair the shambles caused by so many years of neglect.

In the carriage bringing us back to our rooms in the late afternoon. Mr O'Connell began explaining gaily to Mr Dan, though I felt his intention was to embarrass Father Miley, that the women of this town, the Arlésiennes, were regarded as the most beautiful in all of France, being seen as the descendants of the ancient Greeks. Most certainly they all dressed in a distinctive manner being marked out from other French ladies by their habit of wearing large white hats adorned with black velvet ribbons.

There was much talk of this over dinner and little doubt as to Mr O'Connell's mischievous intent in this regard towards Father Miley whom he goaded continuously until the chaplain called upon us to say the Holy Rosary before retiring. They were the Five Sorrowful Mysteries that night, appropriate perhaps for the poor souls whose bones lay in the Aliscamps, but most certainly not for the condition of Mr O'Connell, which continued to improve so much that he planned further exertions for the morrow.

* * *

The weather was now deteriorating rapidly and a messenger from the steamer company had come to inform us that the wind being too high to sail, tomorrow's section of the journey from Arles to Marseilles, a great part of which would be on the open sea, had been cancelled.

Storm or no, Mr O'Connell appeared determined to take an excursion out to the neighbouring countryside, declaring that the continental winds were no more than a draught when compared to the gales he had experienced at his native Darrynane. Doctor Lacour called for rest, but knowing that his advice would be scorned should he give it directly to Mr O'Connell, he spoke to Father Miley and Mr Dan separately. They persuaded the Liberator, not without difficulty, to abandon his ideas for touring and travelling. Thus Mr O'Connell rested all day on Saturday but was still filled with energy and spoke with enthusiasm of the voyage to Marseilles through a region known as Camargo, which was, he assured us, a great wilderness inhabited by flamingos and beavers, with white wild horses galloping across shallow salt pans. This latter confused me, I remember, for pans to me were for cooking in or, more recently, for use when Mr O'Connell needed to relieve himself but was unable to leave his bed. I thanked God this was not the case at present and Mr O'Connell, seeing the mixture of relief and puzzlement on my face, asked what my worry was and smiled when I told him. The "pans" he spoke about, he told me, were large areas of shallow sea which had been dammed and drained to collect the salt which was then purified for human use. For all his faults and his guiles, though he tormented me often with his impetuous demands, I must own that I learned more from the words of my master than from any of the books he allowed me read.

All the while that day the wind grew stronger and brought with it the rain and once more an unseasonal cold but this did not make the Liberator's condition any worse.

He was able once more to receive those representatives of the nobility, gentry and clergy who wished to pay him their respects. This having been done, he simply sat at the fireside talking and joking with Mr Dan and Father Miley. I, as befitted my station, was seated some distance from them. Though unable to overhear their conversation, it was obvious to me that all three of them had begun to relax and to be confirmed in the belief that Mr O'Connell would safely reach Rome, visit his Holiness Pius IX, and return to his duties in Ireland, his health having been saved. For my part I felt that the end which had been brought to his incontinence was the most significant improvement, and one that appeared to have come about spontaneously rather than through the efforts of Doctor Lacour, whose attentions Mr O'Connell had spurned over the past days. Just as the incontinence had served to weaken him in the earlier part of his journeys, its disappearance served to build up his strength almost to the level at which it had been before his illness. The extent of his recovery tempted me to think of my master's promise that he would ensure my freedom from servitude upon his return to Dublin, but the temptation was a fleeting one and was dissolved by my memory of the will and the codicil.

He woke early again the following day and bid me fit him out in his best attire: his good waistcoat and frock-coat and breeches, his silk top hat, his fancy chemise and his shiniest buckled boots. All these were necessary, he told me, in order to impress the people of Marseilles, a large metropolis which had begun to challenge Lyons for the position of Second City of France.

We set off early down the Rhone, the wind having abated. But we steamed through the Camargo without seeing a wild horse or a flamingo or a beaver, viewing only the flat salt pans and the coarse scutch grass with the Rhone and the various branches of its delta making the land look as a series of large islands. Then suddenly the steamer lurched and we were at sea, and a sea which remained disturbed by the high winds of the previous day. Doctor Lacour became violently ill and Mr O'Connell put his mind to imagining all types of vile "cures" which he could apply to the Frenchman, whom he now regarded as being as great an enemy as ever was Sir Robert Peel or the other high Tories of England. The bitterest of herbs, the vilest of injections, the application of leeches by the dozen were suggested to the young doctor as he vomited over the side. The river steamer lurched and rolled and seemed as far from its element in the rough waters of the Mediterranean as Doctor Lacour was in the company of the Irish gentlemen. The Irish group, accustomed as it was to the frequent journeys from Kingstown to Holyhead on Mr O'Connell's visits to parliament in London stood up well to the weather.

## CHAPTER THIRTEEN

# *We Arrive in Health in Marseilles*

Father Miley saw an injustice in the way Doctor Lacour was being treated and sent me to bring him some brandy and a warm coffee to help settle his stomach. This I duly did and by the time I reached the deck again Marseilles was in sight, and what a splendid sight it was!

There was a huge curved bay, as though a giant had taken a bite out of the mountains that stood high along the shore. Set into this bay with sheer rock faces as its inland boundaries were the thousands upon thousands of white houses that formed the city itself. A fall of land from the mountains' edge to the sea exposed the entire city to the passengers of our steamer, each building becoming more distinct as we drew nearer to the shore.

My own time for viewing the great spectacle was limited as I had to go to the hold and see to the baggage along with the servants of the many French and Italian gentlemen on board. I found it hard to leave the deck and the glorious panorama which was being revealed, but my duties had to be attended to and I left my masters to view the scene. Having got everything into order I returned to the deck as our steamer came in through the entrance to the port, which had an ancient fort on either side. Thence we steamed right into the heart of the city where a vast rectangular basin perhaps three quarters of a mile long by 300 yards wide is cut out of the town and forms a bustling port with many fish markets and hotels and restaurants abutting onto it.

Here, I learned from the servants of English merchants resident in the city, are unloaded cereals and furs from the plains of Russia, grains from Turkey, sugar canes from Java and Réunion, oils from Baku, coffee from Brazil, peppers and spices from the Malabars. There were boatloads of live sheep from Algeria and French silk that came down the Rhone from Lyons. More than a quarter of the inhabitants of the city were Italian but there were also a large number of Musulmans from the north of Africa and all in all the city presented an aspect of great animation. It was full of markets and warehouses and ships of all nations arriving and preparing to depart.

On disembarkation the tumult was very great and as usual large numbers of people of quality from the locality were in attendance to pay their respects to Mr O'Connell before we set off by coach sent to meet us by the Hotel D'Orient. A note of welcome was presented to us from the British consulate, which as well as conveying to us greetings on behalf of Her Majesty's representative, inveighed upon us to be exceedingly wary of the robbers, brigands and pick-pockets which infest the city.

By the late evening at the hotel the usual visitors had paid their respects: the bishop and the vicar general, the consuls of the United Kingdom and of Belgium, the prefect and mayor of the city and a representative from the consulate of the United States.

Mr O'Connell held the most animated discussion with the American on the issue of slavery. He had never, Mr O'Connell said, and neither would he ever accept any of the multitudes of invitations he had received to visit America unless the evil of slavery be eradicated. The slave system, he said, "cut at the root of Christianity which teaches us to do to others as we would they should do to us, but you inflict on the slaves that which you would rather die than suffer yourselves."

The American gentleman courteously informed Mr O'Connell that he was from that part of the United States in which slavery was not only forbidden but looked upon with a contempt similar to that expressed so eloquently by Mr O'Connell. They parted on good terms and we all retired early, or so it seemed at first.

* * *

At four o'clock in the morning I was woken by a commotion on the stairwell. Loud words were being spoken in English and French. There was laughter and singing and general merriment. I went to my door and peered out. By the light of the candelabra on the landing I could see Mr Dan and Doctor Lacour with two young women who most definitely did not come from the better class of society. Mr Dan appeared to be searching for the key to his room. He was, I am sorry to relate, drunk. His necktie was askew at the collar of his shirt. Doctor Lacour was bent double with the laughing. The women did not appear to be amused and made some remarks in the

French which I did not understand. By their tone of voice, however, it was obvious they were annoyed.

Suddenly, on the landing above, a door creaked open and Father Miley appeared. The paleness of his face stood out eerily against his long black nightgown. He held a lighted candle in his hand and its flame illuminated the fierce glare on his face. His very presence was like that of an avenging angel. There was instant silence below. The women ran down the stairs. Father Miley pointed to me and said: "Go to your room, Duggan. I shall deal with this."

From my room I could hear Father Miley admonish the two young men in the most severe of tones. Not every word was clear to me but I heard him say "disgrace" and "immortal souls" and "occasions of sin." There appeared to be no response from the two young men.

In the morning Father Miley brought the matter up as I served breakfast. He particularly singled Mr Dan out for criticism. He was, he said, a disgrace to his family and to his country. It was not too bad for the Frenchman, he said, for the morals of the French were known the world over to be lax. It was a scandal, however, that a young Catholic Irishman, the son of the leading Catholic in the English-speaking world should behave in such a manner.

Mr O'Connell tried to come to his son's rescue. He was a spirited young man, he said, who had been locked away from the company of people of his age for the past several months. What could one expect, he asked, under such circumstances? Mr O'Connell smiled as he spoke and I remember that I thought of all the stories of the wild oats he himself had sown, especially in his student days. I recall too that his spirited defence of his son gave me hope that the Liberator's health was truly mending.

Father Miley would have no truck with Mr O'Connell's views. "I would most respectfully remind you, Mr O'Connell," he said, "that your illness has brought you to the point of death on a number of occasions during this journey. For you to condone sinful and shameful practices at a time in which your health is weak would be to risk eternal damnation." There was silence after this.

* * *

When breakfast had ended Father Miley called me to him and gave me a letter for the morning post to be sent to Mr Morgan O'Connell at the house in Merrion Square. He handed me the letter open and hurried off. I was left alone with an hour to spare before the post. I asked myself, should I read it without permission? I remembered my duty and resisted the lure. But I looked again at the envelope and the edge of the letter itself which protruded slightly from it became to me as a bait to a hungry trout. I took the letter out and read it. I remember thinking that I had as much right to know its contents as anyone had.

I copied out part of it which read:

*I delight to inform you that since Thursday last we have observed distinct indications of recovery. I said in my last that the remedies of the Lyonese physicians were telling well, I can now announce with confidence that they have told decisively. All the appearances are of one recovering and recovering steadily. We are now definitely turned towards Rome. His improvement augments – if that were possible – the further we proceed southward.*

*"Marseilles may be called the focus of his popularity in France, so intense has been the anxiety to do him honour at all*

*points. The distinguished by position, influence and wisdom crowd to manifest their respect and admiration.*

So it was, with ladies and gentlemen calling to see us all through the day, some of them returning several times to enquire after Mr O'Connell's health which, we were most pleased to tell them, was all the time improving.

Father Miley and Mr Dan met in the afternoon and decided Mr O'Connell's health was now so good that we should make the quickest possible journey to Rome. I was sent to the offices of the General Navigation Company to purchase tickets on the steamer *Lombardo* which plies from Marseilles to Rome, stopping at Genoa, Livorno and Civitavecchia. I met some difficulty at first but when I showed the letter of instructions in French to a gentlemen who appeared to have some authority I was brought into a private office and the tickets for the journey were written out quickly. The gentleman gave me his visiting card and in good English asked me to convey his best wishes for the improved health of Mr O'Connell.

The plan was for us to rest no more than six hours each at Genoa and Livorno, which was the amount of time allotted for the *Lombardo* to discharge its old cargoes and take on its new ones. From Civitavecchia to the Eternal City, where the arrival of the Liberator was, I was told, awaited with the greatest anxiety, was merely a short carriage ride.

Our hopes were never higher. Father Miley gave praise publicly to heaven saying that the worst was now most definitely over. "We have entered," he said, "on our progress towards complete recovery. Our charge, however, is of a value so inestimable that caution and vigilance must not be relaxed even for a moment."

Mr Dan and I agreed heartily. The only difference in my

view between Mr O'Connell's current condition and his constitution at its most robust strength was that he tired a little earlier in the evenings and rose a little later each morning. The improvement from Hastings to that day had been such that our hopes were at their highest.

Tuesday was set aside to enjoy Marseilles and its environs. A coach was placed at our disposal by the authorities of the city for use as we would wish but with a strong recommendation to travel to the outskirts of the city and take the air. This advice we took with joy, setting out in a party of four, with Doctor Lacour making his excuses and preferring to stay out of sight and one imagines, especially out of earshot of Mr O'Connell whose dislike of him had now almost reached the point of detestation. We travelled along the Corniche, a road that ran along the side of the mountains and was considerably elevated above the sea.

Our journey along the Corniche provided us with the most spectacular views down to the seashore. There we saw the bathing establishments frequented not only by the local inhabitants, we were told, but also by members of the great families of Great Britain who travel to this area annually, as do the nobility of all of Europe, from as far away as St Petersbourg. Members of the Imperial family of Russia had, we were informed, frequently come to this region for the bathing season.

At the Palace Hotel a pleasant lunch was laid on for Mr O'Connell, Mr Dan and Father Miley in the restaurant while I was taken to the kitchens and ate well there of fish soup. As usual they tried to ply me with wine which seems to be in more abundant supply, and cheaper too, than water. I had supped of the wine at other places on our journey and was not taken by it, so I asked for tea.

They provided me instead with an infusion that passed for tea in these parts, boiled water with a leaf or two in it. Just enough to make a stain in the liquid and not enough to give it any distinctive taste.

After lunch we went to the Borely Castle and its adjoining park which contains many exotic plants and trees, with broad lawns and at its southern end many elegant cafés and restaurants where the gentry can dine on terraces overlooking the Mediterranean with splendid views over its islands and headlands. Mr O'Connell partook of an energetic walk in these locations, breathing in the sea air deeply and expressing the view that his strength was returning to him. One could see his heart was full of hope for the first time since we had left home. His eyes were brighter than before, his complexion less pallid and his gait displaying some of its old vitality.

That night, after he had retired, Father Miley, a contrite Mr Dan and I – Doctor Lacour having once again begged to be excused – prayed earnestly that the miraculous recovery being effected by the Liberator should, by the grace of God, be permitted to continue.

* * *

We had a late start to the following day. Mr O'Connell, having taken a long soothing bath, declared that he felt even better than before. He sang the entire *"Gloria in Excelsis Deo"* before breakfasting on coffee and bread in the French manner and calling on Doctor Lacour to examine him now that he was almost back to his full health.

Doctor Lacour asked for his stools immediately but Mr O'Connell said he had none to show him and the

Frenchman warned that constipation could lead to further congestion of his entire system, including the brain, if it were to last longer. Mr O'Connell laughed aloud at this saying that all doctors were mountebanks and thieves who gathered around themselves an air of mystery with which to deceive the more gullible of their patients. Doctor Lacour left in bad temper.

By early afternoon we departed for the port where the *Lombardo* was getting up steam and a reception committee led by the captain awaited us on board.

The change in atmosphere from the French to the Italian was quite marked. The Italian master and his crew expressed their feelings of warmth and generosity towards Mr O'Connell in the most forthright manner without attending to the delicate mannerisms so cultivated by the French and regarded as artificial in the extreme by Mr O'Connell. I could not understand a word the Italians were saying, but by their gestures and their open smiling faces it was obvious that their intentions were to make us as welcome and comfortable as possible. Our journey, we were informed, was to be one of twenty-two hours following the coast of the Riviera past Toulon, Nice, Monaco, Menton, San Remo and Savona before arriving at Genoa at approximately three o'clock in the afternoon of the morrow.

We dined in the Italian style with the captain and his first mate, I being allowed to sit at table with the others. The meal was of macaronis and sauce, which I had great difficulty in guiding from plate to mouth much to the amusement of the Italian hosts and to Mr O'Connell himself. Eventually I had to cut up my macaronis into small pieces and eat them and their sauce from a spoon as though they were soup. Their laughter was one of humour rather than mockery and

I took it in good form. When I had cleared my plate they applauded me loudly and I entered into the spirit of the occasion by standing up and then giving a bow to all those present. I might not have been expert at eating macaronis, I remember thinking to my self, but as for bowing, that was something at which I had plenty of experience.

The meal appeared to give even further strength to Mr O'Connell who went on deck and walked around taking the air before retiring to his well-appointed cabin which, the crewmen told me in halting English, was reserved only for the most important of passengers.

It is odd now to think that not long after Mr O'Connell's death the same *Lombardo* was used by the Italian revolutionaries who despised Mr O'Connell's pacifism, on their journey southwards to Sicily in their quest to relieve his Holiness of his temporal power in the Papal States.

He slept soundly that night in the very bed that was soon to be Mr Garibaldi's. Mr O'Connell, however, was to be spared that knowledge of the future.

# CHAPTER FOURTEEN

## *My Master's Demise*

*May 6th 1847 Genoa*

On time at three o'clock in the afternoon the *Lombardo* pulled in at the Ponte Federico Guglielmo. The local customs officers inspected all our bags in a very meticulous manner despite their knowledge that they belonged to Mr O'Connell and his party and despite the arrival to meet us of the Marchese Pallache, the Governor General of the region, accompanied by the various foreign consuls.

Mr O'Connell had been on deck from an early hour that morning, wrapped in his greatcoat against a stiffening breeze that held no warmth. By the time luncheon was served, the Genoese coast was in sight and the sailors pointed out the snow on the mountains behind the city, a sight which, they told us, was never before seen by any of them at this time of the year. But now, suddenly, as he waited for the customs visit to finish he suffered a violent derangement of the stomach. He vomited once or twice, brushed Doctor Lacour from his presence and insisted that his sudden illness was merely the result of his long sea journey, which had mildly upset his stomach.

It was his first real sign of illness since Thursday of the previous week. At first we were all very upset at what seemed to be at best a setback or at worst the beginning of one of his dramatic declines. After some local attention and drinking of the mineral water of the region followed by a glass of brandy, the Liberator's spirits improved so much that he wanted to proceed to Leghorn at the earliest convenience. We put down his brief illness simply to the sea journey.

Our relief was immense but even so Mr Dan said he preferred that his father should make a short stay in Genoa in order to rest after his sudden seizure. Father Miley, of course, insisted that he should travel on. We were finally persuaded to stay by the consul who informed us the city had, in one Doctor Duff, an excellent English physician. Should Mr O'Connell's condition cause any concern, the consul told us, Doctor Duff would be prepared to attend to him at any hour of the day or night.

This last information swayed the argument. Mr O'Connell himself now opted to stay and glared at Doctor Lacour with a sense of victory, knowing that at least for the period of our stay the Frenchman's medical decisions would be open to challenge.

A messenger was sent to the Hotel Feder and returned with the news that the management would regard it as a great honour should the Liberator of Ireland decide to stay with them. The Marchese Pallache had made a coach available to us and we went quickly to the hotel which was situated very close to the seafront in one of the narrow streets that the Genoese, I was told, call a "*vico*". Some of these lanes are so narrow that two men cannot walk in them beside each other. One must follow the other and if someone approaches from the opposite direction both would have to stand in doorways to let him past.

The hotel was not unlike the Windsor in Paris. But instead of carpets being laid down, its floors were of bare marble of different colours forming a decorative pattern. This was polished to the highest sheen that caused you to fear losing your footing and dealing yourself a painful injury. But despite their lustre the floors were not slippery and my worries in regard to falling were completely unfounded.

Mr O'Connell was completely recovered upon arrival when the management paid its respects in a similar manner to that done by the Parisians, but with a great deal more gesturing and noisiness.

The suite of rooms made available to Mr O'Connell, Mr Dan and Father Miley was spacious and bright with windows looking out on to the narrow streets nearby. The tables bore large ornate jugs and washing basins and soap which had been impregnated with perfume.

The Genoese men had, according to Father Miley, been noted for certain womanish characteristics through the years.

I was put up in a room without windows in the back of the building. But this mattered little for there was a couch in the drawing-room of the suite where I chose to spend my sleeping hours in case Mr O'Connell needed my attention in the dead of night. I used the windowless room instead as a wardrobe for Mr O'Connell's outdoor clothing, getting his topcoat ready against the unseasonable cold.

Doctor Lacour, at Mr O'Connell's explicit request, was

given accommodation on the floor below the main suite and it was obvious that the relationship between the two men was worsening further if that were possible.

There were more macaronis for our supper with a sauce made from tomatoes and minced meat that was not at all unappetising and for this occasion and for other meals it was agreed that Doctor Lacour should be present with the rest of the group. Despite this concession Doctor Lacour and Mr O'Connell exchanged not a single word across the dining table.

But when Mr O'Connell retired the doctor, Father Miley and Mr Dan became involved in an agitated conversation about Mr O'Connell's condition. It was obvious that a major disagreement was afoot, for shortly after the discussion had begun Father Miley sent me off to polish Mr O'Connell's boots for a planned carriage outing in the morning.

On Friday May 7th, I noted in my diary, Mr O'Connell was to go out in the carriage with myself and Father Miley in attendance. Mr Dan would remain with Doctor Lacour with whom he maintained far closer and better relations than did his father. They decided to spend the day exploring the city of Genoa and seeing its many sights having promised first of all to Father Miley that there would be no repetition of their behaviour in Marseilles.

Accordingly Mr O'Connell, Father Miley and I set out after lunch through the incredibly narrow streets with the Liberator in castigating tones describing the filth, squalor and poverty which surrounded us for most of the way as being "worse than France." Indeed it appeared that way, for Marseilles with its white buildings presented a finer and cleaner aspect than the greyer, darker and more concentrated buildings of Genoa. As for filth, squalor and poverty, we had seen enough of this in Dublin before our departure and indeed among the squatters in Derrynanebeg too. Criticising the Genoese for their lack of cleanliness seemed somewhat an exaggeration but Mr O'Connell has ever been given to such.

After some time we departed from the ancient centre of the city, and climbed uphill all the while towards the mount of Acquasola. There in the new park that has replaced a collection of ruined buildings, concerts of music were given on three afternoons of the week at this time of year. Rows of seats were placed around the bandstand upon which musicians in old-style tricorne hats and with scarlet sashes draped across their navy blue uniforms played lively airs from the Italian operas.

Mr O'Connell tarried only a minute or two at the bandstand before setting off for a brisk walk along the edge of the park. I followed him there and the views over the city, its bay and the massive complex of docks, piers and shipyards that made Genoa the principal commercial centre of the Italian peninsula, were exceptionally striking.

The descent back to the city was so precipitate that the horses had some difficulty in keeping their feet especially in turning the extremely sharp and spiralling bends. It was for us an experience that was terrifying, exciting and tiring all at the same time.

We retired early and determined to make the same carriage airing on the morrow.

* * *

Following our second trip to the park at Acquasola on the following day, Mr O'Connell dozed in his room after his outing in the fresh air. It was then that Doctor Lacour opened a discussion with Father Miley and Mr Dan. He repeatedly spoke of the danger of what he called Mr O'Connell's constipation. This he said would cause congestion through the entire body that would eventually reach the brain. The derangement of the stomach he had suffered upon arrival had, Doctor Lacour said, been his body's method of relieving the incipient congestion. There had been no derangement since then and therefore the congestion was increasing again and soon it would reach a stage which would threaten the Liberator's life.

I felt this was wrong. The Liberator's health had improved through the absence of the diarrhoea. His strength had recovered and there was no sign of his health deteriorating. I thought about giving my opinion on the matter but felt if I ventured to do so I could be accused of wanting Mr O'Connell to be constipated so that I would not have to clean him. I knew too that a servant's opinion would first of all not be considered and secondly would be regarded as insolent. I desisted, much as it hurt me to do so and to see my master's health manipulated in such a way.

Doctor Lacour favoured another enema. Mr Dan trusted him and agreed while Father Miley also concurred. It was decided to proceed there and then. Doctor Lacour looked particularly pleased at the decision and I went with him to Mr O'Connell's bedroom.

The plan was as follows: Mr O'Connell was not to be told what was to be done but informed that a general inspection was to be made to determine the extent of his recovery. He was then to be told he was to have an injection and by that ruse he to be taken by surprise with the enema.

This is what was done. It was a dreadful thing to perpetrate on a man who, for all his faults, was possessed of great virtues. A man of important standing throughout the entire continent of Europe, as witnessed by the crowds of people who still followed him around, was sorely humiliated. His roars and bellows, as he was held down by his son and his chaplain to be violated by the French doctor, I can still hear in my mind to this very day.

This operation, I solemnly still believe, had the effect of reducing Mr O'Connell's health to the state it had been in before he had set out from England. I can forgive Mr Dan for what was done. He was, after all, a young and inexperienced man and easily led. He felt too that he was acting to help his father. I had some sympathy for Doctor Lacour at the way he had been treated by Mr O'Connell but the relish he appeared to take at imposing such a drastic measure upon the Liberator was unforgiveable. But above all I was disgusted at Father Miley's part in what happened. I had heard him asking the doctor about what effect the enema might have. He had not been impressed when told it would relieve the pressure from the brain, nor did he seem pleased at the prospect that it would extract poison from his body. It was when Doctor Lacour said that the enema, foul a measure as it might appear, would hasten our departure for Rome that our Father Confessor nodded his approval contentedly.

Mr O'Connell suffered a very bad night from the effects of Doctor Lacour's exertions. His humiliation had not only dealt a blow to his physical strength but had also appeared to have hastened problems with his brain rather than alleviating them. He awoke several times in the night bathed in sweat and muttering to himself. Mostly his words were mere nonsenses but at times he expressed his old fears of death itself or of being buried alive.

Father Miley celebrated the Holy Sacrifice of the Mass next morning in the hotel with the permission and express warrant of His Holiness, something which attracted a great deal of attention from those who worked in the great building. Mr O'Connell, however, knelt throughout with his head bowed and his eyes closed and wiping an occasional silent tear from his cheeks.

After Mass he took to his bed and kept saying to me that he was sure he could not live after the effects of the enema. Again and again he asked: "Duggan, why did you let them do this to me?" I could not answer him. I wanted to answer but I was trapped. My intervention would not have stopped the enema and despite his anger Mr O'Connell would have known this. He wanted to have someone to blame for his plight. I was on hand. I was a servant. Servants did not answer back. I remained silent.

His lunch was brought to him but he refused to eat and chased Mr Dan and Father Miley from the room. Then he put the fear of God in me for the first time since Lyons. His mind was wandering again.

"Duggan," he summoned me, "I earnestly entreat you that under no circumstances should you forget to collect the message for Mr Morgan. It is a bulky parcel but it will benefit his intellect and this is particularly needed at this time. It is the *Cyclopaedia Britannica* in several volumes which shall give young Morgan a knowledge of this world in all its aspects. It is the ideal thing for a fresh young mind, don't you think?" He was talking of his son Morgan as if he were a small boy when at this time he was forty-three years of age, had served in the Austrian Army and in the legion of the other Liberator, General Bolivar in the South Americas. He had also been elected Member of Parliament for the county of Meath.

This was a most distressing turn of events. But when I informed Father Miley, who had come to observe Mr O'Connell's condition, he seemed not to believe me as the Liberator was sleeping soundly and without obvious discomfort. I did not bring the matter to the attention of Mr Dan for he was, as I have said, a sweet-tempered lad and I wished not to disturb him.

When Father Miley departed Mr O'Connell awoke and once more berated me for allowing the enema. He swore he would not eat again, crying that the French doctor was out to kill him. Then he ordered me to go out and collect the false teeth for a Mr Brophy. They were, he said, of vital importance as this man could not speak or eat without them and would die if they were not quickly collected from the depository in South Brunswick street.

It was obvious too that Mr O'Connell's speech had changed. He talked much more quickly and his movements were jerky. Also the diarrhoea had returned, sapping away all his strength and he became a truly pitiable sight.

Mr Dan and Father Miley appeared not to realise how badly his health had deteriorated and they retired to bed at ten o'clock. I stayed up to tend to the Liberator who did not sleep at any time during the night and whose mind became prey to the darkest thoughts of death without proper religious preparation and of an eternity in the fires of hell.

He was no better on Monday morning and swore to me that once again he would not eat to spite "the French pup", as he now consistently called Doctor Lacour. An Italian physician, Doctor Beretta, who offered his services was also turned away by Mr O'Connell. Indeed there would have been no treatment whatsoever without the arrival of Doctor Duff, who had for some time ministered to the English community in Genoa, including many men and women of quality who had retired to these parts in order to effect an improvement to their health.

Doctor Duff was in his late thirties. He was tall and thin, perhaps six foot three and no more than twelve stone in weight. He dressed as a gentleman, his suit well cut, his shoes obviously brought from London and his attire topped off with a tall silk hat.

It was his choice of colour most of all which set him aside as a foreigner. Everything he wore was black or at least of a sombre hue. His light-brown hair and moustache stood out against this background of his clothing just as the black hair and moustache stood out against the light clothes of the Italians.

He made it clear from the beginning of his visit that his views as well as his appearance were English. The Irish, he said, were born to be ruled from their "sister island". Historically they were, he said, "a British tribe" and therefore subject to the rule of the most superior of the "British tribes" to which he happened to belong.

Mr O'Connell, despite having listened to this nonsense, welcomed Doctor Duff's arrival warmly and allowed him to do an examination. In the course of this the Liberator was calm and courteous but did complain of a severe pain in his stomach the onset of which, he said, coincided with application of the enema by Doctor Lacour.

The examination complete, Doctor Duff called Mr Dan and Father Miley to the drawing-room. I brought them coffee and heard what was said. He informed them that Mr O'Connell's health was under great pressure. His pulse was strong and very rapid, his face was flushed which was also an indication of his distress and it appeared to him that there had been chronic bronchitis of some years standing. The most serious problem, however, was that Mr O'Connell was suffering from "profuse and involuntary diarrhoea." Doctor Duff explained that as Doctor Lacour had been Mr O'Connell's physician since we departed from Lyons, he would be prepared to work with him but not to replace him as had been strongly suggested by the Liberator.

Doctor Duff returned to Mr O'Connell who seemed quite soothed by his presence, certainly calm enough to allow him place leeches to the anus in order to relieve pressure. This I could not watch. I turned away because I could not face the humiliation. He was after all, my master. I could not bring myself, for all my hopes of leaving servitude, to see him made inferior to me.

Despite all Doctor Duff's entreaties, Mr O'Connell still refused to eat and worse still would not even drink a simple glass of water, even if it were offered to him by me or by Mr Dan or Father Miley.

When matters quieted down he called me to him again and repeated to me what had now become his most frequent request: "Duggan," he said once more, "you are the only one I can trust. For God's sake do not let them bury me until I am dead." And once again he was unable to sleep for most of the night. He remained quiet for most of the time with the odd distressing moment when he considered himself to be on the verge of an eternity in which his soul would suffer the most awful punishments imaginable.

For a long time he would be peaceful but then he would

tremble and shake himself and mutter words of desperation. "An eternity without a thought," I heard him say as he shuddered. "I won't see them again," I heard him say at another time. At yet another, as I listened closely in case he needed attention, I heard him say the two words: "buried alive."

For most of the night he seemed to fight against the invasion of sleep. It was as though he feared that if he gave in to slumber he might not wake again. It was almost four o'clock before he gave in to his tiredness and slept for a short while.

When Doctors Duff and Beretta arrived for their consultation next day Mr O'Connell was in very severe condition and certainly appeared no better than he had done on the previous day. He seemed, however, to be able to concentrate his mind in their presence and refrained from showing any feebleness of the brain during their consultations. He still managed to retain his darkest looks for Doctor Lacour whom he now cordially detested. His feelings toward Doctor Beretta were a little better, and he still seemed to get on quite well with Doctor Duff. Despite his political opposition to Mr O'Connell on many issues, Doctor Duff had said he valued his professional ethics very highly and would have given the same attention to restoring the health of Mr O'Connell as he would to that of Sir Robert Peel.

As soon as the doctors left, the manic reverie began again. Mr O'Connell summoned me imperiously and asked me had Mr Wyse brought forward his motion and who had seconded it. He seemed convinced that he was now in the Commons in London and was excited, as always, by the activity that went on in that place. Sir Thomas Wyse was indeed one of Mr O'Connell's greatest supporters and had withdrawn from the election in Waterford County back in 1830 to allow victory for the Liberator. Sir Thomas at this time was the member for Waterford City and under very severe pressure from the Young Ireland faction but had also become secretary of the Board of Control for India.

It was strange therefore to hear Mr O'Connell declaim: "Wyse is a madman. Come here to me Wyse, you bloody fool. Where is your motion? Who is the seconder? What in the name of Almighty God are you playing at, Wyse?" It came as a surprise to me, a mere servant, to hear one gentleman of substance speak of another in such a matter. Perhaps this sort of berating was common but if so was usually performed out of earshot of the servant classes.

After luncheon, of which Mr O'Connell once again refused to partake, the doctors returned for another consultation. As God is my judge, they gave him another enema to relieve the "congestion" and this although the diarrhoea continued unabated.

I could not and still cannot understand why Doctor Duff allowed himself to be a party to this savagery. Had he not earlier spoken of the need not to disturb the patient's stomach? But he had earlier also said he would not take over from Doctor Lacour as Mr O'Connell's principal medical adviser. Perhaps this is why he offered a medicinal potion after the enema in order to bind Mr O'Connell's guts together again. But Mr O'Connell refused it, glaring all the while at Doctor Lacour. His persistent cough which had been absent in Marseilles returned suddenly and for some reason which I fail to understand the enema appeared to arrest the diarrhoea instead of increasing its frequency.

The doctors called Mr O'Connell's party together again

in the drawing-room of the suite. Doctor Duff told them that a new symptom had presented itself in the form of congestion of the brain and that Mr O'Connell's refusal to swallow even the smallest drop of medicine was compounding an already very complicated situation. The symptoms they now began to detect were doziness, a flushed countenance and pains in the head as well as his adoption of a particular and peculiar position in the bed as though he were again an infant in his mother's womb. This I had myself noticed, but had put it down to the application of leeches to the anus making him bring his legs up to his belly. We were to look out in the future, they told us, for vertigo, difficulty of speech and a sense of fullness as well as a further strengthening and quickening of the pulse.

Then they left to partake of a supper of lobster and swordfish. As they dined Mr O'Connell returned immediately to parliament where he seemed to address that group of members who supported him and who were known there as his "tail".

Repeal was certain, he told them. In the oratorical tones he used in Westminster he kept repeating the phrase "it is in the bag". He seemed annoyed that no one was there to reply or to applaud his statement for it was after all an important announcement. "They don't seem to be listening, Duggan," he told me on numerous occasions.

"It's in the bag," he repeated again and again in a voice ever decreasing in strength until finally he fell into a light and trembling sleep. It was his first rest in two days. I myself was now on the point of exhaustion from being permanently, day and night, in Mr O'Connell's presence attending to his every need and, most unpleasantly of all, being occupied all the time with cleaning up after his constant diarrhoea.

Doctor Lacour entered as Mr O'Connell dozed and placed leeches behind his ears at which he awoke. On seeing Doctor Lacour depart he declared to me: "Duggan, do not under any circumstances allow the Frenchman even to come near me in the future."

I stayed with him and sat quietly. I could see the sun shining outside and occasionally looked out to the alleyway abutting on the hotel to watch the scenes of great animation that took place each day. A marvellous assortment of fruits was being bought and sold and the brightness of the day and the fullness of life was being enacted before my eyes. Then I would turn back to the room and see it full of darkness and shadow with Mr O'Connell lying pallid and debilitated in his large bed. That one inward glance reminded me that I was inhabiting the land of the shadow of death, a territory at odds with those who created all the busy hustle in the outside world.

My routine was to sit close to Mr O'Connell at all times to listen to his requests. I would clean him up from his diarrhoea and have fresh sheets brought from the hotel's laundry at every turn. I would bring Mr O'Connell the urinal when necessary and I would try to remember anything untoward that happened. It was my duty to report these events to the doctors when they paid their morning and afternoon visits.

On that day, according to the notes I made at the time, his symptoms increased. The diarrhoea was more persistent and he became restless and spoke with a great incoherence, beginning a sentence on one topic and ending it on a matter which was completely unrelated.

Mr O'Connell's room had now become my prison from which the only release appeared when I went out to empty the urinal or bring the dirty sheets down to the launderer. He was an evil-looking man with a hooked nose. He invariably muttered at me under his breath as if to suggest that the filthiness of the linen was caused by some habitual lack of cleanliness on my own part. I had become so lost in my thoughts on my imprisonment that when the doctors came for their evening visit I had very little to tell them. I had forgotten to note the frequency of the diarrhoea or the number of times he had used the urinal but I was able to report his increased restlessness and his incoherence of speech.

At Doctor Lacour's insistence they performed yet another enema.

* * *

On the morning of Thursday May 13th Mr O'Connell was almost completely delirious and did not recognise either Father Miley or Mr Dan when they visited. Ominously one of the predictions made by Doctor Duff had come to pass: Mr O'Connell's voice had become scarcely audible, more broken and weaker even than was reported on the occasion of his last speech to parliament.

Once again that is where he considered himself to be. He rallied his supporters. He spoke of deals to be done with the Whigs. He talked of his hatred for the Tories and especially for Sir Robert Peel and Mr Disraeli, whom he regarded as untrustworthy for having changed his religion, he believed, to enhance his political career.

They say that when approaching death the minds of many people turn back to their youth and this surely happened to Mr O'Connell. Suddenly, sitting there on my own I heard him speak in Irish, the first tongue he had spoken in his childhood in Kerry and I called in Mr Dan who understood the Irish as well for, though I understood the tongue from my own Tipperary days, I felt that my record of what was being said would not be accepted.

Mr Dan had to strain to hear him and then turned away with the tears in his eyes. "He is reciting," he said, "from the great poem *Caoineadh Airt Uí Laoghaire*, written by his aunt, his father's sister Eibhlín Dhubh Ní Chonaill. I heard him say these words:

'*Is gránna an chóir a chur ar ghaiscíoch,*
*Comhra agus caipín.*'

In the English it could have been put this way:

'*It is an ill-looking rig-out for a hero,*
*A coffin and a cap.*'"

Once again when the doctors came for their late visit he had pulled himself together and spoke coherently once more and in English, which caused less embarrassment.

Doctor Duff informed Mr Dan and Father Miley that all Mr O'Connell's symptoms had increased. He had developed a great tendency to sleep but a light sleep which did not refresh him and from which he was very easily roused. His breathing was embarrassed, his circulation difficult and his pulse indistinct and these symptoms and his tendency to further incoherence all indicated a congestion on the brain.

When they had left he called me and once again pleaded that he should not be buried until after it was absolutely certain that he had died. Then he questioned the existence of heaven or hell. "We face," he said "the bleak prospect of an eternity in which we shall be unable to speak, or see, or touch, or smell, or hear, or taste or think."

I immediately informed Father Miley of this despair in which Mr O'Connell found himself, as I feared that should he pass away in such a condition that the fires of hell would surely lie in wait for him. Father Miley came and comforted him and helped him to pray and to trust in Our Lord Jesus Christ until, close to midnight, he spoke of walking down the Strand in London and of setting out for Ireland on the morrow. Then he dozed off to sleep.

He awoke on Friday with a strange blister, which had developed at the back of his head. The doctors said this was of little importance. This time Doctor Duff, who had now assumed the role of principal physician, had brought with him not only the hated Doctor Lacour and the ineffectual Doctor Beretta but also Doctor Viviani who, they said, was the oldest and most respected medical practitioner in the city of Genoa.

There was much consultation and examining of stools and piss. The earthenware pots containing the material that had so recently been inside the Liberator, they raised to their noses and peered into at close range, in the manner of gentlemen sniffing and admiring glasses of important wine.

There was a determined period of nodding and shaking of heads and then a large basin was called for which I procured from the kitchen of the hotel. Mr O'Connell's left arm, that nearest the heart, was extended out of the bed with the basin held under it. Doctor Duff severed a vein at the bend of the arm on the inside and bled Mr O'Connell into the basin for several minutes. And I knew that Doctor McCabe so long ago in Hastings had been right in his judgment that Mr O'Connell would die before he reached Rome and in my mind I cursed those who did not heed him.

The bleeding so weakened Mr O'Connell that he ceased his incoherent conversations in the English and Irish languages and began to doze again.

The doctors retired across the street to consult with each other and went their separate ways leaving us in peace until their evening visit. In their absence Mr O'Connell called me again but this time only to refer to his diarrhoea and the state of the sheets by whispering to me in the weakest voice: "We will be disgraced before we leave this house." As night wore on his condition became more feeble by the minute and in the early hours of the following morning his prostration was extreme.

* * *

### Saturday, May 15th 1847

At two o'clock in the morning his breathing became distressed in the extreme and his thoughts concentrated solely on leaving this world on good terms with his Maker. Then he calmed down and prayed and did not express his usual fears about being buried alive.

Father Miley sent to the Cathedral Church of Genoa for the Viaticum and even the aged and infirm Cardinal Archbishop raised himself from his sick-bed. He joined the vicar-general of the diocese and a large contingent of the clergy and laity of the city. Although it was the dead of night they set out in procession from the cathedral to the Hotel Feder.

The Eucharist was carried under a canopy, thurifers cast incense into the night air, the hymns and prayers that marked the end of a life were recited. Shutters were clanked open and latches lifted by those awakened to the sound of the *"De profundis clamavi ad te Domine"*. I knew the sombre hymn. *"I have cried to you out of the depths, O Lord."* At first I heard only the notes of the hymn in the distance. As they came nearer the clank of the chain on the thuribles reached my ears. Then I began to hear the dull but persistent noise of feet against stone, and finally as the music of the hymns and the sound of the chains and the noise of the feet grew louder the scent of the incense finally invaded my nostrils.

Soon they were on the staircase and as I glanced out the window I saw that all the shutters of the street were open. There were faces at the windows, some curious in mien but most of them apparently aware of what was in progress. The sign of the cross was being constantly made by many of them.

In the Feder the priests and the doctors were soon at their work. As Father Miley applied the chrism and holy oils, the doctors put cataplasms, large poultices bound in wool and plaster, on his thighs. These made him so uncomfortable that in the presence of the doctors he asked me to remove them.

For every move the priests made to prepare him for the next life the doctors made a countermove to keep him in this one. He greeted the administerings of the priests with feeble attempts to pray and at one state managed to say the prayer of St Bernard of Clairvaux which is also known as the *Memorare*. He began the prayer himself:

*"Remember O most gracious Virgin Mary, that never was it known that anyone who fled to thy protection, implored thy help or sought thy intercession was left unaided."*

He then appeared to forget the rest of the prayer and

Father Miley had to help him along: *"Inspired by this confidence I fly unto thee, O Virgin of Virgins my Mother,"* Father Miley said.

Mr O'Connell repeated the words breathlessly before remembering the final part and saying in a weak whisper but of his own volition: *"To thee do I come. Before thee I stand, sinful and sorrowful. O Mother of the Word Incarnate despise not my petition but in thy mercy hear and answer me. Amen."*

The Sacred Host was the only matter consumed by him in more than two whole days and even that he managed to swallow with the greatest of difficulty.

At four in the morning when the doctors and the priests had gone and Father Miley and Mr Dan had left me alone with him, he called "Water, water!" but when I brought the water to him, he brushed it aside and pointed to the floor. I brought him the urinal then and he made water in it without my assistance looking at the quantity as usual.

When the doctors came again at daybreak they said they still had hope that he would survive the crisis. But Father Miley told them: "I have no hope save that of heaven."

All the same Doctor Viviani tried an application of leeches to the temples and Mr Dan, the poor young man, broke down and cried like a baby for the first time in this most trying of journeys.

Mr O'Connell went quiet then and at noon I managed to eat a cold lunch while he slept. At three in the afternoon he called me again and his voice was so weak that I had to place my ear almost in his mouth to hear him say: "As yet I am not dying." The calmness which came over him seemed to indicate a resignation that his life on earth was drawing to a close and he confirmed that he knew this by calling Father

Miley at five o'clock and saying to him: "I am dying, my dear friend."

At eight in the evening the sun set out at sea, out at the west where Ireland was. Mr O'Connell became almost completely still, the fierce pain in the abdomen either having deserted him or his strength having ebbed so much that he could feel nothing.

When the sun had gone, Mr O'Connell departed. I cannot forget the sound. It was for all the world like the gurgling noise of the final emptying of waters down in a drain; just as the last portions of his life sank from Mr O'Connell, Doctor Duff placed a mirror to his mouth and pronounced him dead.

## CHAPTER FIFTEEN

# *Disembowelment*

As Giambattisa Ballieri walked across the Piazza delle Fontane Marose every bell in Genoa was ringing. The large bells of the large churches and those of the cathedral of San Lorenzo boomed out their bass voices, the tenors and sopranos of the smaller chapels and oratories tinkled in obeisance. From his sick bed the aged Cardinal Archbishop had ordered the bells rung to mourn the death of Mr O'Connell in the Hotel Feder down at the waterfront.

Ballieri was on his way to the Feder, his long, narrow black case with its silver fasteners placed under his left arm, his fat brown bag held firmly by the handle in his right hand. He had one stop to make on the way where the upper city began its tumbling progress towards the sea.

In a narrow vico, just off the Via Luccoli, was the atelier of Ferruccio the cutler, well-known to Ballieri in his position as chief surgeon in the Hospital for Incurables.

Ferruccio was a cantankerous old man in his eighties, a

hunchback with a flat almost no-nosed face who always dressed in black and was reputed to be the ugliest being in Genoa. Ballieri knew the sort of ill-humoured reception his unannounced visit on a Sunday morning would engender. The cutler answered the surgeon's knock cursing the "stronzo Irlandese", the Irish turd, who had shattered the peace of the Genoese morning with his cacophony of bells.

"I was expecting you," he told Ballieri. "When a big knob like the Irishman dies they call on the chief surgeon to work on his body."

"Well, here I am, Ferruccio, and you are not surprised, eh."

"Surprised?" Ferruccio asked. "I have a surprise for you. This Irishman is the biggest fish ever to fall into your net. You will want your gruesome tools to be at their best, their sharpest. You don't want that Englishman Duff to make snide remarks, do you? You will want every incision to be perfect, will you not?

Ballieri nodded slightly.

"Well, it's Sunday," growled Ferruccio, "and I want double the usual fee and I want it in advance."

Ballieri, with the financial astuteness for which the Genoese were noted, had expected this and palmed a small red velvet tie-bag of coins to the old artisan. Ferruccio opened it and counted. "You anticipated my request, I see, and you want them all sharpened," he said. "The amount you have tendered is exactly that required."

Ballieri opened the long rectangular case and placed the array of instruments on the counter. There were knives of many sorts: some with long thin blades, others with blades that were short and squat, some blades flat, others corrugated. One, for all the world like an apple-corer, was used for extracting samples from the organs of the dead.

There was also a great shears for opening up the breast bone, a contraption of ingenious craftsmanship made by Ferruccio himself, and capable, just like the deep-toothed saw which accompanied it, of being telescoped to a size small enough to fit inside the long, narrow black case.

"There will be time as well as money involved in this. An hour at the least."

Ballieri said he would go for a walk and return in forty-five minutes, putting the pressure on Ferruccio who he knew would have the job done in that time.

He walked briskly to the broad Via Roma where the Caffè Andrea Doria was opening its doors. The talk of the early comers, mainly elderly men of the professional and propertied classes, was of O'Connell and of the bells. Some, the most self-contained, the most smug, spoke of how one of the most famous men on earth had come to breathe his last in Genoa or "La Superba" as most them, without the slightest hint of modesty, called their city.

Ballieri ordered a coffee and a square of cake. The old men eyed him, for they knew who he was and had a fair idea of the mission on which he was bound. He knew they found him a menacing sight: a strangely-shaped man, full of physical paradoxes, ridiculously low in height yet with an immensely strong-looking torso. His forearms, bulging thick with muscular strength, and his hands, small and delicate and long-fingered, filled the onlookers with terror.

He used a knife to carve the cake into small, bite-size pieces and did so accurately and above all with such lightning speed, that all the old men looked away in unison, thinking that some day, all too soon, those very hands might go to work on their own bodies.

He smiled to himself at his little practical joke, left a few centesimi for the waiter and set off for Ferruccio's workshop once more. The tools sat there gleaming in their case, all but a knife with a long and tapering blade. Ferruccio held the handle down on the bench lightly forming a fulcrum between the thumb and forefinger of his right hand. With his left he pressed the tip of the blade until a bead of blood appeared on his index finger.

Below the blade sat a gleaming apple. Ferruccio let the blade fall under its own weight to slice the fruit so neatly in two that when the halves were pressed together again the apple appeared perfect and untouched. This had been the way he had always demonstrated his work to Ballieri. It had become a gruesome ritual.

Ferruccio winked as he placed the knife in its allotted place in the bag. Ballieri nodded, placed the case under his right arm and set off down the Via Luccoli which became the Via Soziglia, which in turn became the Via Degli Orefici, the street of the goldsmiths, at different and lower levels of the city on its journey towards the sea.

Before the Piazza Banchi, with the waterfront Palazzo di San Giorgio and the Hotel Feder in sight, the sound of the bells became particularly intense. The tenors of Santa Maria delle Scuole Pie and San Pietro pierced the skull through the left ear, the Basso Profondo of Santa Maria delle Vigne boomed in from the right.

The laneways that led to Santa Maria delle Vigne were filled with the artisans of the archdiocese bearing black drapes for the altars, faldstools for the leaders of society, reams of sacred music for the choir and black vestments edged with gold thread for the priests who would say the Mass over the Irishman's body.

In a workshop not far away on the Vico Torre San Luca a

heavy lead coffin was being placed into another, larger coffin of polished hardwood. The lead coffin was lined with Lyonese silk and a drape of crimson Genoese velvet had been prepared to cover them both. In an attic off the street of the goldsmiths an engraver was etching the words for the coffin's silver plate.

In another attic on the same street another engraver was inscribing a silver urn in which O'Connell's heart was to be placed and sent to Rome. It had been decided that, just as the dead Robert Bruce had his heart sent on to Jerusalem when he died before his pilgrimage had been complete, so the Liberator's body should return to his western island and his heart go on to the Eternal City to be enshrined there forever.

* * *

Doctors Lacour, Duff, Beretta and Viviani were waiting with Father Miley for Ballieri in the hall of the Feder to accompany him to the room in which O'Connell had died. The body had been placed on a low table to accommodate Ballieri's lack of height. The tall Duff towered over the surgeon, even the dapper Lacour appeared of greater than average stature by comparison.

The five men donned back-to-front white coats, each helping the other to tie the garb firmly into place. The knives were taken from the long, narrow, black case and placed in line on a low bench.

Duggan, the Irishman's servant, was called to fetch the necessary basins of water, and the operation began with Ballieri piercing the skin in the region of the solar plexus with the lower blade of the great shears. At once a vile odour filled the room. But thoughts which had concentrated momentarily on the stench were soon diverted as the little barrel of a man summoned up all his strength to snap the breastbone and open the body of Daniel O'Connell to the world.

Bit by bit, piece by piece, the interior of the Liberator of Ireland was taken out and examined. As the five men stood in a rough circle round the corpse, dipping their hands in, pulling a organ out, one of them standing at his full height, the others bending down steeply, Ballieri briefly glimpsed the scene through one of the room's mirrors. The doctors, he thought, presented a picture that looked remarkably like small boys on a seaside outing extracting crabs from a pool. He grinned at this for a moment before concentrating once more on the job in hand.

Lesions were noted in several organs, the catarrh that remained in the right lung was inspected with great care by Duff. Lacour, with his obsession with the bowels and stools, unwound the long tube of O'Connell's intestines as though it had been a coiled snake. He sniffed at its contents before proclaiming he had detected the vestiges of a former inflammation.

In his hands now, Ballieri held the heart about which he had read so many metaphors in the newspapers. It had been large with generosity. It had symbolised O'Connell's love for his country. It was to be sent to Rome as a token of O'Connell's faithfulness to the church. It was nothing like this now he thought. There had been no difficulty in detaching it from the veins that bound it to the body.

Ballieri placed it in a small copper casserole purloined from the hotel kitchens. It lay there, larger than a calf's heart and smaller than that of an ox. It looked as though it was being readied for the oven.

Then came the sound of metal sawing through bone. Ballieri was at work on O'Connell's head. The brain, the seat of the great man's intellect, was about to be revealed in an operation of the utmost delicacy. The surgeon sliced all the way round through the skull stopping just short of the brain. Then he tapped the head sharply to ensure all connections had been broken, lifted off the top of the head like a hat and placed it on the bench beside the knives.

No one was prepared for what was to be revealed. All of them had been present at the opening of bodies and heads before. They expected to view the trite and crumpled greyness of the human brain that had been a commonplace in their medical experience.

What they were presented with made them gasp. O'Connell's brain was bright crimson in colour. It was gorged with blood throughout its entire extent. Here and there it had become as soft as jelly. Doctor Duff pointed to the membranes which had become inflamed and thickened. A joint diagnosis of "congestion of the brain" was reached unanimously and without delay.

Ballieri now opened the fat brown bag. Here were needles and catgut wound into a ball and syringes and little phials of coloured liquid. What Ballieri had put asunder, he would bind together again.

First he pulled out the organs and had them placed in a large basin. Then his hands moved round the body as neatly as those of an expert seamstress as he sewed the wounds and incisions together. Just as the halves of the apple had matched perfectly, so too was the top of O'Connell's head replaced. A red, gluey substance used to bind the bone together again was wiped away to reveal a perfect union.

The syringes were then filled with the liquids from the

phials and injected in to the body at specific locations, many of them still bearing the suction marks of the leeches. The silversmith's apprentice had arrived with the urn at precisely the right moment. The surgeon injected the heart with balm, plopped it in the receptacle and placed it on the window ledge. He noted the inscription:

*Daniel O'Connell*
*Natus Kerry*
*Obiit Genuae*
*Die XV Maii 1847*
*Aetatis Suae Ann. LXXII.*

As though to condescend to Duff he slowly translated the words into English: "Daniel O'Connell. Born in Kerry. Died in Genoa on the 15th day of May 1847 in the 72nd year of his age."

The doctors, in a strange ritual, turned their backs to each other and helped themselves out of their gowns. A hotel servant slid the innards of the Liberator from the basin into a sack and removed it from the room.

Perfumed candles were lit to rid the room of its stench.

The attendance of the medical profession on Daniel O'Connell, Liberator of Ireland, had come to an end. His mortal remains had been emptied of their offal. What was left had been embalmed. His heart had been readied for its grisly journey to Rome. The doctors now donned their street clothes and headed out for a final luncheon together at the Ristorante Cambio on the Piazza delle Vigne.

The tiniest trace of O'Connell's blood could be observed in a crevice of the print of the middle finger Ballieri's left hand as he expertly dissected a brace of quail. The four other doctors complimented him on his carving, which left not a trace of flesh on a single bone of the small birds' carcasses.

The entrails of other men who had departed this life in the city of Genoa – but not Mr O'Connell's, for his name was too respected – were jokingly compared to those of the little birds which lay on the surgeon's plate. Laughter resounded across the square and a toast in the wine of the Cinque Terre was proposed to the expertise of Ballieri, his knives and his potions. As they raised their glasses to the squat surgeon he saw a group of men in long scarlet soutanes and glistening white surplices emerge from the main door of Santa Maria delle Vigne and walk slowly, long white candles in their hands, in the direction of the Feder.

Ballieri mused, as he ate, on the next rite to be performed on the body of Daniel O'Connell. It was a ceremonial designed to prepare the corpse for its return to ashes and the soul for the eternity that, Ballieri had been told by Miley, had instilled such morbid fear in the Liberator over the last months. The leaden coffin, cased in wood would be brought to the hotel room and Mr O'Connell's embalmed body placed in it with lighted candles at each corner so that on this Sunday the religious and lay people of the city could file past the Liberator's mortal remains.

The entire community of the city's Jesuits passed the diners, marching from the Church of Sant' Ambrogio in their black soutanes. From the Annunziata del Vastato, the bearded Capuchins, their brown robes tied at the waist with white cords, came to pay their respects. All the while, from the moment of O'Connell's death to his removal from the Feder to Santa Maria delle Vigne, the bells of every church in Genoa tolled their solemn and remorseless dirge.

* * *

Mr O'Connell's heart having been placed in the silver urn, his body having been laid out in its coffin and the wake having been attended by large numbers of the city's clergy and laity, I was given a brief respite from my duties and allowed to rest in my own room for the first time since we had arrived in Genoa.

It would be no exaggeration to state that I had reached the very point of exhaustion, but sleep did not come easily. My mind raced all the time, trying to piece together the confused events of the past days into a logical order.

The business of Mr O'Connell's heart being removed and sent on to Rome, is something I am still not clear about. It has become the accepted belief now that Mr O'Connell willed his body to Ireland and his heart to Rome, but I was with him through all of his death agony and I cannot remember him do this. I did not hear the phrase, so often quoted since: *"My body to Ireland, my heart to Rome, my soul to heaven"* in the course of my attendance upon the Liberator.

What I do remember is Father Miley telling Mr Dan about Robert the Bruce and his heart being sent on to Jerusalem after he had died while travelling on a pilgrimage to the Holy Land. I can only assume that the separation of heart and body was decided upon by Father Miley, rather than by the Liberator himself whose last hours were taken up in prayer and the insistence that he not be buried alive.

I was sent to order the urn for Mr O'Connell's heart, and for this I was grateful as it allowed me to depart from the mustiness and the depressing atmosphere of the death room for the first time since the murderous enema had been perpetrated upon him.

The brightness of that Sunday morning will remain in my

mind as long as I live, coming as it did after the half-light I had lived in for the best part of a week. Becoming part of the noise and bustle I had occasionally witnessed from the hotel room windows, also served to brighten my spirits. I worried about feeling happy on so sad an occasion. But even though I had lost my master forever it was also true that a great burden had been lifted from my life.

I took the opportunity of taking a short walk along the magnificent crescent-shaped waterfront from which eight vast piers extended into the sea. The sea air refreshed me before I turned to walk back to the hotel and Sunday Mass.

I slept fitfully after the Mass said by Father Miley in the death room, for the bells continued to toll without cease and one particular subject continued to prey on my mind. In Lyons almost a month previously Mr O'Connell had promised me he would mark his gratitude to me my ensuring I would be forever independent of servitude. I knew that in order to have that promise fulfilled I should, as soon as was respectably permissible after Mr O'Connell's death, remind Mr Dan and Father Miley of the Liberator's intentions in my regard.

But I could not bring myself to do so as events unfolded with great rapidity and even had I plucked up the courage to bring my self-interest to their attention, I could not have managed to find the time. I did realise, however, that the death of my employer had now left me without employment and that on return to Ireland I should have immediately to seek another position.

Had I known my job would turn out to be the one I now have, I would surely have been driven to the depths of despair.

In the meantime my duties included ensuring the safety

of the urn which contained Mr O'Connell's heart as well as attending to the needs of Father Miley and Mr Dan. I also had to arrange for the journey onwards to Rome via Leghorn and Civitavecchia and post letters to Dublin, London and Rome in order to confirm that the Liberator had died. Whatever free time remained to me I used to rest on my bed and finally to sleep.

The solemn high Requiem Mass began on Monday at Santa Maria Delle Vigne at eleven in the morning. This church was chosen for the ceremonies not only because of its proximity to the Hotel Feder but also because it was one of the principal churches of the city of Genoa. It was situated in one of the small squares that characterise the city. When we arrived, a full half and hour before the ceremonies were due to begin the square had already filled with people anxious to view the arrival of Genoa's most important personages.

The Church's interior darkness was magnified by the black drapes that hung everywhere. I counted twenty-four altars at which the simultaneous Masses were being said and thought of the great importance put on Mr O'Connell by the Italians.

Mr Dan and I attended at the altar at which Father Miley was the celebrant, whence we could see clearly the main Mass at the church's high altar.

The Church, Father Miley had told us earlier that morning, dated from the 11th century. This, he said, made it older than any in Dublin save Christ Church Cathedral. There were several ancient statues and crucifixes and it presented an extremely solemn picture as the gentlemen in their darkest attire and the ladies, heads covered in black lace, filled every available place. The choir of the Cathedral of San Lorenzo augmented that of the church itself. Tears came to my eyes, and I saw them too in the eyes of Mr Dan, at the beauty of their performances and from the fact that many of Mr O'Connell's favourite hymns were included in their repertoire.

The *Stabat Mater*, his true favourite, was exquisitely rendered and brought Mr Dan almost to the verge of breaking down but, young man though he was, he pulled himself together and bore up well through the rest of the ceremonies.

The requiem lasted for an hour and a half with all the main sections sung slowly rather than spoken. It might have lasted longer had not the Cardinal Archbishop, due to the feebleness of his age, given an encomium of just ten minutes, quite the shortest of such eulogies I had heard at a funeral Mass of any person of importance. On this occasion I was relieved as, I think, were the others and, as the oration was given in Italian it was beyond my ability to understand it even to the slightest degree.

The Cardinal had invited Mr Dan and Father Miley to a reception in his palace after the funeral and I was to go with them to attend to their needs. On leaving the church of Santa Maria Delle Vigne all three of us expressed to each other a certain feeling of emptiness, a feeling that something had suddenly gone from us. The departure of Mr O'Connell from this world had already made its impact, leaving each one of us, but particularly Mr Dan, perturbed and saddened at his loss and perturbed at the very thought of a future without him.

There was also a new and different feeling on which we remarked. It was one of peace and tranquillity and it was not until we had almost arrived at the Archbishops palace that we realised how it had come about. The bells had stopped ringing. Genoa, for a brief time, seemed as quiet as a glen in Kerry.

At the reception, I stood in the background with the Cardinal's servants, while Mr Dan and Father Miley sipped some light white wine with the old man for not more than five minutes. Each of them went down on one knee to kiss his ring and then departed back to the Feder again on foot.

I was sent to the office of the Compagnia Generale di Navigazione with a detailed letter from Father Miley. This informed them that Mr O'Connell's party wished arrangements to be made for the transportation of his body by sea to the port of Dublin at the earliest convenience. Letters from Dublin would follow to confirm this.

I also posted mail from Father Miley and Mr Dan to the Irish College in Rome, to Mr O'Connell's family in Ireland and to the *Freeman's Journal* in Dublin giving an account of Mr O'Connell's death.

We had the rest of the morning to ready ourselves for the arrival of the steamer before setting off for Livorno and Civitavecchia and onwards by land to Rome. We were seen off on the quay by the Marchese Pallache and the foreign consuls who had greeted us upon arrival and our bags, other than the one containing Mr O'Connell's heart, were taken away for us to our cabins by members of the crew.

The urn was committed to my personal care. I kept it in my cabin and slept a shifting and erratic sleep for fear it might be stolen or mislaid.

The journey took us ten hours through the night on a sea as calm as glass and at breakfast next morning Mr Dan and Father Miley recounted how soundly they had slept. I mentioned nothing about my restless night.

On our arrival at Livorno we were forced to remember how much our importance had diminished since the death of Mr O'Connell. After weeks of travel in the course of which our every arrival and departure was greeted by large crowds of people we arrived for the first time at a city, and a considerable one at that, where no crowd waited for us at the quay. A single priest had been sent by the bishop to welcome us ashore and to ask if we had any special needs.

We took some time to look around the town before the *Lombardo* set off again. We presented an odd picture. The sight of three men with pale Irish faces, walking aimlessly around the town was hardly a normal one in these parts. As I was carrying with me the silver urn containing Mr O'Connell's heart, and worried in the extreme about my responsibility in this regard, I must have surely appeared the oddest of the three.

# CHAPTER SIXTEEN

## I See the Fireflies of Tuscany

The memories of my visit to Rome run into each other now. At first it looked disappointing. There were many beggars on the streets, many buildings in ruins. It appeared to me that His Holiness, the temporal as well as the spiritual ruler of Rome, was faring better at caring for the souls rather than the bodies of his charges.

Our journey to meet Pius IX at the Quirinale palace was short enough from the Irish College. At one stage, I cannot remember now if it was on our journey to the audience or on the way back, we caught sight of the massive grey dome of the Basilica of St Peter's in the distance.

Situated on a hill the Quirinale was not, at first sight, as impressive as I thought it was going to be. But when we went inside the grandeur was overwhelming. There were huge oil-paintings of the Popes which took up all the space from the ceiling to the floors of the corridors. I was allowed to accompany Mr Dan and Father Miley through several of the magnificent ante-rooms which led to the Pope's reception room. I was told then to wait in the final antechamber until they returned from their audience.

They spent what seemed to me to be the best part of an hour with His Holiness. I was taken completely by surprise when the Holy Father accompanied them from his chambers. He stood not ten feet from me but he did not appear to see me. The Pope was dressed in white robes from his shoulders to his feet, upon which he wore soft white shoes. A white skull cap was placed on the back of his head and a gold cross hung from a chain round his neck.

After the Pope had bade Mr Dan and Father Miley goodbye I followed them silently through the suites of rooms. At each door stood members of the Swiss and Noble Guards with bands of black crepe bound around the right arms of their colourful uniforms as a mark of respect to Mr O'Connell. Yes, even in the Pope's own quarters, Mr O'Connell was being mourned. I wondered at the time what his small-minded enemies would have thought of this. Would they at last have known the measure of his importance, or would they simply have sneered at the attitudes of those they considered "foreign"?

As we approached the courtyard where our carriage was to collect us, Mr Dan and Father Miley seemed filled with excitement and were so anxious to recount what had happened that I, their sole listener, was told of the meeting with His Holiness in the greatest detail.

Having made their formal obeisances to him, the Irish visitors who were accompanied by Monsignor Cullen, the rector of the Irish College, were bade to be seated at either side of His Holiness.

Mr Dan, at the Pope's right hand, told me he was taken

very much by surprise when the first words spoken by His Holiness, translated by Monsignor Cullen, were: "Since the pleasure of seeing and embracing the hero of Catholicity was not reserved for me, let me have the consolation of embracing his son." Mr Dan was asked to stand and Pius IX held him in a warm, fatherly embrace which caused him, he confessed to me, to blush with extreme embarrassment.

"The death of Mr O'Connell was blessed," the Holy Father then told them, referring to the pious manner in which the Liberator had passed from this world. His Holiness also recalled that he had "read with extreme consolation the letter in which his last moments had been described".

This letter had been sent by Father Miley to Monsignor Cullen who appeared to be on such close terms with the Pope that he was able to pass the letter on to him.

The Pope, I was told, was at pains to describe Mr O'Connell as "the great champion of the Church – the father of his country – the glory of the Christian world".

As we waited for our carriage to arrive, Monsignor Cullen joined us briefly and told us that as a man with some knowledge of the Holy Father's temperament, he could say that had the Supreme Pontiff been "a bosom friend of Mr O'Connell's he could not have spoken of the illustrious deceased with greater warmth of affection".

His words seemed stilted and formal despite the warm message he was delivering. Father Miley winced when Monsignor Cullen indicated his closeness to the Pope. I look back on that scene now in the knowledge that the two men became important figures of the Church. Father Miley, as I have said, went on to be rector of the Irish College in Paris but he was, of course, outshone by Monsignor Cullen who was to be Cardinal Archbishop of Armagh and later of Dublin. And when Cardinal Cullen took charge in the capital, Father Miley was moved from Paris to become parish priest of Bray in County Wicklow.

As we drove home silence reigned. Father Miley and Mr Dan seemed to be lost in reflection on their meeting with Christ's vicar on Earth. As for myself, it was my duty to speak only when spoken to, and much as I wished to hear further details of the encounter, I remained, like the others, silent.

* * *

We all dined together that evening and it was decided that we would spend the next days seeing the sights of the Eternal City and visiting the places of religious importance. It was our duty, after all, Father Miley said, to complete the pilgrimage we had begun. I was to accompany Mr Dan as a companion rather than as a servant. At first I felt this to be a compliment. I was flattered at the remarkable compliment paid to me, a simple servant, by a Doctor of Divinity, the confessor to the Liberator of Ireland and a man who had so recently been received in audience by the Holy Father.

My pleasure must have been obvious for Father Miley then clapped me heartily on the back and Mr Dan extended his hand across the table in a gesture of friendship. It was the first time in all my years in the O'Connell household that I had shaken the hand of a member of the family and I felt so confused and flustered that my spoon shuddered and shook as I tried to bring my soup to my mouth. Father Miley laughed at my clumsiness, not in the jovial way that the Italians had laughed at my attempts to eat their macaronis but in a superior, smug sort of fashion.

His laughter cut deeply into my feelings of satisfaction and attainment. Doubts and suspicions began to cool the glow of camaraderie and friendship. Slowly I recognised that my new-found equality was merely a signal of what was to come. I was no longer a servant for I no longer had a master and without a master I no longer had employment of any sort.

I spent the rest of the meal musing in silence. I retired early and thought things over in bed. I was, I realised, being given a false equality at least until I returned to Merrion Square where Mr John and Mr Morgan and Mr Maurice would decide my fate. I realised that I would be turned out on the world with no assistance.

At first I felt I should raise the matter of Mr O'Connell's solemn promise to me in Lyons. But the Liberator's death had invalidated that promise and his family would not be bound by it. By raising the matter, I felt, I would probably just be creating problems for myself. I knew only too well as a witness to his will and its codicil that no benefit from it would accrue to me.

At all events Mr O'Connell's management of his financial affairs had always been catastrophic and even if my name were included in the will and codicil as a beneficiary I doubted if there might be enough money left to share out between his family members and those other people named in the documents.

* * *

I decided therefore to enjoy my freedom in Rome and to take the opportunity to visit the famous places for I knew that the chance to do so would scarcely arise again.

Mr Dan and I first went the Irish Franciscans at the little Church and college of Sant' Isidoro on a hill in the centre of the city and they appointed a Friar from Wexford to guide us round the various places of interest. In one church we saw the pillar at which Our Lord was scourged in the course of his passion, at another church there was a charnel house, filled from floor to ceiling with the bones and skulls of martyrs.

We saw too the Basilica of St John Lateran with a marvellous statue of the flayed St Bartholomew holding his skin in his hand, the skin being made of stone as the statue is, but appearing to be as flimsy as gauze.

And we went up the holy staircase, the Scala Santa, on our knees praying aloud on each step for the repose of Mr O'Connell's soul and we visited the huge Basilica of Saint Peter where the Pope presides as vicar of Christ and head of the universal church.

Not far away by coach, but a little too far on foot because of the steep climb, we made the most special visit of our free days in Rome to the little Church of San Pietro in Montorio. Here in front of the altar, lay the tombs of The O'Neill and The O'Donnell who, like Mr O'Connell, had failed in their quest for independence and had died far from home.

As this place would have been of special interest to Mr O'Connell had he survived to reach Rome, we tarried a while, prayed for his soul again and engaged the Spanish Franciscans who administer the church to say a series of masses for his soul.

All the while as we toured the city, workmen, at the command of the Sovereign Pontiff, were erecting special edifices and artisans, painters, sculptors and other artists were exercising their ornamental skills, to prepare for the funereal services to mark Mr O'Connell's death. A splendid temporary basilica was erected near the church of Sant' Andrea della Valle where the main ceremonies were to be performed: sixty feet in height it stood, adorned with tablets in bas relief depicting scenes from Mr O'Connell's life. I recognised many of them instantly, for I had myself participated in them.

His triumphal tour of Dublin in his grand carriage following his release from prison was most accurately portrayed right down to the appearance of his grandchildren on the lowest tier of the great contraption. He was shown entering parliament for the first time, addressing his great meetings at Tara and at Mullaghmast, where he was crowned if not as King of Ireland, certainly as leader of the Irish people.

We saw a temporary tomb built at the Basilica to contain the urn in which his heart reposed and this was surrounded by a large angelic figure representing religion.

Father Miley, in a letter to Mr Morgan, written that night and read surreptitiously by me before the morning post, was full of praise for the efforts of the Romans.

*You can have no notion, he wrote, of the spirit with which the Roman people, properly so called, have combined to render this magnificent compliment to the Liberator of Catholic Ireland all that it should be. Nor is it alone that the mere echoes of his renown have told on the ears of this posterity of Kings and Martyrs, they have become indoctrinated with the great principles of our unequalled chief. If I may express myself they have become thoroughly Irish. They now know our position – the perils over which we have triumphed, the perils still more menacing which we have yet to overcome.*

On the first day of the funeral ceremonies the temporary basilica was thronged by all the important people of the city with the students of the Irish and Scots colleges ranged round the altar and to one side those of the College for the Propagation of the Faith dressed in white from collar to ankles and representing every nation of the earth.

Mr O'Connell's heart, which had been such a worry to me in the short period it had been my duty to mind it, was placed in a special tomb of *papier mâché*. It had been made to look like a stone sepulchre and inscribed with the citation: *For Daniel O'Connell, immortal through great deeds, the safeguard and protector of the kingdom of Ireland; for his distinguished services to the Christian commonwealth, the last due offices of the dead have been performed by the nobles and people of Rome. Whether you be a guest or a citizen, as you approach this sepulchre, supplicate heaven with a pure mind for peace and repose for his matchless spirit.*

Mr Dan and I seated ourselves while priests at the twenty special altars prepared to offer simultaneous Masses.

The Pontifical Mass at the main altar was offered by Archbishop Girolamo dei Marchesi d'Andrea, a nobleman of Italy. The orchestra of the Philharmonic Academy Rome under the baton of Maestro Andrea Salesi, provided the music. The hymns were sung by a choir of one hundred Roman boys. The urn containing Mr O'Connell's heart was given a formal blessing by the Archbishop of Imola, His Eminence Cardinal Baluffi. We were indebted to the master of ceremonies who whispered these important informations to us in the course of the ceremonies.

It shocked me to see that the Roman people appeared to

have little respect for the holy sacrifice. They talked animatedly with each other throughout the ceremonies, gesticulating and continuously pointing out Mr Dan as the son of the Liberator.

They were silenced, however, by the arrival of Father Gioacchino Ventura, reputed to be the greatest orator in Christendom. On this the first day of the solemn ceremonies he preached for an hour and three-quarters on the theme of "Daniel O'Connell causing the triumph of liberty through Religion."

Neither Mr Dan nor I have any understanding of the Italian but a student of the Irish college, appropriately from the County of Kerry, was allocated to translate the oration. He whispered his words in Mr Dan's direction and I was able only to pick up parts of what he said. Indeed towards the end of the speech the young man's concentration, and ours, had begun to falter.

On the second day of the ceremonies another Cardinal and another Archbishop presided. Father Ventura's oration on this occasion was shortened to an hour and fifteen minutes on "Daniel O'Connell causing the triumph of Religion through Liberty." The young Kerry student did far better at the translating on this occasion. But even so I must admit that the oratory which brought raptures to the Italians and indeed to Mr Dan, was far too complicated for a person of my humble occupation, with many references to subjects and persons I had never heard of.

I do remember, all the same, that Father Ventura was hopeful that Mr O'Connell's success in gaining emancipation for the Catholics of Ireland and Great Britain had led to a situation in which the day was approaching when the Mass would be said in St Paul's in London and that a future British monarch would himself be a Catholic. To me this merely illustrated that while Father Ventura's had a great way with words, he was not well endowed with common sense.

His description of Anglicanism too as "this scandalous exercise of the royal rights of a Christian sovereign," did not, I must say, coincide with Mr O'Connell's views of tolerance between those of different faiths.

At all events I found the depictions of Mr O'Connell which hung inside the church a greater attraction than the oration of Father Ventura, though it must be said that the people of Europe and most especially of France thought otherwise. I afterwards learned that its publication and sale, the proceeds of which went towards relief in Ireland, raised more than one hundred thousand francs.

I heard also that many leading Catholics of the continent opposed the ideas put forward linking religion and liberty because in their view the standard of liberty had been soaked in so much blood that it had been completely debased. But Mr O'Connell, and I have known him long, had learned totally to abhor bloodshed since the time of his duel with Mr d'Esterre a full thirty-two years earlier.

The truth, I must own, is that my attention was fixed on a phenomenon which the Kerry student had pointed out to me before the first of the ceremonies had begun. To the right of the main altar, in full view of the public, there was a corpse in a glass case. It was, I was told, the body of Cardinal Joseph Mary Tomasi who had died more than one hundred and thirty years earlier, and had not decayed. This was believed to be a sign of his sanctity, though I must say that to me he looked like a waxen model as he lay on his back, dressed in his cardinal's scarlet.

All the same I could not take my eyes away from the dead

man. His feet faced me but I could see his waxy hands and the two dark orifices of his nostrils appeared to stare at me all the time. Sometimes in my dreams to this very day I see this sight again.

My obsession with the uncorrupted corpse was such that Mr Dan had to elbow me in the ribs to signal the end of the final day of the ceremonial when the urn containing Mr O'Connell's heart was formally presented to Monsignor Cullen.

That night at dinner in the college refectory it was decided that Mr Dan and I should travel back together to Ireland by coach and rail as far as possible by the overland route. This would be quicker than using steamer travel between continental destinations and suitable to both of us who were in good health.

Father Miley was to stay in Rome for another few days but he too would be back in Dublin for the arrival there of Mr O'Connell's body and its burial in Glasnevin cemetery.

We set out in gloomy mood for Civitavecchia where we spent the first night. From there we went along the coast of the Maremma, a region of misty swamps where annually the malaria claims hundreds of victims due to the foulness of the air, then onwards to Grosseto and Sienna.

* * *

It was a bilious attack upon Mr Dan in Sienna, which took some time for the local doctors to put right, that caused us to travel to Florence by night. We had to allow the diligence to go ahead with the other passengers while Mr Dan was being treated with the magnesium waters of a local spa, and we needed therefore to hire a private coach for the rest of the journey.

Otherwise I would not have seen the fireflies. I was not sure at first what they were and neither was Mr Dan. An entire field appeared to be aglow with lights which darted to and fro and in all directions.

We thought at first that it might have been the will o' the wisp which is reported to have been seen on the bogs of Ireland and Scotland. Then we feared it may have been some evil and unholy supernatural manifestation.

The coachman laughed at us. He kept repeating the word "lucciole" and finally, the coach having been stopped for some time, he took a small glass jar with him into the field, collected some of the darting lights into it, replaced the lid in which he punctured an hole or two with his travelling knife, presented the jar to us and continued on our journey to Florence.

Now it was we who laughed. Like children we giggled and screamed at the lights which flashed in our jar and upon arrival Mr Dan placed it on the mantelpiece of his room when it cast almost as much light as a good beeswax candle.

Mr Dan called me to his room on the following morning with an edge of disgust on his voice and an uncommon paleness on his face. The jar that twinkled in the night just a few hours previously was now seen to contain a host of the most ugly-looking insects crawling around inside the glass, most with a great deal less vigour than when they had first been collected, some of them already dead.

We opened the shutters of Mr Dan's room and allowed the surviving flies go free in the air of the city. But for all my life thereafter I have held in fascination that night in the Grand Duchy of Tuscany. I appear to have a natural leaning towards an interest in the animal kingdom, as my attraction towards the lizards in the cemetery in France had previously indicated.

# CHAPTER SEVENTEEN

## *I Return to the Black Fever*

The return journey through France and England took a similar route in reverse to our previous travels, forcing us to relive the days of Mr O'Connell's illness in London.

From London we set out for Dublin having now been almost half a year away from Ireland. The journey through England and Wales was a familiar one which we had travelled so often on Mr O'Connell's trips to and from parliament. Everything seemed as it had been when we left and after a calm crossing from Holyhead, dawn broke with a view of Ireland.

The hills of Wicklow peeped up through the mist and gradually the coastline to the south of Dublin began to emerge with the great harbour walls of Kingstown standing out like the pincers of a crab ready to catch us and draw us into our homeland.

But our arrival brought to us a great sense of shock. The quay was lined with hundreds, perhaps a thousand, of the most unfortunate people I have ever seen. The wails of the frantic women filled our ears. The babies they held close to them were like small skeletons, their heads appearing huge in comparison to their shrunken bodies. Some men looked for all the world like the corpse in the glass case in Rome, only their clothes, several sizes too large, indicated that they once perhaps had been strapping labourers.

Others were swollen with the dropsy to such an extent that their jackets had burst open. But most of them were pale, hungry and eager to leave for places which could afford them food and shelter. A dull groan emanated from the crowd as though their voices responded in unison to their awful fate.

It was a strange thing to have travelled through Italy and France and England where people lived frugally but decently and then suddenly arrive in a land of starvation, pestilence and absolute calamity.

Our own coach was at the pier to meet us and it took us directly to Merrion Square but not without seeing scenes of the most appalling misery. The entire city appeared to be home to masses of beggars of the most destitute appearance imaginable. They had swarmed in from the famished countryside in search of a means to keep body and soul together.

The closer we came to the city the greater the number of wretches we saw. Our driver told us they had been streaming in from the west and that the eastern part of the city had been spared the most harrowing scenes. Merrion Square itself was relatively free of the unfortunates.

* * *

At the house young O'Brien prepared a bath for me below stairs with several large pots of water boiled on the stove. Some of the master's own bath salts were provided and I soaked myself for almost half an hour until the cooling water took the comfort from the bathing.

I then managed some hours of sleep before lunch. Having eaten, I took up my position below stairs and shared my news with the rest of Mr O'Connell's staff. I told them, as I have told you, of the events which had taken place since we left Ireland in January. I chose to leave out some of the more unpleasant details of Mr O'Connell's illness. They listened in silence, tears being drawn from the eyes of the women and grave expressions appearing on the faces of the men.

My story, despite its sadness, had some bright points, such as Mr O'Connell's recovery in Avignon and the magnificent tributes paid to him all along his journey and the great ceremonies in Genoa and Rome. But the tale they had to tell me was one of unremitting horror. After what had appeared to be a bounteous and unblemished crop, the potatoes when dug out had been found to be nothing but a stinking, rotting mass. This had happened right throughout the country; there were no areas immune from the disaster as they had been in the past. Worse still the typhus and the relapsing fever was taking hundreds if not thousands of people daily. The roads into Dublin were crowded with unfortunate wretches trying to escape from the horrors of the countryside.

Hundreds of them had died by the roadside and special teams of corpse-gatherers had once again been formed to collect and bury the dead, Mrs Twomey the cook told me.

Nash, the coachman, said the fever hospitals of Dublin had been filled to overflowing with sufferers from the different pestilences which had manifested themselves as a result of the great hunger. Tents had been set up at the fever hospital in Cork Street in order to deal with the overflow of numbers, but even these measures were not enough and hundreds of people were sent away to spread the fever through the pestilent warren of little streets in the poorer quarters of the city.

If Mr Dan and I had thought the scenes at Kingstown to be horrifying it was because we were, I was told by Lyons the clerk, unaware of the more dreadful situations which prevailed in other parts. In the port of Dublin ten times that number of wretches could be seen waiting for transport to Liverpool where they would take what we were told were now called "coffin ships" to Canada and the United States.

Miss Larkin the housekeeper added that people who lived in the more salubrious areas of the city were afraid to go abroad in daylight for fear of catching a disease for which there was no cure. As far as the typhus was concerned the physicians were divided as to its cause. Some felt it was due simply to the lack of nutrition from which the victims had been suffering, others thought that lice spread it quickly through the poorer sections of the population in recent months.

Be the cause what it might, the stories of how those unfortunates suffered shocked me to the core. My fellow servants spoke of people turning dark-skinned from the fever which the country people now call *An Fiabhras Dubh*, the black fever.

Young O'Brien whose family was from west Cork, described the great suffering there, where the victims broke out in dreadful sores all over their bodies. Sometimes their fingers and toes fell off due to mortification and at all times the disease was accompanied by a most unbearable odour which, our cook told me, was the means by which the Lord informed us to stay away from these people lest we get the diseases ourselves.

The relapsing fever was not regarded as being as bad as the typhus, but was accompanied sometimes by a jaundice, which made its victims yellow all over. This fever came and went over a long period of time and it was believed that some unfortunates were suffering from the typhus and the relapsing fever at the same time.

I was warned by Nash that there were certain places in Dublin into which I should not travel, these mainly being where the poor people lived or certain outskirts, mainly to the west, where sufferers of the famine fevers had gathered to rest before attempting to get to the port to sail for Liverpool or the Americas.

The worst part of the city, I was told, was that close to the fever hospital in Cork Street and to the South Dublin Union workhouse in James's street as well as the neighbouring destitute districts such as the Coombe and St Patrick's Street, Thomas Street, Francis Street and Meath Street and the adjoining lanes and alleyways where people lived crowded lives in great proximity to each other and where funerals thronged the streets daily.

That night my sleep was filled with horrors from my journeys in France and Italy and from what I had heard from my fellow servants in the great house in Merrion Square. Only the thought of the fireflies gave me solace. I forced them into my mind and they drew me away from the thoughts of horror.

\* \* \*

In the morning at breakfast downstairs a message was sent to ask me to attend in the drawing-room at four o'clock. It was the call for which I had been waiting. Of all the servants I was the only one specifically employed to work for Mr O'Connell. The others were employed to work for the household and the household still existed. Mr O'Connell had died; so, therefore, had my employment.

Coming up to four o'clock I donned my best clothes, polished my shoes and scrubbed my hands once more before I felt ready to go above stairs. When I knocked on the drawing-room door at precisely four o'clock on the watch Mr O'Connell had given me the previous Christmas, it was Mr John's voice that bade me enter.

I took this to be a bad sign. Of all Mr O'Connell's sons, Mr John was the most narrow in his outlook. He would be less charitable in disposing of my services than would the others and, although he was only Mr O'Connell's third son, his influence with the others was strong. His answer to my knock seemed a message to me that his views had prevailed over those of the others.

His enemies, of whom there were many, thought of him as extremely rigid in his views and unable to adapt to changing situations. While I was always loyal to Mr O'Connell when he was attacked by the Young Irelanders, I felt there was no small amount of truth in the statement of Mr Gavan Duffy with regard to Mr John. "His father," Mr Gavan Duffy had said, "began with a dozen followers and increased them to millions. He began with millions and reduced them to a score or a dozen."

Seated round a table when I entered were Mr John, Mr Maurice, the eldest of the O'Connell sons, the bluff soldier

Mr Morgan and the young Mr Dan who looked away when I greeted him.

Mr Maurice, a director of the National Bank, spoke with some authority as the eldest. His words were confined to thanking me for the long and faithful service I had given his father in good times and in bad.

Mr Morgan said he would like to add his voice to the thanks given by his elder brother. "Duggan," he said, "you have been an example to the other servants by your diligence and loyalty to our late father. I can only congratulate you on your work over the years."

Mr Dan was silent. He knew what decision had been made but his status was so junior that even if he had the strength to disagree openly with his brothers, his voice would not have been heard. For my part I had worked it out for myself and I wished the brothers would hurry and give me the bad news quickly.

It struck me at the time that of all the strength of character, of all the brilliance of intellect possessed by Mr O'Connell, of all his ability to act on ideas conceived in his own mind, only a fraction had been passed on to the next generation; and even this had been divided out among his children with the daughters, to my mind, inheriting more than the sons.

On the other hand, Mr O'Connell's occasional duplicity, so highlighted by his enemies in England, seemed to have been augmented greatly in the next generation and concentrated, to differing degrees, in the characters of his sons. Mr John could be termed the chief inheritor, with the innocent Mr Dan receiving least of this unwelcome characteristic.

The pause after Mr Morgan's congratulatory statement seemed to last forever. I looked out the window across the street towards the park. A group of young ladies were enjoying an afternoon walk apparently unaware of the dramas being played out in the poorer quarters of the city which they had probably never visited, and for certain unaware of the smaller drama which was going on a few yards away from them.

"You will be aware," Mr John said, "that upon the death of my father, your employment automatically ceased. Indeed, and I would be obliged if the following information does not go any further, it seems likely that the family will have to sell this house in order to meet the debts incurred by my father. So not only yourself but the entire household staff will have to look out for new employment."

"Yes sir," I replied. But I was unexpectedly overcome by a strong temptation to mention Mr O'Connell's promise made to me in front of Mr Dan and Father Miley in Lyons. I looked at Mr Dan and he looked away again, his face suffused in a blush which almost matched the terracotta paintwork on the drawing-room walls.

I kept silent.

"In your case, Duggan," Mr John continued, "in order to show our appreciation for your devotion to our father, we have decided," and at this he nodded towards Mr Maurice, "to make a payment to you as a token of our gratitude and to keep you in our employment until the funeral ceremonies in Dublin have been completed. We have also asked the Archbishop of Dublin, Doctor Murray, to use his influence in finding you another suitable position. That is all, Duggan. Thank you."

He handed me two envelopes, one of them a large official manila type and the other small white and scented. The larger of the two contained a cheque for twenty-five guineas made out to me and drawn on the National Bank in Dame

Street. The smaller contained a joint letter from Mr O'Connell's daughters: Miss Kate, Miss Ellen and Miss Betsey, expressing their gratitude for what I had done in the service of their father. They dissociated themselves, I felt, from the decision taken by their brothers by referring to my "unnecessary departure" and assured me that I should be a welcome visitor in any of their houses should I be passing their way at any time.

As I left the young ladies strolling on the park side of the square burst into a peal of laughter. The hall was flooded with sunshine from the fanlight as I walked towards the stairs which would lead me down to the people of my own station and I could feel the welling of tears behind my eyes.

Below stairs the staff was lined up as if for a military inspection, each one with a questioning face. "I am to leave you after the obsequies," I told them. "All possible efforts will be made to find me a job elsewhere."

Butler nodded and handed me a note which I took to my room. It was from Father Miley informing me of his return and asking me to attend to him in the course of the obsequies which were to take place next week. The O'Connell brothers had, he wrote, agreed to this and by the time the ceremonies would take place he would, he hoped, have some news from the Archbishop regarding my new employment.

* * *

It was not yet five o'clock, no duties had been assigned to me on that day and as the weather was fine I determined to take a walk in the city.

Out on the square the young ladies stood and chatted with each other, still full of youthful happiness. The trees and bushes were in full greenery, the sun still shone and the people of this quarter sauntered leisurely around the park's perimeter. All was style and elegance compared even to the streets of Marseilles and Genoa yet not so far away there was another world to which I felt drawn.

I turned left at the end of the square and then walked into Stephen's Green. Here people of quality also took the air as I passed the Earl of Iveagh's house to cross the bottom of Harcourt Street, turn right after the Earl of Clonmell's and enter Wexford Street. Now the crowds were thicker and less well dressed and further on in Kevin Street the children played without shoes.

The Dean of St Patrick's strode from the gates of his deanery into Kevin Street and was followed by a band of ragamuffin boys who jeered him for his dress and in turn begged alms of him.

In the warren of lanes and alleys the usual unpleasant smell of poverty and insanitary living conditions was augmented by an even stronger and more sinister odour which I was later to recognise as that of the typhus.

Arriving at the hovel which was my destination, the home of a Tipperary family with whom I was acquainted in the old days, I found its windows broken. The smashed panes had in some cases been covered over with brown paper. One of them was stuffed with an old hat. I felt a tug at my britches. A small girl of about ten, unwashed and dressed in rags looked up at me. "The Kellys," she said, "are took to the Union."

# CHAPTER EIGHTEEN

*My New Life Begins*

There was a great stir of movement about not long after dawn on that August morning. It was the almost silent motion of people on foot, all heading in the same direction, downhill to where the river broadened enough to take a ship. The signal of this early animation had been a plume of black smoke from the chimney of a steamer from Italy in Dublin bay. I had seen it myself from the top window of the house on Merrion Square and I was out and about early before the ceremonies began.

From the heights of the old city I saw men in cloth flat caps and women in long black dresses form a silent moving mass of darkness punctuated here and there by the blood-red coat of a soldier.

From just north of the river another silent horde, its children unshod, had a shorter journey to the quay in front of the 18th century palace of the Custom House where the vessel was due to dock. From further afield fine equipages drove the comfortable from Rathmines and Rathgar in the south and from the villas of Howth, where the plume of black smoke had first been seen out to sea, and from Clontarf and Sutton in the North. From Kingstown in the south-east the trains had been full all morning.

All had come at the bidding of that plume of smoke from the ship, which carried the Liberator's body from Genoa.

Every available boat and smack and launch and ship had taken to the waters of the river for the occasion. Further down-river a vast crowd of the famished, fever-stricken and tatterdemalion paupers from the West of Ireland on board a ship they had boarded for the first stage of their sad journey to North America were as excited as those on the shore.

They heard the news in their own tongue that the body of the Liberator had entered Dublin bay and a loud wail of Gaelic keening filled the air. The wretches keened again on the river itself when the ship which they had boarded to take them away from Ireland forever passed the ship which brought O'Connell's remains to the soil of Ireland for all eternity.

I took my place on the platform on the Custom House Quay a good hour and a half before the coffin was due to be taken from the ship. The timetable had been worked out in advance. Signals to and from the ship had confirmed the schedule. Everything was organised in dispassionate and businesslike fashion and this seemed to have its effect on me. The grief and sympathy I felt might engulf me on this day were completely absent. These passions were spent in Genoa and Rome. Here in Dublin I felt like a detached observer.

I was one of the first to take his seat on the platform and I was joined eventually by cousins and in-laws of Mr O'Connell. Members of his immediate family were among the last to arrive and were seated immediately in front of where I sat.

I recognised it, in a detached way and without emotion, as a truly historic scene and was at pains to concentrate on what was happening and to observe all the people and the events as keenly as I could. As a result I can still picture the scene in my mind.

Mr Maurice as the liberator's eldest son and his wife Mary Frances, were in the first position. Alongside them were: Mr Morgan, dressed in his uniform as an officer in Bolivar's Irish Legion, Mr John and his wife Elizabeth, Mr Dan and the O'Connell daughters Kate, Nell and Betsy with their children. Mr James O'Connell, the liberator's youngest brother, Mr John O'Connell, his second brother, his cousin Mr Charles O'Connell a resident magistrate, his nephew Morgan John O'Connell and a host of persons of the O'Connell cousinage all of whom had their lots improved by their relationship with the Liberator, and at first placed near me, pushed their way to the front.

The entire hierarchy of the Catholic Church in Ireland was also seated at the quayside, their colours ranging in downward degrees of importance from the scarlet and purple of the prelates, to the white surplices and black soutanes of the priests selected to officiate at the ceremonies, to the all-black clerical suits of those who merely attended as onlookers.

As the ship approached one could perceive on the foredeck a miniature church of wood, draped in heavy black velvet, edged with gold embroidery and looped with large silver tassels. As soon as the vessel pulled in to the dock, sailors removed the curtains at the side of this temporary mausoleum to reveal to the view of those near enough to see, Mr O'Connell's huge coffin, the same one in which I had seen his remains placed in the Feder Hotel in Genoa and which had been sited in front of the altar of Santa Maria delle Vigne. Huge brass candelabra were sited at each corner and the dais on which the coffin rested lay covered in crimson Genoa velvet.

Upon seeing this coffin the entire assemblage fell to its knees. Half a million right hands flashed in unison in making the sign of the cross. The Liberator – and not, I reflected, without an element of triumph – had returned to his devastated country. No doubt this occasion engendered differing emotions among those who were present. I am sure I was the only one whose mind invoked once more the picture of Doctor Lacour unwinding the intestines of a body for which all respect had been cast aside.

It was surely true that an act of sacrilege had been committed on what, after all, we had been taught to believe was the "Temple of the Holy Ghost". If the body of such a great man as Mr O'Connell had been so treated, how could we expect any great respect for our own bodies after their souls had departed?

The ceremonies which followed were carried out with great solemnity by the clergy and the faithful who, I supposed, were paying their own due tribute to Mr O'Connell. To me the ceremonies seemed totally out of place. This was not the Liberator I had known and served but a body sullied by scalpels, its heart in Rome and its innards left for the Genoese hounds and rats to consume at their will. It was a tainted, tarnished and defiled corpse which lay in that majestic coffin and I, unlike almost all the others in the half-a-million-strong assembly, had seen that debasement taking place.

The coffin with what remained of Mr O'Connell was carried ashore amid scenes verging on barbarity. Some of the more emotional members of the throng grabbed at the black cloth in which the wooden mausoleum had been draped and ripped it into shreds. They grabbed it for a memento of the occasion, as though it were a holy relic of some long-dead saint, with an indulgence attached to speed them more quickly to their salvation after their deaths.

It was a shocking and distasteful scene. For a moment it seemed as though the wild panic would cause serious injuries or even death to those who had lost their composure. The screams of mourning turned to those of terror but the voluntary stewards from the sodalities of the city and the men of the Sherriff's contingent managed, thank God, to calm them.

When the crowd had finally quieted, the procession formed. It moved slowly to the Church of the Immaculate Conception in Marlborough Street, the pro-Cathedral of the Catholic Church in Dublin. The interior had been completely draped in black to receive the coffin. A short service was held at which the coffin was placed on a massive catafalque before the altar. It was to remain there for four days before the burial, to allow the people of Dublin to file past and duly pay their respects.

That afternoon the house in Merrion Square was thronged with people. As in the case of most funerals for a man of Mr O'Connell's years, those not so closely related as to be consumed with grief, behaved as though at an important social occasion. Those who had not seen each other for some time, embraced and shared reminiscences; those who harboured deep-seated enmity towards each other kept their distance so as not to debase the occasion by their anger.

Though given a place with the family in the short procession from the river to the church I was, once back in Merrion Square, regarded as a servant again and I busied myself with ensuring the comfort and sustenance of the visitors.

Towards evening when the numbers began to thin out, Father Miley called me into the presence of Doctor Murray of Dublin and Doctor MacHale of Tuam and introduced me to their Graces. The Archbishop of Dublin had, I was informed, been kind enough to use his considerable influence to obtain a post for me as a porter in the South Dublin Union. I would, I was told, start work there on Thursday morning, the day after Mr O'Connell's burial.

The Archbishop smiled what to me seemed a forced smile and told me I was indeed lucky to have obtained such a position for there were many seeking work around Dublin at this time. He used the words South Dublin Union in a manner hitherto unknown to me, saying them slowly and deliberately and completely without the terror with which the name instills in the common people of the city. The very thought of becoming an inmate in this house of terror, a daily threat to the ordinary citizen, could not possibly have entered the Archbishop's mind.

I kissed the ruby ring on the soft hand extended to me, thanked Doctor Murray for his solicitude on my behalf, bowed and backed away into a corner of the room where I was immediately asked to fetch more drinks for some guests who had just arrived from Kerry.

It took some time for the news to take effect on my mind and busied as I was with seeing to the needs of the guests it was not until I retired late that night that I had the opportunity fully to consider the fate in store for me. I knew the Union was an awful place, everyone in Dublin knew that apart, it seemed, from the Archbishop and the young ladies who daily walked and chattered in the park at Merrion Square. I knew, at all costs, that I would live there in better conditions and with better food than the unfortunate wretches who inhabited it. I did not know how many hours I would be expected to work each week, nor how much I would be paid for my labours. A person of my station does not question an Archbishop on these matters.

In the days remaining before the funeral, I took the little spare time I had to walk down James's Street, past the Union's front gate and round the perimeter to the back entrance near Rialto. The complex covered a vast acreage with residential wings, infirmaries and a mortuary chapel from which funerals issue of a much humbler degree than the one I was soon to attend. All of these buildings were constructed in a dismal grey stone which gave the place a physical aspect to match its gloomy reputation.

On Wednesday morning the city was even more crowded with people than on the Monday of the arrival of Mr O'Connell's body. Those people from the remoter areas of Ireland with some physical strength and personal finances remaining to them, had now had enough time to travel to Dublin to mark the return of the Liberator to the soil of Ireland.

The carriage in which I travelled was, once again, that which contained some grandchildren of the Liberator. The sight, which caught our eyes upon entering the church, was astounding: I had been told that more than a thousand priests would attend but the sight of them in special pews roped off from the rest of the congregation was extraordinary. The white of the surplices and the black of he soutanes seemed to turn the mass of men into one vast being, like an immense magpie stirring occasionally and then quieting down.

The mournful tones of the Solemn Requiem echoed through the pillared church. As the incense rose heavenward and the deep bells of mourning rang out, the city became suddenly drenched in a downpour of rain.

The words *Miserere Nobis*, "have mercy on us", resounded again and again in the course of the liturgy. When the great coffin was brought to the doors, the men in the vast crowd outside doffed their hats. That single sweeping movement struck me hard. *"Hats off for Mr O'Connell!"* had been the cry of the Dublin tradesmen in the days of his political ascendancy. Those who did not obey the command in those times showed their opposition to the Liberator and walked the streets at their peril. Now all hats were off for the dead leader and the jubilant cries of yesteryear were absent. The dreadful silence was broken only by the hissing sound of the rain sweeping along the footpaths.

The triumphal carriage, last paraded round Dublin in pomp and ceremony after Mr O'Connell's release from prison, had been brought out for the occasion, its three tiers of seats empty of passengers to mark the sense of loss that pervaded every mind in the host of mourners. The final procession of Mr O'Connell through Dublin began. The City Marshal led the way on horseback followed by the men of Dublin's fifty trades on foot and with the triumphal carriage immediately behind them.

After them came the holy confraternities in their robes, the society of St Vincent de Paul, the Brothers of the Christian schools.

Then came the coffin on its bier and our series of mourning carriages. The lead horse of each carriage was led by a mute from the city's institution for the deaf and dumb. This was the tradition, heaven know why, for the funerals of great men. The members of Dublin corporation with the High Sheriff, the judges of the various courts and the aldermen and councillors of Limerick, Waterford, Kilkenny, Drogheda, Clonmel and Sligo formed up behind us.

We made our way very slowly into Sackville Street where the crowds had grown immensely in the time, which passed during the Requiem. The roof of the General Post Office swarmed with people, Nelson's Pillar too had been used as a vantage point for the occasion and we followed the bier at slower than walking pace towards Carlisle Bridge, down Westmoreland Street and along Nassau Street to Merrion Square where the traditional pause was made outside the house of the dead man.

All the windows at Number 30 had their blinds down and their shutters bolted closed. The O'Connell arms were hung from the central second-floor window. The noise of the carriage wheels having stilled, we could hear in the distance the ships of many nations in the river sounding off their foghorns to pay their final respects to our Liberator.

In St Stephen's Green, a further vast crowd awaited us, all so quiet in comparison to the times they came on the streets during Mr O'Connell's lifetime, all dressed in their darkest funereal clothes. A black mass of people relieved occasionally by the movement of white handkerchiefs to the eyes and cheeks of the ladies.

Here the political affiliations of the inhabitants of the great houses could be determined by their appearances. Blinds were drawn on those whose owners supported Mr O'Connell, or opposed him but wished to pay their last respects or, and I am sure there were a large number in this category, who were afraid that leaving their windows clear might provoke such anger among the populace that an attack might ensue.

Only one or two were defiant and not only kept their blinds up but lit their chandeliers as though to celebrate the fact that their enemy was no more.

The scene on Harcourt Street with its noble curve of fine houses was similar to that on the Green. Blinds were drawn, umbrellas raised against the increasing intensity of the rain and heads were bared.

The cortege then doubled northwards down Camden Street, Wexford Street, Redmond's Hill, Aungier Street and South Great George's street where the spectators were thicker in number, the men in bowler hats or cloth caps and the women in colourful dresses, these being, I knew, the only apparel they owned. Black armbands and diamond-shaped patches of black felt sewn to a sleeve replaced the full mourning wear of the wealthier streets.

At the end of George's Street we turned left into the broad Dame Street and paused for a short while before the City Hall whose columns were draped in black to pay respect to Mr O'Connell, who had been the city's first Catholic Lord Mayor in centuries. Then we wheeled right into Parliament Street, crossed the river into Capel Street, heading northwards through vast crowds all the way, the streets lined six to ten deep with people who seemed undeterred by the rain which had now reached tempestuous proportions.

Bolton Street shone in the rain, the black horses gleamed and seemed to glide into Blessington Street, dividing the sea of umbrellas in its path as it reached the North Circular Road and proceeded to its, and Mr O'Connell's, final destination.

At Glasnevin we dismounted and formed up in front of a huge circular plot, the work upon which had begun shortly after news of Mr O'Connell's death had been received in Dublin and now flowers were already strewn in vast numbers around this circle. In its centre lay a deep vault seven feet in height and fourteen feet long, reached by a flight of twelve steps and entered through an iron door with a brass plate bearing the single word: "O'Connell."

Mr O'Connell's coffin was placed on a massive slab of rough granite, lit by a pair of gilt candelabra and surrounded by the priests and the boy's choir from the pro-Cathedral. Being at the front of the huge crowd with Mr O'Connell's family I could see right into the tomb and watch the religious ceremony being performed therein.

I remember noting to myself how different this must have been to the funerals of the wretches who were being buried daily. I remember thinking on Mr O'Connell's worries of being buried alive to be suffocated by the surrounding earth, when here he was, well and truly departed from this life, being placed underground in a room almost the size of his study in Merrion Square.

The choir of Marlborough Street church sang the "*Benedictus qui venit in Nomine Domini,*" and finally the "*De Profundis clamavi ad te Domine.*" Silently I recited the English words of each hymn to myself: *"Blessed is he who comes in the name of the Lord"* and *"Out of the depths I have cried to thee, O Lord."*

Then the priests and choir removed themselves from the tomb to the Music of the *"Miserere"* and one of their number locked the iron door with a huge key with the sound of absolute finality.

I found myself completely alone in a vast crowd of people whose faces I had known over the years. I became detached from men and women who had looked me in the eye in the reception rooms of Merrion Square but who had automatically excluded me from their memories as a servant and therefore not worth remembering.

As the crowd dwindled I made my way towards the cemetery's iron gates to see the coaches with the O'Connell children depart without me. I began my journey alone to the city.

Down the Circular Road and into Sackville Street the silence, which had permeated the city during the funeral procession, dissipated slowly. Here and there an emaciated beggar pleaded for alms. Ragged men from the west played heart-rending slow airs on their flutes and penny whistles, their caps thrown down as a challenge to passers-by with pence in their pockets.

The buzz of talk, the clip-clop of horses' hooves, all the sounds of the city which had seemed muffled by the crowds earlier in the day, were now returning. Dublin had lost its leader but was already beginning to turn its back on him. There were other more immediate problems to be faced. The victims of hunger and disease continued to flood in from the countryside. They tried either to find sustenance or a passage out of a country which once they loved but which now aroused in them such fear of death that they were fleeing in their droves to any country that would take them.

I crossed Carlisle Bridge and walked down Burgh Quay past the Corn Exchange buildings. For many years they had housed Mr O'Connell's political headquarters, and they were now controlled by Mr John and declining daily in strength. The building had its shutters closed in mourning but outside its door stood a blind peddler of ballad songs offering his latest composition to the public at threepence a sheet.

He stood there and declaimed his work to the passing throng. The crudely-wrought verses told the feelings of those who lived on in this land of despair. Their only hero, their bright hope, had left them and the hunger and the sickness stayed on.

I stood a while and listened to the pathetic dirge so poorly written, a silly ditty in comparison to the great lament of the O'Connell family, *Caoineadh Airt Uí Laoghaire*:
> "In ninety-eight he viewed the state
> Of this lovely island, I declare,
> With grief oppressed he came from the south,
> And he was elected in the County Clare,
> They first seduced him and then abused him,
> But he confused them till they gave o'er,
> The oath of allegiance he refused to take,
> But our noble Dan is now no more.
> The Emancipation without hesitations,
> To our lovely isle he soon brought o'er,
> Our clergy crowned him with a wreath of glory,
> When he sailed to old Erin's shore,
> Our Chapel Bells they do ring melodious,
> When no scorpion dare cross the door.

*Quite broken-hearted from us he departed,*
*The Pride of Kerry and Old Erin's shore,*
*To Mullaghmast and likewise Tara,*
*As a modern Moses he led us, you see,*
*Tho' we were pursued by the proud and haughty,*
*In the land of promise he left us free,*
*A shout is gone from Dingle to Derry,*
*Along the Boyne, the Liffey and the Nore,*
*And all repeat in mournful accents,*
*Our noble leader brave Daniel is no more."*

Once again I could not bring myself to feel the sorrow which so many of my countrymen shared. I must have looked stern in the company which had gathered round the ballad singer for he cursed me and pointed me out as a member of the Orange party whose members would be haunted by Mr O'Connell's ghost for all eternity.

I stepped briskly away, Mr O'Connell's haunting ghost at my shoulder, as it has been these fifteen years. At Merrion Square I entered though the rear, went to my room and packed my belongings for my new start in the morning. I had not realised how little I owned: three white wing-collared shirts, two pairs of black shoes, one suit cut in the style of the serving classes, one walking-out suit, a few handkerchiefs, some stockings and underwear. These and the suitcase into which they were packed, the twenty-five guineas given me by Mr O'Connell's sons, my diary of our journey to Rome and back, and my own personal memories, these were all I had to show for my years of service with the most famous man in all of Europe.

At dusk, in my walking-out suit I ventured onto the streets again, those streets of the Liberties where the people swarmed in their hovels, destitute, dying and doing everything possible to avoid being sent to that place in which I would start my new life in the morning. In the maze of streets that surround St Patrick's Cathedral, the sharp smell of this poverty was everywhere.

A peeling door here and there was adorned by a crude, romantic and idealised portrait of Mr O'Connell riding through Dublin in his triumphal chariot; the man who saved the people of Ireland, their hero, their prince, their strong arm against oppression. Under the arch at Christ Church and down Michael's hill into Winetavern Street I walked and from the drinking houses the pathetic new ballad *"Our noble Dan is now no more"* along with some songs of the lewdest nature were carried out on to the night air.

Across the river the mighty edifice of the Four Courts, the scene of many of his greatest triumphs stood in its majesty. To my left, up St Michael's Hill the streets led to my new destiny, to the house of terror which was to be my home for the rest of my life.

The rain, which had persisted for most of the day, had stopped. A clearance was coming in from the west. The sky was clear, a little wind whipped up waves on the surface of the river, the moon was out and sparkled on the water and I saw my fireflies of Tuscany again.

# HISTORICAL FOOTNOTE

Following the ceremonies in Rome the silver urn containing the heart of Daniel O'Connell was placed in the crypt of the Church of Santa Agata dei Goti. Four years later, in the course of a return visit to his home country, Mr Charles Bianconi, a friend of O'Connell's, saw the urn and felt it deserved a more important location.

Bianconi, who had become a very wealthy man from his horse-drawn public transport network in the pre-railway age in Ireland, offered to pay the cost of a fitting monument to contain the urn.

He consulted with Father Tobias Kirby, who had succeeded Cullen as Rector of the Irish College. The celebrated sculptor Benzoni from Bergamo was commissioned to execute the work in Carrara marble.

The Gaelic theme of the *aisling* was chosen with a tearful young princess, representing Ireland, holding an urn in her hand and being consoled from above by an angel. Below this O'Connell was depicted at Westminster refusing to take the oath by which Catholics were banned from membership of parliament.

The urn containing O'Connell's heart was placed in the

wall of the church behind the monument, immediately behind the urn in the hand of the young princess. The monument and, it was presumed, O'Connell's heart remained in place for seventy-one years.

In October 1926 the Irish College was transferred from Santa Agata dei Goti to its current location on Via Santi Quattro. The Archbishop of Armagh and Primate of All Ireland, Cardinal O'Donnell, wrote to the Rector of the time, Monsignor John Hagan, that there was a "strong feeling that O'Connell's heart should not be left behind".

Work on removing the monument began in September 1927. When the marble sculptures were taken away from the north wall of Santa Agata the urn containing O'Connell's heart was not to be found. It remains unaccounted for.